The Far-Enough Window

Or

The Reclaiming of Fairyland

John Grant

Illustrated by Ron Tiner

BeWrite Books, UK
www.bewrite.net

Published internationally by BeWrite Books, UK.
363 Badminton Road, Nibley, Bristol. BS37 5JF.

Text © John Grant 2002
Illustrations © Ron Tiner 2002

The right of John Grant to be identified as the author has been asserted in accordance with sections 77 and 78 of the Copyright, Designs and Patents Act 1988. The right of John Grant to be recognized as the sole author is further asserted in accordance with international copyright agreements, laws and statutes.

British Library Cataloguing in Publication Data.
A catalogue record for this book is available from the British Library

ISBN 1-904224-79-2

Also available in eBook and cd-rom formats from www.bewrite.net

Digitally produced by BeWrite Books

This book is sold subject to the condition that it shall not, by way of trade or otherwise, be lent, resold, hired out or otherwise circulated without the publisher's consent in any form other than this current form and without a similar condition being imposed upon a subsequent purchaser. No part of this publication may be reproduced, stored in a retrieval system, or transmitted in any form by any means electronic, mechanical, photocopying, recording or otherwise without the permission of the publisher, BeWrite Books, UK.

This book is a work of fiction. Any similarity between characters in its pages and persons living or dead is unintentional and co-incidental. The author and publishers recognize and respect any trademarks included in this work by introducing such registered titles either in italics or with a capital letter.

'Yes, but to come into the past . . .'

'Not the past,' said Mustardseed. 'Haven't you been listening, Robin Goodfellow? The past is a place that no longer exists. It's a collection of likelihoods that might, if they're lucky, come to be the present. At the moment, sitting here in front of us now, you're nothing more than a figment, Robin Goodfellow. Although,' she added not quite under her breath, 'an extremely becoming figment.'

'And you say I was – will be – your friend?' said Robin Goodfellow, turning abruptly to Joanna.

'You said you were. That was why I followed you through the Far-Enough Window – because I thought you were a friend.'

'I wish,' said Robin, fretting at the front of his cap, 'I wish I knew a little more about this Far-Enough Window – I wish I knew anything about it.'

'But you will know,' said Joanna. 'When the time comes. You'll know because I'll have told you about it.' She smoothed her gown over her knees, thinking that, even if the sunlight were only an imitation of the real thing, it shone on the white cloth very pleasingly.

'Hrimfaxi,' said Mustardseed, suddenly becoming very businesslike, 'told us that there was a gateway from here into the reality of Fairyland. I don't suppose, Robin, you know anything about it?'

'A place where reality clusters,' said Robin Goodfellow slowly. He stretched as if yawning, though his face was alert. 'I'm tired of all this heavy talk. The world was made for play and dance, and, though tomorrow may be made for thunderstorms to fill, perhaps the thunderstorms will be good enough to forget to come.'

About the Author

The author, Paul Barnett, is best known by his most frequent *nom de plume*, used in this work, John Grant, under which name he has written over fifty books, both fiction and non-fiction. Among the latter are two standard authorities in their fields: *Encyclopedia of Walt Disney's Animated Characters* (1987; third edition 1998), and, with John Clute, *The Encyclopedia of Fantasy* (1997), for which he received the Hugo, Locus, Eaton, Mythopoeic Society and World Fantasy awards. He has also received a rare British Science Fiction Association Special Award and been shortlisted for the British Fantasy Society Award, Bram Stoker Award and the 2002 Chesley Award. His novels include *Albion*, *The World* and *The Hundredfold Problem*. For younger readers he has written the twelve novels in the Legends of Lone Wolf series, tied to the gamebooks by Joe Dever, as well as retellings of *Frankenstein* and *Dr. Jekyll and Mr. Hyde*. Married to Pamela D. Scoville, owner of the Animation Art Guild, he is Commissioning Editor of Paper Tiger, the world's leading publisher of books on the art of the fantastic, and US Book Reviews Editor of *Infinity Plus*. His most recent books are *Enchanted World: The Art of Anne Sudworth*, *Perceptualistics: Art by Jael* and *Masters of Animation*. His quasi-mythology *Dragonhenge*, illustrated by Bob Eggleton, is to be published in Fall 2002. His latest novel, *The Far-Enough Window*, is the first John Grant work to be published by BeWrite Books.

For Pam, with love.

And with a note of thanks to J. Eddy Fink.

Acknowledgements

Thanks to my daughter Jane, who had to put up with me while I was writing this book – and made sacrifices as a result. Further help came from John Clute, Paul Hamilton, Robert Kirby, Pamela D. Scoville, Ron Tiner, Colin Wilson and Joy Wilson: thanks, friends. Special thanks to Keith Barnett, Carolyn and Malcolm Couch, Rikki Horn and Ron Tiner for pulling me through a bad patch: my gratitude to them is unlimited. Thanks to Neil Marr for falling in love with this book and for giving it the kind of detailed, sympathetic edit it needed.

Contents

1	Joanna's Diary	13
2	The Lampeter Wing	43
3	Goodfellow	59
4	Far Enough	73
5	In the Hall of the Fairy King	111
6	Forgotten Fears	159
7	Was or Might Have Been	197
8	The Threefold Queen	237

Everything is true in the truest of all possible worlds.

Once upon a time, what happened did happen, and if it had not happened this story would never have been told.
> – Andrew Lang, *Stan Bolovan*, 1904

'I'm rather out of practice,' said he; 'but that's the way my part ought to be played.'
> – Rudyard Kipling, *Puck of Pook's Hill*, 1906

The Far-Enough Window

Or

The Reclaiming of Fairyland

One

Joanna's Diary

All children, except one, grow up. They soon know that they will grow up, and the way Wendy knew was this. One day when she was two years old she was playing in a garden, and she plucked another flower and ran with it to her mother. I suppose she must have looked rather delightful, for Mrs Darling put her hand to her heart and cried, 'Oh, why can't you remain like this forever!' This was all that passed between them on the subject, but henceforth Wendy knew that she must grow up.

– J.M. Barrie, *Peter Pan*, 1911

On the second day of the new year Joanna woke to find bright sunlight pouring into the room. Its whiteness, draping over the dressing-table and the bookshelves and making the mirror seem incandescent, matched her waking mood. She felt as if, during the night, a cold draught of air had blown through her mind, tumbling away cobwebs from all the corners and polishing all the surfaces until they gleamed.

She sat upright in bed and put her arms around her knees, looking at the daylight. A glance at her watch told her it was half past nine – Mrs Ruggeley had let her oversleep again. No wonder she felt so completely rested ... and hungry, though the slight ache of hunger was something to

be enjoyed: it seemed somehow apposite alongside her sensation of clear-headedness. She let her eyes run across the carpeted floor to the upright chair over whose back she had put her dress, neatly folded, the night before. It would do another day – certainly Mrs Ruggeley thought so, or she would have tiptoed in during the night and put a fresh one in its place.

Joanna sat there a few moments longer, enjoying the warmth and the brightness and her own feeling of well-being until her bladder insisted she get up. Leaving Knolly Mutton propped up against the pillows, his little teddy-bear arms jutting out towards the ceiling, she padded through to the bathroom and used the loo, then looked at herself in the mirror.

Her hair was still tousled from sleep, its long strands making impossible shapes that she quickly combed away with her fingers. The peppering of freckles across the top of her nose and her cheekbones was in fine fettle today, reminding her of a cluster of russet wallflowers. She rubbed the heel of her hand against her eye, smiling at herself, then stretched her two arms towards the corners of the bathroom ceiling, head thrown back, standing up on her toes as if she were trying to fly.

She would go down to breakfast in her dressing-gown and slippers. Mrs Ruggeley wouldn't mind, and there was no one else in the house today. There hardly ever was.

That brought a frown to her reflected face as her body relaxed. It was nice to be able to wander around the house half-dressed, but it would have been even nicer if Daddy had been here for Christmas and New Year as he had promised her the last time she'd seen him, in summer. Christmas dinner had been a matter of merely herself and Mrs Ruggeley, plus Mudgett the gardener – there to make up the numbers but obviously resentful that he'd been forced to enter the dining-room, which he normally considered out of bounds. They sat around a turkey that was too large, wearing paper hats and frantically pretending to be merry. Afterwards there had been presents – a big pile for Joanna, a few for Mrs Ruggeley and just a couple (one each from Joanna and Mrs Ruggeley) for Mudgett. He at least had the grace to look delighted with his new tobacco pouch and pipe-knife, paid for by Joanna out of her own allowance although, obviously, actually purchased on her behalf by Mrs Ruggeley. Joanna's own presents had been mainly the usual: perfumes to add to the unopened collection on the bathroom shelf, clothes that might or might not ever be worn, books – plenty of books, which were always welcome – and videos, bits and pieces of cosmetic equipment whose purposes Joanna could only guess at . . . and, from Mrs Ruggeley, a leather-bound diary.

Coming back into the bedroom, Joanna saw the diary lying on her dressing-table, and smiled again. She'd never had a diary before. The moment she'd unwrapped it and realized what it was she'd flown to the old housekeeper and hugged her roundly, kissing her on both wrinkled cheeks. Mrs Ruggeley had hugged her right back, her eyes moist – although it seemed she was also faintly surprised, as if she hadn't known how *wanted* her present would be.

For Joanna's main gift Daddy had given her an electronic keyboard. It was something she'd vitally desired during the summer. Now it lay in the music-room and she religiously went in there every day for a quarter of an hour to practise on it, wishing it were the piano's keyboard under her fingers but not wanting to seem disloyal. It was fun for a while to play Bach's two-part inventions on bells or jazz saxophone, but...

The diary, on the other hand, was *hers*. She ran her palm across the textured leather cover, tooled gaudily in something like gold, and pressed her thumb against the elaborate brassy lock; the little key was on a thin chain around her neck, where she'd worn it ever since Christmas Day.

She scrabbled under the bed for her slippers, which were black and stiff and embroidered in turquoise and daffodil-yellow. Last night, after coming up to her room, she'd kept herself awake for an extra half-hour to cover the creamy page headed JANUARY 1: MONDAY with her best writing, recounting not so much the events of the day – because as usual nothing much had happened – but the thoughts and ideas that had come into her head during it: her reflections on life, and on her allotted place in it. She had been very tired when she'd finished, and worried that she might clumsily blot the paper, so she'd held the shaft of her Osmiroid fountain-pen extremely tightly, until her fingers hurt. Standing in her dressing-gown and slippers in the morning light, she flexed her right hand to banish the memory of last night's stiffness.

After breakfast she would read what she'd written to see if it were worthy of the leather cover and the soft, fusty-smelling paper.

She was at the bedroom door, just about to open it, when she thought for the first time to look out of the window. The sight drew her across the room to press her hands against the cold glass.

Snow had fallen during the night to lie in a smooth, deep

carpet across the gardens and the drive and the stables and the distant wall. Everything she could see had been turned into the decorations on top of a birthday cake, simplified models carved out of icing. Mrs Ruggeley had left the car in the drive overnight, and it had become a white toy, so that Joanna half-expected Knolly Mutton to wind down the window and wave to her. The stables were sugar-coated gingerbread, looking as if they were very warm inside – which they probably were, because the witch living there would already have the oven lit in case any little children called by. The telephone wire was a thin strand of treacle toffee, splashed here and there with little dollops of icing.

The glass in front of her eyes steamed up and she turned away. Later she would build a snowman, and maybe Mrs Ruggeley could be persuaded to help her – or Mudgett might start a snowball fight, which would of course see Mrs Ruggeley retreating to the door at high speed to stand there shouting dire threats and warnings at Joanna and Mudgett and Mr Dogg romping in the snow. Afterwards Joanna and Mr Dogg would have to sit steaming in the kitchen, she in her underthings and he in his wet fur, until Mrs Ruggeley was satisfied that neither of them was likely to die of pneumonia.

As she wound slowly down the stairs, feeling the open space of the hall coming towards her, Mr Dogg came lolloping up to greet her, shaking his head and his tail in counterpoint, his tongue flapping out of his great toothy mouth. She paused to make a fuss of him, fumbling his head in her hands and tickling behind his ears, then carried on down the stairs more rapidly, with him boisterously jostling along beside her.

The kitchen was warmer than the rest of the house,

although the same chilly light poured in through its window. Mrs Ruggeley had been making something with nutmeg in it.

'It's all right for some,' said the housekeeper, turning round from the cooker. 'Half the day's been and gone while you've been lying up there snoring.'

There was no sting in the words, and Mrs Ruggeley's arms were open to embrace her. Mr Dogg rubbed himself against their legs, then trotted off to the corner of the kitchen to see if Fortune had thought to place anything interesting in his bowl. Joanna allowed herself to be smothered in Mrs Ruggeley's ample softness. The housekeeper was past middle-age and had perhaps once upon a time been slender, but not now. Her bosom was a pneumatic cushion loosely covered in flannel: Joanna had never been able to visualize it as two separate breasts, although presumably it must be. Bushy grey hair – the one part of Mrs Ruggeley that wasn't always trimly presented – struggled, not wholly unsuccessfully, against the pins that crimped it into a bun. Complicated networks of wrinkles spread out from under her eyes across the tops of her red cheeks.

'It's not yet ten o'clock,' said Joanna, laughing. 'The cock forgot to crow. The alarm didn't go off. Your watch is wrong.'

Mrs Ruggeley gave an exaggerated sniff. 'Excuses,' she said primly.

'Besides,' said Joanna, 'I was up late last night. Writing in my diary. The diary you gave me. I'm a chronicler now, thanks to you, Mrs Ruggeley.'

'Samuella Pepys,' said the housekeeper, letting her go.

'Joanna Evelyn, I thought,' said Joanna, puffing out her chest. 'When the spring comes I shall spend all my time in the garden, redesigning it completely until it looks like Sayes

Court, and writing about it every night so that future generations can wonder at my artistry, and . . .'

'You'd better have breakfast first,' observed Mrs Ruggeley. 'You can't go off and be of historical significance without anything in your tummy.'

Joanna giggled and pulled a stool out from beneath the kitchen table. Mrs Ruggeley's habits in the kitchen took after her hair rather than the rest of her, and Joanna had to push aside a couple of goo-smeared bowls and a leaking bag of flour to make a space in front of herself.

'That animal needs a bath,' said Mrs Ruggeley, opening the fridge door. 'And I'm not giving it to him.'

'This evening,' said Joanna. 'I'll bath him then. It'll be something to do. But I want to take him out in the snow as soon as I'm dressed.'

'Here's the milk,' said Mrs Ruggeley, putting the jug down in front of her. 'There's plenty of porridge in the pot.'

Joanna helped herself at the cooker. The smell of the oats made her suddenly hungrier, and she added a second ladleful to her bowl before taking it back to the table.

'So that's the plan for the day, is it?' said Mrs Ruggeley, sitting down opposite her. 'Making a fool of yourself in the snow with that animal until you're both wet through and filthy. If your father were here he'd soon put a stop to – '

The woman stopped, realizing she'd said the wrong thing. Her face crumpled as Joanna bent to concentrate on her porridge.

'Do you think Daddy deliberately avoids us here?'

Joanna had asked the question a thousand times, sometimes in different words, sometimes screamed at the top of her voice, other times, like now, in a low voice, barely above a mumble. What she really meant to ask was 'Do you think Daddy doesn't love me, that really he can't stand me?' but she'd never been able to say that, even to think it, in case the words made doubts crystallize into reality.

Mrs Ruggeley became suddenly effusive, standing up and coming round the table to rest her arm around Joanna's shoulders.

'Don't you be so silly, my lass. Your father adores you – anyone looking at the two of you together when he's here could see that. You remember him being here in the summer, don't you? You're the bright light in the sky that makes the day dawn, as far as he's concerned. It's just that . . . he's a very busy man. A very important man. When people are as important as he is they're hardly ever allowed to do what they want. If he had his way, he'd be here with us all the year round, or he'd be taking you with him wherev – He'd have you by his side the whole time. So stop being mawkish, girl, or the wind may change and you'll be stuck with a face like a prune forever.'

Joanna knew that most of what Mrs Ruggeley was saying was true. She let the continuing flow of words wash over her, ignoring their individual meanings but hearing their general sense. Like her question, the reply changed in its details but had been spoken countless times before. The truth of the matter was not that her father didn't love her – even though that was the misgiving which frequently nagged her – but that he loved her too much. After what Mummy had done to him . . . and to her . . .

She couldn't remember her mother's face or anything else about her except the way it had felt to know that she was there – either right there in the room or somewhere nearby, ready to come if Joanna called. Then, one day, all that had changed. Joanna, aged two (or so Mrs Ruggeley had told her), lay in bed listening as Daddy and Mummy shouted at each other, slamming doors and breaking stuff, and when she woke up in the morning it was to be told that Mummy was leaving, that Mummy was packing up her things at this very moment and would kiss her goodbye before she went. And then there was the knowledge that the house had suddenly got so very much bigger, with one person less in it.

Daddy had sat on the end of Joanna's bed that night and explained everything to her, except that he'd used words she didn't understand. Every time she'd asked him the one really important question – when would Mummy be coming back? – he'd just looked upset and said, 'Darling, you haven't been listening . . .', and started all over saying strings of words that didn't mean anything.

Mummy never had come back. She sent birthday presents – usually money – and something special and silly for Christmas, but even this had stopped after a few years, round about the same time that Joanna had begun to wonder if Mummy had ever really existed or if she were just something out of a favourite story book which Mrs Ruggeley had often read to her when she was too young to read it for herself. By then, even if Mummy had returned, Joanna would hardly have welcomed her: she and Mrs Ruggeley had become the very firmest of friends, and the only person who could, occasionally, make Joanna look outside the glow of that friendship was Daddy.

Except that he wasn't home very often. He never had been there much – Mrs Ruggeley had once enigmatically told Joanna that this was the real reason why Mummy had had to go away – but now his business seemed to keep him away for weeks and then months at a time, leaving her with Mrs Ruggeley and Mudgett and a succession of female tutors who came for a few months at a time and then, for one reason or another, left again.

She ate a few more spoonfuls of porridge before pushing the bowl aside.

'We could go into the village,' she said sourly. 'We could put on our warm things and get into the car and go down to the village and look in the shops and maybe buy something or have a cup of tea and a rather unpleasant cake somewhere, and then we could come home again and talk about all the things we'd done and at night, before I got into bed, I'd have something to write about in my diary.'

Mrs Ruggeley, stopped in mid-flow by this sudden announcement, looked down at Joanna's upturned face.

'No, lass, you know we can't do that,' she said quietly. 'If it were up to me we could go to London or beyond every day of the week – perhaps even to Paris once in a while – but I gave my word to your father, and I can't break it. He wants you to stay here, and me with you; and I said that's what I'd do. It was a promise, dear heart, and you know promises should never be broken.'

'Oh,' said Joanna in a little disappointed voice. Of course she'd known what Mrs Ruggeley would say, but it still *felt* like a disillusionment to hear it spoken. 'Oh.'

Mrs Ruggeley hugged her again, pressing Joanna's face into her midriff.

'It's because your father loves you so much that he wants us to take such good care of you.'

'I wish,' said Joanna, feeling tears come at last, 'I wish my father loved me less.'

The anticipated snowball fight never materialized, but that afternoon she and Mrs Ruggeley built a large fat snowman with an old naval cap on his head and a carrot for his nose, and he looked very fine until Mr Dogg came along and piddled on his side. Then, after Joanna had called in to the stables to see that Rapscallion was well and that Mudgett had fed him, they dug the old sledge out of the garage and took turns pulling each other on it across the main lawn to the Willow Copse, beyond which there was a long steep slope just perfect for sledging down. Mrs Ruggeley chose not to 'risk breaking my legs, like some damn' fool of a girl' but stood at the top of the slope yelling steaming encouragement in the chilly air as Joanna went whooping down the hill and plodding back up it again, time after time. She tried to persuade Mr Dogg that he'd like to be tied to the sledge to drag it to the top of the hill, but the old mongrel was too wily to be having any of that, instead whoofing off through chest-high snow to investigate the mysteries of the copse. Twice she fell off, landing face-first in a drift; the second time she was laughing so much that she didn't notice her ski hat had filled up with snow until she crammed it back on her head, and that made both of them laugh all the harder.

It was nearly dusk, and snow had started lightly falling again – the flakes dancing in the grey air like the sparks above a bonfire – by the time they trudged back to the house, Mr Dogg walking ahead of them with his head down, tired after his important explorations.

As they came into the house Joanna suddenly realized that

she'd forgotten to read her diary, as she'd promised herself she'd do that morning.

'You're not going upstairs like that,' said Mrs Ruggeley firmly. 'I'm not having slush and muck trailed all over my carpets, thank you very much, my miss.'

Joanna followed her into the kitchen and obediently stripped off her coat and her boots and her woollies and her dress and her thick knitted tights, and sat on a wooden chair in front of the Aga stove, rubbing her hair with a big pink towel. Mrs Ruggeley tugged off her own boots, grunting, and put them beside Joanna's on an old newspaper to dry out.

'Hot soup,' said the housekeeper, opening one of the cupboards and peering at a shelf. 'We have oxtail or cream of mushroom or mulligatawny or . . . oh, dogfood, how did *this* get up here?'

'Mulligatawny,' said Joanna. It was what she always chose – less because she liked the soup than because of the name. When she was smaller she'd thought it must be made from Irish tigers.

A few minutes later, sitting with the mug steaming in her hands, the soup still too hot to drink, she asked Mrs Ruggeley: 'Why did Mudgett go into town?'

'He didn't.'

'I thought you said . . .'

'He was going to, but as soon as he looked at the way the snow was heaped up around the gates he decided to leave it 'til tomorrow. No sense getting the car stranded miles away from home. He walked into the village instead to get his tobacco – the other things can wait.'

'What other things?'

Mrs Ruggeley looked vague. 'Oh . . . just things.' Joanna

could see she wasn't being mysterious – the woman didn't know and wasn't much interested. 'I think he said something about needing some oil for his machines.'

'Why doesn't anyone ever come to visit us?'

The housekeeper looked startled at the sudden change of direction. 'My, you're a one for questions today, aren't you, Joanna?'

'But why?'

'Your father doesn't like it.'

'But he's not here. He's hardly *ever* here.'

Mrs Ruggeley sat down at the kitchen table, resting her mug of soup on a dirty plate in front of her. 'That doesn't make any difference: it's his household, and I'm his housekeeper, and you're his daughter, so we do things the way he wants us to do them.'

'But why doesn't he want us to have visitors? All the people in my books go visiting each other the whole time – they seem to spend most of their lives doing that. So why don't some of them, just sometimes, come to visit *us*?'

'Because your father doesn't want them to,' said Mrs Ruggeley wearily.

'But *why* not? I get so lonely, and . . . oh, it's not that you aren't the best friend anyone ever had, Mrs Ruggeley, and it's not as if I didn't love you with all my heart – you know that I do, dear, dear Mrs Ruggeley – it's just that . . .' Joanna knew she was beginning to flounder, and she took a gulp of her soup to give her an excuse to start the sentence again. 'It's just that, in a way, it would be nice to see people around who I *didn't* like quite so much, just as a contrast, if you know what I mean . . .'

'You'd like a bit of a change from just me all of the time, is what you mean,' said Mrs Ruggeley. 'Don't worry, dear heart: you're not hurting my feelings. It's only natural you should want to see other people – maybe someone your own age, for once.'

Joanna was startled. She knew in a theoretical way that not everyone was older than her, like Mrs Ruggeley and Mudgett and her tutors and Daddy, but the knowledge wasn't something that ever *felt* very true. That hadn't been what she'd been thinking of at all.

'I don't mean – ' she began.

Mrs Ruggeley held up a hand. 'Whether you meant it or not, it's true: you *should* be having friends who're more the same age as yourself. I wish I . . . But your father won't allow it. I said to him when he was here in August, I said . . . Maybe when he's next here – I'd expected him to come for Christmas, and I was going to raise the subject with him again, but . . .'

Joanna took some more soup. The hot spiciness of it made the rest of her feel warm. The side of her shift closest to the front of the Aga was getting uncomfortably hot, and she turned around on her chair.

Mrs Ruggeley seemed to take Joanna's thoughtful silence as a continuation of the question, because she suddenly began to speak again.

'Your father blames the world for what your mother did to him,' she said rapidly, talking to the far corner of the kitchen rather than to Joanna direct. 'He couldn't believe that the woman he'd wooed and married could have done any such thing – that something must have possessed her, turned her into a different person from the one she'd been. And, since your father isn't so silly as to believe in evil spirits or demons or ghosts, he concluded that it was the world itself, the society in which the two of them moved, that had ousted her own mind and replaced it with itself. Mixing in the world, being corrupted by its ways, learning to think the way it thought, letting herself be dissolved by it until there was nothing really of herself left; that's what your father thought – thinks – altered your mother.'

Mrs Ruggeley put her face in her hands – not weeping, but as if she didn't want to be here listening to herself. 'After your mother went, he mourned her as if she'd died – because that was what truly, in his heart of hearts, he believed had happened: that she'd died some while before, only no one had noticed because this stranger who looked like her and talked like her but *wasn't* her had taken her place.

'And then he saw you, lying in your cot and waving your arms and gurgling at him, and he said to me, "Harriet," he said, "I couldn't bear for that little girl to be lost to me the way her mother's been – I couldn't stand for the world to destroy her the way it's destroyed her mother, crushing her *real* self out of existence. That would be more than mortal man could bear, Tettie," he said – sometimes he calls me Tettie, you know – "more than mortal man could bear."

'So now you know,' said Mrs Ruggeley, raising her head.

'But I *don't* know,' said Joanna, wrinkling her forehead. 'You haven't told me anything at all! What was it Mummy did to Daddy? What do you mean, "the world ousted her real self"? She looked out of the kitchen window, half-expecting to see the snow-shrouded bushes of the garden creeping towards the house, ready to leap through the glass when she wasn't expecting them so that they could destroy her soul.

'Maybe it was just his way of speaking,' said Mrs Ruggeley

reluctantly. 'Maybe all he was trying to say was that there hadn't been any evil in her heart until other people came along and put it there. And he knew there wasn't any wickedness in you, either – but that you might not stay that way if you listened to what other people would tell you. He loved – loves – you far too much to ever run the risk of that happening. So he decided you should be kept away from the rest of the world until . . . until . . . whenever.'

A silence hung between them. Joanna took a mouthful of lukewarm mulligatawny soup, not realizing she was doing so until she heard the slurp.

'Is it very unusual?' she began hesitantly, then started again in a louder voice: 'Is it very unusual for people to live the way we do?' None of the people she read about lived away from the world – unless they were hermits, and different – but she'd always thought it was just that no one ever wrote books about people like herself because nothing ever happened to them.

Mrs Ruggeley looked as if she'd rather the question hadn't been asked. 'There isn't really any such thing as "unusual" when you're talking about the way folk live their lives,' she said, obviously prevaricating. 'Everybody's different, and does different things – which is just the way it should be.'

'Have you ever heard of anyone else living like us?' said Joanna firmly, leaning forward. She didn't like to see her friend squirming this way, but she sensed the answer to her question was important.

'No,' said Mrs Ruggeley after a long pause. She stared at the backs of her hands as if examining them for symmetry with each other. 'No, love, I can't say as I have. Now, your soup must be cold by now, so I'll – '

'Stop!' said Joanna. 'Stop dodging away from telling me things I need to know. It's like you were stealing bits of me when you keep avoiding my questions. Please, dearest Mrs Ruggeley...'

The housekeeper stood looking down at the kitchen floor. For a moment Joanna had the illusion that their rôles had been reversed, so that she was now the adult and Mrs Ruggeley the child. 'Please,' she repeated softly.

'You're right,' said Mrs Ruggeley. She took a deep breath. 'You're seventeen now, and that's old enough – far *too* old – to be told everything. Oh' – she wrung her hands together – 'how I wish your father were here!'

'I spend most of my life wishing Daddy were here.'

'Touché,' said Mrs Ruggeley with a sigh. Looking distracted, she walked across to the stove and opened the lid on one of the hot plates. 'It's too late now, and I'm too upset, and Mudgett'll be here in a minute wanting his supper – heavens, but you'd better be running and getting some proper clothes on before he appears! So I'm not going to talk about this any more tonight. But in the morning, I promise you – in the morning I'll sit down with you and tell you everything I know. You'll just have to wait until then – not one more word out of me you'll get tonight, my best-loved one.'

'But – '

'Clothes!'

Neither Joanna nor Mrs Ruggeley could think of much to say over supper – lamb chops fried in cider and herbs, with

THE FAR-ENOUGH WINDOW

boiled potatoes and tinned peas – and Mudgett never spoke a lot at the best of times. So the meal passed in a succession of stifling pauses broken by blurted inconsequentials or the sound of Mr Dogg snuffling in his basket. Afterwards Joanna volunteered to wash up, but Mrs Ruggeley would have none of it, saying she wanted the kitchen to herself for a couple of hours so she could get things sorted for once. Mudgett sloped off towards wherever Mudgett generally sloped off towards. The housekeeper hugged Joanna tightly for a few seconds, then told her to go upstairs to the television room and watch one of her Christmas videos; Mrs Ruggeley would bring her some cocoa later.

Joanna did as she was told – it hardly occurred to her to do otherwise – and picked listlessly through the heap of brand-new videotapes with their brightly coloured sleeves. Daddy never remembered exactly what he'd given her – she suspected, anyway, that he sent one of his secretaries out to buy the presents he gave her – so as usual a few of the tapes could be immediately discarded as duplicates of ones she'd watched dozens of times before. One of them was *The Sound of Music* – most Christmases and birthdays he gave her *The Sound of Music*, as if it were the one, unique movie that a girl of seventeen could be relied upon to enjoy. She put the new copy tidily on the shelf beside the others. Even their sleeves were identical. *The Aristocats* – another repeat.

She picked up one of the unfamiliar tapes and desultorily read the back. *The Red Balloon* was 'charming' and a 'classic for all time' which could 'hardly fail to capture the imagination of any viewer from eight to eighty!' She wrinkled her nose: at least *The Red Balloon* was short, which gave it her vote.

But, as she watched it, she discovered that for once the sleeve's hyperbole was right. She lost herself entirely in the simple tale, becoming the little boy chased through Paris's alleyways by the gang of urchins who wanted to burst his friend, the magical red balloon. And at the end, as all the balloons of Paris rallied to the place of the murder to raise the boy aloft, she felt his sudden surge to freedom.

When the movie was over, she sat in silence for some minutes, blankly watching the empty tape as it spooled towards the end of the reel. Then she grabbed up the remote control from the floor beside her overstuffed armchair, rewound, and ran *The Red Balloon* for a second time, unconcerned about the tears that wet her cheeks. Mr Dogg came whuffling in and jumped up beside her, settling himself half on her, but she hardly noticed.

This time, when the word *Fin* had come and gone on the screen, she switched off the monitor at once. Leaving the tape rewinding, she shoved the mongrel off herself and went downstairs.

'I'm going to bed,' she said, leaning against the frame of the kitchen door. 'It's been a long day.' She smiled ruefully. 'No need for cocoa.'

'But it's only nine o'clock. Are you sure you're all right?' said Mrs Ruggeley, screwing up her eyes. 'You've been crying, haven't you? What's the matter?'

'Nothing. Just a soppy movie, that's all. And I'm tired because of being out in the snow this afternoon. I need to sleep – though not before I've written up today in my diary,' she added. 'I still haven't got round to reading what I said about yesterday.' Her smile became a grin. 'I do hope it's not the most awful garbage.'

THE FAR-ENOUGH WINDOW

'Poor love. It's been quite a day for you, hasn't it?' said Mrs Ruggeley. 'I don't mean just the sledging, I mean –'

'I know what you mean,' said Joanna. 'It's been quite a day, as you say. All the more to write about.'

She kissed the housekeeper and went upstairs.

Joanna forced herself to undress before opening her diary. The restraint wasn't difficult, for she wasn't certain she was calm enough yet to write anything. Mrs Ruggeley's 'quite a day' had been the understatement of the year: not only had there been the discovery that no one else in the world lived like this, unless they had been locked away because they were terribly evil or had offended someone terribly evil, like the Man in the Iron Mask, but there had come to her, at the end of *The Red Balloon*, the sudden discovery that things needn't and shouldn't be like this. She wasn't a prisoner, the way she understood that word: she was somebody free who happened to have been thrown into a cage. That the bars of the cage were made of love rather than steel didn't alter the principle: she was a bird who floated high and unconstrained on the breezes of the sky, except for the fact that she wasn't doing that *right now*. Or had ever done it.

She sat on the edge of her bed in her clean flannel nightie, the blue-and-brown-and-white-checked gingham dress she had put on before supper now folded carefully over the back of the chair. She put her hands under her bottom and rocked backwards and forwards on the bony pivot. The Man in the Iron Mask was released from his bondage because he had friends outside the prison who determined that this injustice should be rectified. The Prisoner of Zenda – much the same. In every other story she could think of where innocent people had been imprisoned, they had escaped because of someone from outside coming to help them. Like Charles Darnay in *The Tale of Two Cities* – except that nobody had come to release Sydney Carton, and she remembered only too clearly what had happened to him.

She didn't know anyone in the outside world apart from Daddy, and he was her gaoler.

Picking up Knolly Mutton by one paw, Joanna went across to sit in front of the dressing-table. She reached up to click on the striplight over the mirror, then fished out the diary's brass key from where it hung on its chain between her breasts. The lock and the key were very tiny, and she fumbled a few times before finally the clasp popped open.

She had managed to fill a whole page yesterday, but it had been difficult. She wondered if a page would be enough for today.

Tucking her hair back behind her ears, out of the way, she leaned forward and began to read.

Today is the first day of a new year, and I have promised myself (and Mrs Ruggeley, who kindly gave me this diary) that I shall keep a true record, each day and every day, of the events of my life. But first, dear reader (although I suspect there never shall *be a dear reader), let me introduce myself to you. My name is . . .*

Her handwriting was small and neat and, even though the ruled lines on the page were close together, she had no difficulty reading what she had written. At the end of the first long paragraph she sighed, patting the slightly furry-feeling page. Not a word out of place, no crossings out, and not a spelling mistake that she could notice. At the same time, it was hardly Charles Greville – although perhaps he too had started off this way, giving all sorts of boring details about his age and his height and his weight, but years later had crossed this stuff out and left only the juicy bits for other people to read. That was what she would do, once she was free of the house and had become famous in the outside world.

She started to read the second paragraph, and almost at once her mouth dropped open. This was nothing at all like she remembered – she couldn't recall having written the words, and it certainly wasn't a true record of what had happened to her yesterday. She wasn't sure, twenty-four hours later, exactly what *had* happened yesterday, because it had been just a day like so many others before it, but she knew that it had never been like this.

She turned over the diary to look at the cover, as if in some way she might have picked up the wrong one. Then, perplexed, she held the page up to the striplight, examining the handwriting closely. If someone were playing a trick on her, it was a very nasty trick – it was an invasion of her most personal self. But the forgery of her handwriting – if it was a forgery – had been meticulously executed, and the style of the writing seemed to be very much her own. It was as impossible to believe that she had not written this as to believe that she had. But who could have performed the counterfeit? Who would have *wanted* to? She stared accusingly at her Osmiroid fountain-pen, lying still capped beside her hairbrush, as if it might have waited until she was out playing in the snow and then unpicked the diary's lock to falsify the page.

She read on.

. . . and I climbed all the way to the attic in the Lampeter Wing, where I'd never been before. It was full of old junk. I tried on a hat

made of straw with a broken feather sticking out of it, but as I pushed it down on my head the crown disintagrated, so I threw it away and had a lot of trouble getting the bits out of my hair. But most important than that . . .

She tutted at 'most important than that'. It was the sort of mistake she was always making, and always it was so obviously a mistake to her afterwards.

. . . was that there is a little window in the end wall made of thick glass that has glooped down towards the bottom so it is a bit like a lense. The window is circular with a cross of lead holding it all together. You can look through the window out over the whole of the front garden. (I think it is going to snow tomorrow, because some of the clouds looked very heavy, they are probably full of snow.) I saw several cars drive by on the other side of the wall, then one of them slowed down at the gate and it was Mrs Ruggeley coming home from doing the shopping.

The lense bit at the bottom is interesting, if you look through it at the correct angle it makes the front garden go different colours and shapes. I made Mrs Ruggeley go different colours and shapes as well when she was climbing out of the car and bringing the shopping into the house, it looked very heavy and I felt a bit guilty being up there just watching when I should have been down with her helping.

But I still haven't got to the most important part of all, which is what he told me about the window, which is called the Far-Enough Window because of the things that it does. Tomorrow I will go back up to the attic to see him again, and the window, and to see if the window can really do the things he says it can, because if it really can, then it really will have earned it's name of the Far-Enough Window, like he said. But tonight I am tired and I am getting to the bottom of the page so I will stop now, dear reader, and tell you more tomorrow when I hope there is more to tell.

THE FAR-ENOUGH WINDOW

She put the diary down, open at its single written page, and stared at it. The Lampeter Wing hadn't been used since the times when Mummy and Daddy had thrown big parties; she could still bring back into her mind the noise and commotion and loud, pounding music. Nowadays, though it wasn't locked up or anything, no one ever went there – or, at least, she didn't, and she would be surprised if Mrs Ruggeley or Mudgett did either. She didn't know if the rooms there were still furnished, or if they'd been cleared out after Mummy had gone. If there really was an attic at the top of it, in the little turreted tower at the northwest corner of the house, it would undoubtedly be every bit as dusty as the writer – as she – had said it was.

But her mind was wandering away from the central riddle. She could swear that she hadn't written anything last night about the Lampeter Wing – but *somebody* had, and the only person whom that *somebody* could be was herself, Joanna. Oh, wait: there was the person she'd mentioned as 'he'. Infuriating! Nothing more than that: just 'he'. Obviously when she'd been writing about him she'd known exactly who 'he' was, and it had never occurred to her that she might forget. Or was it possible that 'he' could have written the diary entry, mimicking her handwriting – maybe even borrowing her body? She remembered what Mrs Ruggeley had said about the world coming into and possessing Mummy's body, like an evil spirit, and she shivered despite the central heating. Maybe 'he' was an evil spirit?

She didn't want to write in her diary tonight – she was frightened even of touching it. She thought about going back downstairs and asking Mrs Ruggeley about what was going on, and for a moment the prospect of the warm kitchen and Mrs

Ruggeley's soft, comforting bosom seemed very attractive; but then she realized that Mrs Ruggeley couldn't know anything more about this than she did, and would simply make a huge fuss and not solve anything. (She tried not to think about an even worse possibility: that Mrs Ruggeley, her one dear friend, might in fact know *everything* about this.)

Let's take stock. She knew for a certainty that she hadn't gone to the Lampeter Wing yesterday – and she hadn't done it today, either: today she had woken late, had eaten breakfast, had bathed for ages, had practised for a while on her electronic keyboard, had read and giggled over Macaulay's essay on Robert Montgomery, had eaten lunch with Mrs Ruggeley and then gone out with her to build a snowman and play on the sledge. Afterwards she had sat in the kitchen, drying off, while Mrs Ruggeley had begun to tell her a little about how Mummy and Daddy had stopped living here together and how she had become confined by Daddy's love for her. Then she had quickly changed into her checked dress in time for supper with Mrs Ruggeley and Mudgett. The last thing she had done was to watch *The Red Balloon* twice in a row before coming up here to get ready for bed and read her diary.

There simply hadn't been time to go to the Lampeter Wing today. As for yesterday? She'd been occupied doing other things all day long: she knew that, although none of the things had been important enough to remember individually. Bathing, reading, music, videos ... If there was an attic in the Lampeter Wing (presumably there must be), and if that attic had a window called the Far-Enough Window and there was somebody there called 'he' who knew about it, then they had spent the day unvisited by her.

THE FAR-ENOUGH WINDOW

She switched off the striplight over the dressing-table mirror. She moved to close the diary, then stopped: she'd leave it open. Bad enough to think that someone might come in here to write in it while she was asleep, without them having to dig in under the bedclothes to find the key. She opened her bedroom door a few inches and gave a low whistle. A few moments later she heard Mr Dogg lumbering heavily up the stairs: he wasn't really supposed to spend the night in her room, but Mrs Ruggeley usually turned a blind eye to this breach of the rules. The mongrel appeared in the doorway, his eyes bright and eager, and she fisted the top of his head.

Then she climbed into bed and pulled the bedclothes up to cover herself completely, leaving until last one arm, with which she reached out to turn off the bedside lamp.

Mr Dogg waited until she was settled, then hauled himself up onto the bed and slumped on top of her feet.

A short while later they were both fast asleep, ceding the room to the full moon's light.

'Was my mother a "fallen woman"?' asked Joanna the next morning at breakfast. Her mind had been working away at the problem while she dressed.

'Yes,' said Mrs Ruggeley, 'you could put it like that. But not while you're eating a boiled egg.'

'Like Hetty Sorrel?'

'Later.'

Joanna glowered. It seemed that Mrs Ruggeley had, ever since yesterday afternoon, wanted to consign everything to that vague place called 'later'. And her boiled egg was overcooked: Mrs Ruggeley had told her a hundred times that it was unhealthy to have them soft-boiled, because of the risk of salmonella, but that didn't change the fact that Joanna liked them runny, so that they overflowed their broken rim of shell when you stuck your toast soldier into them.

'I may be busy, later,' she said airily.

Mrs Ruggeley snorted.

Back up in her room Joanna stole another look at the page for JANUARY 2: TUESDAY. She was almost disappointed to discover that it was still blank. When she'd found it that way on waking up this morning she'd somehow assumed the mysterious diarist – for sleep had brought the conviction that it couldn't have been her who'd written JANUARY 1: MONDAY – had been wary of disturbing her, and had decided to wait until she was safely ensconced in the kitchen having breakfast.

As she brushed her teeth she wondered what to do with the morning. Mrs Ruggeley had clearly disbelieved her when she'd said she might be busy, so it was important she should be. But she didn't think she'd be able to keep her mind on practising in the music-room, and she wasn't in the mood for books or videos. Going for a walk was out of the question because the air was full of a niggling drizzle and the snow had melted into greasy grey slush.

When she came out of the bathroom she glanced at the open diary once more, and was astounded that the obvious solution hadn't occurred to her before: investigate the Lampeter Wing.

She had a vague feeling that Mrs Ruggeley would forbid the venture if she knew about it, so Joanna quickly plotted out a route to the northwest corner of the house that would keep her well clear of the kitchen and the housekeeper's own apartments. She would stick to the first floor as long as possible, then duck down the back stairs that led to the old gunroom. If she nipped across the broad expanse of the rear hall without being seen she would be safely at the base of the northwest wing – and after that there was certain to be no one to interfere with her plans.

Except, possibly – she chewed absently at a fingernail – 'he'.

Still, standing here worrying about that wouldn't get her anywhere. She pulled on a pullover on top of her dress (still the checked gingham one from yesterday, but she'd really hardly worn it) because the central heating didn't reach that far and so the Lampeter Wing was likely to be freezing cold. She stuffed a torch into her pocket. Mr Dogg would make good company, so she whistled for him from the landing. While he was making his wheezing way upstairs she turned on an afterthought back into her bedroom, closed the diary, and checked that it was locked. Then she put it into the bottom drawer of the dressing-table and arranged a scattering of her smalls on top of it.

'Now,' she said to Mr Dogg, 'you and I are going on a very big adventure . . .'

Two

The Lampeter Wing

The Phoenix did begin to sing. She lifted her head and the plumes changed from white to gold and from gold to orange. As the song increased so as to shake the very house, the plumes changed from orange to scarlet and lo, they were no longer plumes but flames . . .
– John Masefield, *The Box of Delights*, 1935

She soon tugged off the pullover and knotted it around her waist. There might be no central heating here, and the air might in reality be chilly, but making progress through the Lampeter Wing was hot work. She felt like an archaeologist opening up a pyramid after five thousand years had passed. Wallpaper had peeled to form snatching limbs of brittle fabric; floorboards and stairs had rotted through – sometimes leaving great holes from whose depths came dark, fetid stinks; sometimes, even worse, they hadn't quite rotted away but were waiting for her to put her weight on seemingly intact timber. The electricity had been cut off in this part of the house, so it was lucky that instinct had told her to bring her torch. There were cobwebs everywhere, and plenty of live spiders as well, their eyes sometimes glinting in the beam of the torch. Once she had stopped, heart pounding, her mouth open ready to scream, before she had realized that the spectral figure rushing along the dark corridor towards her was in fact the dried-out husk of a moth, twirling in a spider's web only a few inches from her nose.

She opened one of the doors leading off the central corridor and the torch showed her a split-open horsehair sofa crawling with maggots. After that she left the doors closed.

Picking her way through drifts of dust and heaps of fallen fittings, telling herself to ignore the orchestra of individual drip-drip-dripping noises that seemed to be, near and far, all around her, she finally reached the base of the stairs that must eventually lead to the tower. Mr Dogg had got there some minutes before, less concerned about possible hazards; his tongue wobbling loosely out of the side of his jaw, he sat waiting for her and visibly wondering why she should be taking so much time over the exploration of this wonderful virgin territory.

'You've got to be joking, Mr Dogg,' she said, shining the torch up into the gloomy stairwell. 'You might be able to get up there, but it looks lethal to me.'

Mr Dogg cocked his head, his eyes on her face as if he understood what she'd just said.

'Oh, you think I'm just being a fusspot, do you?'

She told herself that the mongrel nodded in agreement.

'Well, we'll have to see, won't we, who's right and who's wrong.'

She took hold of the bottom of the banister and gave it a good shake. There was a disconcerting creaking noise from further up, but the banister seemed sound enough as long as she didn't try to put too much weight on it. The treads of the stairway were another matter, though: someone must have economized on the original carpeting, for the material had worn away almost entirely, leaving just traceries, like the veins of leaves, on the plain wooden surfaces. There were enough loops of threads still surviving, however, to make her sure to trip if she didn't watch what she was doing with her feet. The wood itself looked healthy enough – perhaps its distance above the ground had saved it from the worst effects of the damp – but she remembered how she had already been nearly plunged a couple of times through floorboards that had seemed firm just to look at. She reminded herself sternly to take every care as she climbed.

'Now, you'd better stay behind me, Mr Dogg,' she said. 'If you go running ahead, darting around the way you do, you're bound to come a cropper.'

The dog looked up at her, wanting her to get a move on.

Her hand locked onto the banister, she took a first tentative step, pressing the tread with her foot before letting it take her full weight. In the same check-and-step fashion she moved slowly up a further few treads, the dog still sitting at the foot of the stairs looking at her in evident perplexity, wondering if this were some new game, played according to incomprehensible rules.

'Come on,' she said. 'Come to heel.'

Resignedly Mr Dogg rolled off his haunches onto his feet and clambered up alongside her. She could see he was impatient to go leaping ahead of her, but he sensed enough of her instructions to keep himself back.

'Good boy. Wise old boy.'

She was still terrified of what she was doing, but now the terror was being coloured by excitement at the adventure of it all. The image of the archaeologist investigating the pyramid came back into her mind: that must be a terrifying experience, too, never knowing if a stone door might heave suddenly open and a dingy-shrouded mummy come leaping out at you with murder in its ... no, not in its heart, because they used to cut out the heart and other organs, didn't they, when they were mummifying people. She vaguely remembered having read Howard Carter's book where it told you all about the process of mummification – she'd read it with an entranced, sick fascination a couple of winters ago, wishing the gale coming through the cracks in the windowframe wouldn't make the curtains billow out just *so*, and ...

Crrreak!

She came back to the present in a rush, looking down aghast at the treacherous wooden stair beneath her right foot. She'd been just swinging her weight onto it, but luckily the noise had woken her out of her daydream. Joanna withdrew her foot as if a beast were snapping at it.

There was an odd, hoarse sound in the air, and she realized it was her own breathing. If she broke a leg or anything here it might be days before Mrs Ruggeley or Mudgett thought to come to the Lampeter Wing to look for her. She squatted down beside Mr Dogg and put her arm around his hard-haired shoulders.

'You'd run and fetch help for me, wouldn't you?' she said, more to hear the sound of her voice than anything else.

He slapped her cheek with his tongue.

'I'll take that as a "yes",' she said properly, drawing herself upright again. 'Come on. We'd better see if the tread beyond is OK.'

It was, and they restarted their painstakingly slow ascent.

When they came to the first landing her mood cheered. There was pallid sunlight spilling in through the windows at either end of the short hall, and the air no longer stank so oppressively of damp; instead there was the slightly tart, cleanly tang of old cobwebs and dust. The carpet underfoot was badly faded but still, in most places, whole: it had once showed colourful starbursts of roses or chrysanthemums, she guessed, but now the flowers were pale yellow overcooked cabbages. The walls were clean in the places where they weren't festooned in spider-webs. On a side-table some toppled ornaments gleamed mutedly from beneath layers of dust.

'Nothing a few hours' hard work with mop and brush wouldn't deal with,' she said. 'Eh, Mr Dogg?'

She looked around the little hall and felt herself beginning to grin. She had been putting the best face on things largely in order to keep the dog's spirits up, she told herself, but in fact it was true: over the course of a week or two she could clean this place up and make it her own, a home within a house, somewhere to which she could retreat safely in the knowledge that it was truly hers – *her* territory, to which Mrs Ruggeley and Mudgett might come for visits but not as of right.

She still remembered to test each footstep ahead of herself as she made her way, the dog in tow, down the hall to where the dark well of the stairs rose once more. She found herself humming the opening bars of *Eine Kleine Nachtmusik*, and allowed her voice to open up until she heard echoes from further up the tower joining her in chorus.

The next rise of stairs was of stone, rather than wood. She was surprised, and paused, disconcerted. Then she recalled Mrs Ruggeley telling her long ago that the house, though old, had been built around the remains of a yet older construction. The turret in the northwest wing must belong to the original building. In entering the Lampeter Wing she had, in effect, been stepping a decade and a half into the past; now she was travelling back centuries in time. The thought made her skin tingle and the fine, soft hairs on the backs of her forearms rise.

'Better into the past than the future, though, Mr Dogg,' she said. 'At least we won't find any Morlocks.'

But you might, said a tiny voice inside her, *come across some ghosts.*

She shook her head, silencing the little voice. Ghosts were things confined to the pages of books by M.R. James and Sheridan Le Fanu, books that smelt fustily arcane and which she didn't read when Mrs Ruggeley was around, on the grounds that they would probably be disapproved of. Ghosts and demons and hobgoblins and banshees didn't exist in the real world any more than fairies did: Mrs Ruggeley had always been quite firm on that point, and Joanna believed her ... although yesterday Mrs Ruggeley seemed to be giving credit to the idea of spiritual possession ...

No: the housekeeper had been speaking figuratively.

Setting her chin, Joanna began to climb the stone stairs. Speaking figuratively was a thing grown-ups did a lot: Joanna must learn to do it more often herself. Here there wasn't a banister as such: instead a tubular metal bar, fastened to the wall by circular braces, spiralled up into the darkness ahead of her. The steps were slippery in places, so she clutched the metal determinedly, reaching out with her other hand to grasp the collar of Mr Dogg, who was once more showing signs of wanting to go skittering ahead.

'You've been patient so far,' she admonished him, 'so you can be patient just a little while longer.'

As she came around the curve of the spiral she chanced a look upwards. Grey illumination was infiltrating the gloom. That must be the windows at the top of the tower – the little square windows she had seen so often from outside the house but never really thought about. Their dull, doubtful light seemed to be an awfully long way above her, but presumably it couldn't really be very far.

Wait a moment. There was something she'd just been thinking . . .

Yes. That was it. The turret windows were square, but the entry in her diary had said that the special window – the Far-Enough Window – was round. She didn't remember ever having noticed a round window from the lawn.

Maybe the unknown writer had been wrong about that, she thought. After all, if he or she was a dishonest forger of other people's journals, then it was asking a bit much, was it not, to expect him or her to be punctilious about the facts – assuming the trespasser knew them in the first place.

Confused by her own thoughts, she shrugged and continued upwards.

The turret room, when she came into it, was another pleasant surprise. Although there was the usual cloak of dust everywhere, the chamber was otherwise empty, and warmer than she'd expected it to be. 'Perhaps,' she said to Mr Dogg, who was leaping around, puffing up clouds of dust that made both of them sneeze, 'perhaps the top of the tower is too far from the ground to feel the cold.'

She checked the windows at once. They were filthy – mainly on the outside, as she discovered when she tried to wipe a pane clean with her bunched pullover – and let in the sunlight only after a struggle. Significantly, though, they were rectangular, just as she had recalled.

Now that she and Mr Dogg had arrived here and discovered that the attic was nothing at all the way the false diarist had described it, she was at a loss what to do. It was only half past ten, far too early for dignity to allow her to reappear in the main part of the house, and the turret chamber was hardly packed with diversions. She gave the windowpane another rub with her pullover, but saw she was making very little impression on the grime. On the other hand, she thought, with a bit of luck she might be able to get one of the windows to actually *open* . . .

The first catch she tried was so badly rusted that it came away immediately in her hands, but the next was made of sterner stuff and, after much groaning, slowly turned. She shoved at the window and it swung outwards on its hinges.

The slushy ground seemed a very long way away. Joanna looked down at it across a bridge of steeply sloping grey-tiled roof and a clogged gutter. Turning her gaze outwards, she could see the estate wall and the road beyond it – so many cars, and all in different colours! They were, most of them, also a different shape from the square black vehicle in which Mrs Ruggeley and Mudgett plied to and from the village or wherever else they went in the outside world. On the other side of the road was a field with some big brown animals she thought for a moment must be horses, like Rapscallion, but

THE FAR-ENOUGH WINDOW

then realized were cows. Somehow she'd always thought from the pictures she'd seen that cows were about the same size as an extra-big Mr Dogg, but now she could see that they were positively huge – as tall as Rapscallion and ever so much fatter. Further away than the field with the cows in it was a different field where the sods of grass had been cut away to show the grey-brown earth beneath. In the middle of this field was a tall metal structure, like a giant spider on four complicated stilts, with wires – telephone wires, she swiftly concluded – leading to others like it. And further away yet there was a hillside, with some grey and brick-red houses nestling against it and a thin line of road snaking up it. Fields crawled over much of the hillside, thickets and copses over the rest. Glinting reflected light told her there was quite a lot of traffic on this distant road as well.

She squinted upwards to where a pale sun hung in the sky, a hem of cloud swathing its lower half.

The world was a far bigger place than she had ever expected, and she knew what she was seeing was only the tiniest part of it.

There was a squeak from overhead. Mr Dogg whined, and rubbed himself against her legs, his tail still. He was looking upwards intently.

Joanna froze, then slowly turned her head.

There was no one else in the room, no movement except the dust-motes pirouetting in the shafts of feeble sunlight.

But there had been a sound – a slight, furtive sound. It hadn't been her imagination. And it had come from somewhere above her.

'A weathervane,' she said to Mr Dogg. 'Just a weathervane, blowing in the wind.'

She was pretty certain she was lying, though. She'd have seen any weathervane atop the tower if there'd been one.

The mongrel was still staring towards the ceiling and, unhappily, she let her gaze follow his.

The ceiling had once been painted in some dark colour, and at first she couldn't distinguish the darker rectangle in its centre. Then she saw it.

'A trapdoor, Mr Dogg. It's only a trapdoor.'

She tried at first not to let herself think that trapdoors didn't squeak. The trapdoor must lead to a further attic, one she hadn't suspected existed – perhaps the counterfeiting diarist had been correct after all? Yes, and the account had mentioned a window . . .

'There's a window up there,' she told the dog. 'It must be open – that's what it'll be. Rusty window-hinges squeaking as the wind rocks them.'

Mr Dogg didn't relax his stance. Neither, she noticed, did she.

'There can't be anyone up there. No one's been in this room for years – you can tell by the dust – so how could – ? Oh, let me see: the window's open, all right, and pigeons or bats have made their nests there. How would you like a pet pigeon or a pet bat to come and live with us and share your bowl, Mr Dogg?'

The mongrel didn't seem reassured.

'Bats are like mice, only with bigger ears, and they fly,' she explained. 'Pigeons are . . . well, you know what pigeons are because you've chased them often enough. And they're good to eat, as well. If there are pigeons in the loft we'll be able to come here and get one every time we feel like pigeon pie for supper. Won't that be a fine thing, Mr Dogg?'

THE FAR-ENOUGH WINDOW

Still Mr Dogg didn't ease. Somewhere in his ancestry there might be a trace of gundog.

It isn't just pigeons and bats that live in attics, Joanna, said that infuriating little voice inside her head. *Sleeping Beauty climbed up into an attic and found the evil Witch with her spinning-wheel and spindle . . .*

She was getting up there, if she could. Witches and suchlike belonged in the same place as ghoulies and ghosties and long-leggety beasties: in books or videos, or in the cluttered museum of the imagination. She was going to prove that to herself – she was going to try to find a way of reaching the attic to demonstrate beyond all reasonable doubt that there was an entirely rational explanation for that squeak they'd both heard . . . and the new overhead noise that made them both start.

But reaching the loft might be something easier said than done. If she stood right up on tiptoe she could just touch the ceiling, but she certainly wouldn't be able to open the trapdoor, much less to pull herself through the opening. Her heart sank at the thought of going all the way back down the treacherous stone steps to find a chair, then bringing it up here again.

She took the necessary few paces to reach the middle of the room, directly under the trap. Mr Dogg tappingly accompanied her, his eyes never shifting from the ceiling.

Close up, she could see there was a small brass ring, blackened by age into near-invisibility, hanging from one edge of the trapdoor.

'Ah,' she said. 'I think it's supposed to open downward – '

Joanna tugged the ring, and the trapdoor seemed to jounce in its frame. She pulled harder, and this time she both felt and heard pulleys and counterweights reluctantly dragging themselves into action.

'Stand back, Mr Dogg!' she cried, retreating herself as she gave the ring one last mighty lug.

With a scraping and a clattering, what she'd assumed to be a trapdoor suddenly swung downwards, revealing a complex of wooden and aluminium spars and struts. When the whole construction had slumped down by an angle of about forty-five degrees it seemed to take on a life of its own, for suddenly there were all sorts of extra movements going on inside the network of beams. With a hideous, painful screech, parts of the device began to slide towards Joanna and Mr Dogg, so that they both yelped, stepping quickly backwards.

Dust and unidentifiable scraps of something flowered in the air, so that Joanna put a hand up to shield her eyes. The floor shook as the heavy weight of the apparatus impacted on it, and she felt Mr Dogg jerk his shoulder against her knee.

She lowered her hand cautiously.

A flight of wooden stairs – more like a ladder, but with a handrail – was in front of her. Though she knew that all those intricate shapes must somehow collapse into each other, ready to be drawn out again at a moment's notice, still it felt as if the staircase had been brought into existence out of nowhere, by magic. What was creepiest of all was that the treads themselves, unlike anything else she and Mr Dogg had encountered since venturing into the Lampeter Wing, were free of dust: the aluminium was pitted by corrosion, but the woodwork glowed a varnished yellow.

The trap in the ceiling was now a broken rectangle of bright grey light. Joanna guessed the topmost loft must have a cupola.

THE FAR-ENOUGH WINDOW

She braced her shoulders, and looked down at Mr Dogg, who was quivering – though whether with fear or excitement she couldn't tell.

'This is it, my trusty friend,' she said. 'Time to go and find out if it's bats or pigeons or . . . whatever it might be.'

After a moment's hesitation she began to scale the stairway. If she went up with the same slow, plodding caution with which she'd ascended the other stairs in the tower she thought there was a good chance her nerve would break before she reached the top, so she climbed briskly, her brogues going click-click-click on the wood. Mr Dogg reared up, putting his forepaws on the third step, clearly unable to work out how he could follow her. He began to whine, but she shushed him absent-mindedly – because now she was entering the attic.

At once she knew this was exactly the place the unknown diarist had described. There were those exact same heaps of historical junk – dating from long before the Lampeter Wing had been closed off: she could see that at a glance. She wasn't terribly confident of her ability to date styles and fashions, but the clothes draped over the edges of the ancient leather trunks looked as if they must date from some time before the Second World War. Propped in a corner was what looked like an old walking-stick that had lost its handle. A lampshade slumped against the wall like a giantess's discarded summer bonnet. And there, sure enough, was a filthy old grey straw sun-hat with a broken feather in its band.

Despite the brightness of the air up here, the attic had only one small window.

Circular. Leaded in the form of an upright cross. The thick glass distorted with age to form a lens at the bottom.

The window that the sham diarist had called the Far-Enough Window.

The window that made things happen.

As the straw hat disintegrated in her hand, Mr Dogg set up a new whining beneath her. She came back to the rectangular hole in the floor and looked down at him. He was staring upwards anxiously, his ears flat back against his skull; clearly he felt his duty was beside her, but the steps presented an impassable barrier.

'I'll be down in a moment, Mr Dogg. I just want to ... look around for a while. Wait for me. I'm all right.'

He still looked worried, but he dropped back obediently to sit at the foot of the ladder, his tail out like a long comma on the floor behind him, his brown-and-white face still upturned, his soft eyes with their yellow whites pleading with her not to tarry. His right paw lifted a few inches off the floor as if he were preparing to beg for a tidbit.

'I'll be down in a moment,' she repeated once she was sure he was settled. Then she turned away to examine the remains of the straw hat as if they might contain some vital piece of information that would explain all this.

Perhaps the secret lay with the thing that was 'most important than that' – the Far-Enough Window.

She raised her eyes and stared at it. From here it seemed innocent enough – just an ancient assemblage of gravity-distorted glass and brittling lead. Through it she could see the top of the distant hillside that rose behind the village. The lower part of the image was split into strange curving shapes that were both natural and unnatural. She moved her head from side to side, and the shapes ripplingly transmuted in response. It was an arresting effect, but there was nothing especially strange about it. Nothing abnormal. Nothing mystical. Nothing supernatural. Just elementary physics at work in the real world.

She crept closer to the window and reached out to touch it with the tips of her fingers. The glass was cold and hard, as one would have expected it to be. Reassuringly commonplace.

Emboldened, Joanna stood right up beside the window, looking through it at something very much like the scene she had observed from the chamber downstairs where Mr Dogg waited. When she tried to look downwards at the house's grounds the optical aberration of the bulging glass took over, making homely shapes seem alien – much as the thick fall of snow had yesterday transformed the car and the stables. She wished Mrs Ruggeley would come out of the house for some reason and be distorted like a character in a cartoon movie. Joanna grinned as she visualized the components of the housekeeper's body all dancing to a different tune.

But she couldn't stay here any longer. She'd promised Mr Dogg that she'd be only a moment and, although the mongrel had no sense of time except when feeding was involved, a promise was a promise. She gave the contorted, slush-covered lawns a final look and started to turn away, promising herself she'd come back here another day – preferably tomorrow – preferably *many* other days . . .

There was a breath on her neck. She dropped the torch.

'You can stay as long as you like,' a light voice said. 'Mr Dogg doesn't mind. I've spoken with him.'

Three

Goodfellow

Night and silence: who is here?
— William Shakespeare, *A Midsummer Night's Dream*, c1594/5

The world swung in a sudden loop, and she felt herself sway.

'Don't be frightened,' said the voice urgently. A hand caught her by the waist. 'There's nothing to be frightened of.'

'I . . . I . . .'

' "Aye-aye" is what the sailors say – or is it the little lemurs? But it's certainly not what a girl – what a young woman should be saying. She should be saying "Hello" and "How are you?" and "What is your name?"'

'But . . .'

'Come over here and sit down on this nice stout trunk that's been to Baltimore and back, and many other places too if the labels don't lie. Wait 'til the air stops tasting like cold treacle and you can see a bit more clearly, then we can start our conversation all over again as if it had never begun, only this time on a more equable footing.'

'You surprised me,' she said crossly, following the gentle pressure at her waist and flopping down on the battered leather trunk. Despite her giddiness, she turned her head to try to see the stranger, but the patch of darkness she'd thought was him proved to be one of the shadows in the far corner of the room.

'You can't see me until I've told you my name,' said the voice. 'Can't be helped: it's one of the rules. And I'm sorry I startled you. I had to come all of a sudden because it's hard to find the other side of the Far-Enough Window, which hides where it wishes to, and because you didn't give me proper warning exactly when you were going to look through it again, and I wouldn't have come at all if *you* hadn't.'

'I don't know . . . I don't know what you're talking about.' Joanna was suddenly mortified to discover she was on the verge of bursting into tears.

'But the day before yesterday – '

'The day before yesterday I wasn't here,' she said firmly, gathering her resources. 'Somebody else might have been here pretending to be me, because the same person pretended to be me when they were writing in my diary. But it wasn't me. I was doing something else entirely.'

Her head was beginning to clear now, and with the dizziness the threat of tears was receding.

'You should let me finish my sentences,' said the voice, taking on a tinge of severity. 'What I was about to say was that your ghost was here the day before yesterday – except then, while you were speaking so waspish just now, I remembered that, silly me, of course you knew nothing about that.'

'My *ghost*? But I'm not dead!' She began to giggle. Maybe

she'd had a faint spell, standing there by the window, and was imagining this voice. It certainly seemed to talk the sort of nonsense she liked to make up for herself.

'I can't be held to blame for your ignorance. Everyone has at least one ghost, whether they're still living or have died – or haven't yet been born, for that matter. I think it's just stubbornness on the part of you humans – the Comelatelies are just as bad, but in a different way – that you refuse to recognize any ghosts until after people have died, and even then you do your best to ignore them most of the time. And the worst of your madness is that you unequivocally, positively, definitively decline to recognize your own ghosts, or listen to any of the things they try to tell you. Even Mr Dogg, who you think is so stupid, knows his own ghost: you've seen him talk to it, though you'd rather pretend he's dreaming of chasing rabbits or he's having one of his funny, doggy turns.'

'You're talking nonsense,' said Joanna, still giggling. She put on her best Mrs Ruggeley voice: 'Absolute tosh, my dear girl, absolute tosh. Now come and have a biscuit.'

'*Aren't* you going to ask me my name?' said the voice wistfully. She swivelled abruptly in an attempt to see the speaker, but once more all she discovered was a pattern of shadows. 'We've already been introduced, you know, somewhere else, though of course you remember nothing of that. But be assured: it's not embarrassingly forward of you now to ask my name. And it's impossible for us to hold a rational conversation when you can't see me.'

'I'm not certain it's possible for us to hold a rational conversation at all,' said Joanna. 'I think you're just a figment of my imagination – something I've half-remembered out of a book by Lewis Carroll. Or even Edward Lear. And you talk so strangely, and such rubbish.'

'Whether or not I'm a figment of your imagination is absolutely beside the point – it wouldn't make me any the less real even if I were, which I doubt. And if you think that *I'm* the one who's talking rubbish – why, you ought to listen to yourself for a change. Now: ask me my name, or I'll have to be off about my business.'

'All right,' said Joanna, sitting alertly on the edge of the trunk. 'Tell me your name, Mr Voice, and let me see what you're really like.'

'Which of my names would you like to hear?'

She groaned histrionically. Her imagination was playing silly bug– Oops, *there* was an expression Mrs Ruggeley had told her she was never supposed even to *think*, but the sense of it was true.

'Whichever name you think I'd like you best by,' she said wearily.

'Oh, such a choice, such a choice,' said the voice fussily, 'and all of them good ones. Let me think, let me think – yes, one of the Robins! Robin's such a nice name – I can tell that you like it. Lots of your favourites are called Robin: Robin Hood, Robin Redbreast, Robin Oig McCombich, Batman's Robin, Robin of the Green, Cock Robin . . .'

'Robin Goodfellow,' said Joanna automatically. 'Puck. Of Pook's Hill. *A Midsummer Night's Dream.*'

The voice was silent.

She looked around the attic. She seemed to be entirely alone. The presence – whatever it had been that was speaking to her – was gone. Her imagination had suddenly run out of invention.

THE FAR-ENOUGH WINDOW

Then the voice spoke again, right against her ear.

'It *wasn't* supposed to be a guessing game,' it hissed. 'Now you've spoiled the nice surprise.'

She turned in that direction, and this time there was no abrupt dissolution of a half-seen shape into a contrivance of shadows.

At first she thought the figure standing before her was a normal young – no, older than young – man, but then she saw that his shoulders were no further from the ground than Mr Dogg's. He was dressed in tight-fitting hose and a jerkin of some felt-like material, coloured half the green that leaves are in the summer and half the yellow some of them become in the autumn. He wore a hat or a cap made of the same cloth as his jerkin, its brim extended out into a peak in front of him. To the front of his cap was pinned a peacock's feather, almost as long as he was tall and curving backward over his shoulder. The expression on his thin, sharp-cornered face was not unfriendly, but he seemed a little peeved.

'You *are* Robin Goodfellow,' she said incredulously.

'None other,' said the little man, giving her a half-bow. 'I would say "in the flesh" but that's a turn of speech that's open to misinterpretation.'

'Puck,' she said. 'You're the most vivid daydream I've ever had, and I've had a few, I can tell – '

He made an irritated gesture with his hand. 'If you and I are to be friends, young Joanna, we must get rid of this silly fiction that I'm nothing but a product of your overheated imagination. I'm as real as A, B, C. I'm as real as your toes at the other end of the bath, or the extra spoonful of sugar you sometimes put in your tea when you think no one's looking. I'm as real as the air you breathe or as your own two hands.

I'm as real as – Oh, there are more things I'm as real as than there are stars in the sky, and I don't propose to stand here counting them off for an empty-headed girl. Here – take my hand and feel how real I am.'

He reached out and Joanna obediently took his hand. It was cooler than her own, though not cold, and the skin felt drier and less flexible than hers or Mrs Ruggeley's or Mudgett's. It felt a little like textured parchment, and she fleetingly wondered if it smelt the same.

'*Now* are you convinced?' said Robin Goodfellow.

'I have a very powerful imag– ' she began slowly – then, seeing his face cloud, added quickly: 'No, I was only teasing. Of course I believe you're who you say you are. It's just that I've never met a sprite before. You shouldn't have expected me to take on board your existence just as easily as that.'

Am I going crazy? she thought, although the possibility didn't seem terribly worrying. *All the way up to this attic I was telling myself ghosties and bogles and goblins didn't exist, and now here I am thinking I'm talking to a hobgoblin . . . and if I believe* that *then I have to believe in ghosts as well, and . . .*

'Some humans refuse to accept us as real even after they've met us a hundred times,' conceded Robin Goodfellow. 'So I suppose you're doing better than many.'

Something was troubling Joanna.

'A little while ago,' she said, 'you called me by my name. Yet I haven't told it to you. How did you know?'

'Because your ghost . . .' Robin began. He shrugged.

'Because my ghost told you – the day before yesterday,' she said flatly. It was easier to say than she'd expected it to be. 'And what was my ghost doing up here, then?'

'It was coming to look through the Far-Enough Window,

of course.'

'Yes, but – '

'To make sure it would be safe for you to do the same today. Are you always so slow to catch on, Joanna?'

'There's no need to be rude. Just because a person doesn't know something doesn't mean they're stupid.' She let go of his hand – she hadn't realized she'd been holding it all this time, as if he and she had known each other for years – and folded her two on her knee.

He laughed, and again he gave that little shrug which seemed capable of expressing so much.

'I am humbled,' he said.

'You could be quite a nice person, you know,' she said carefully, 'if you didn't spend all your time mocking people who see things . . . differently from the way you do.'

'I see their failings too clearly,' he admitted.

'I would,' said Joanna, 'have no particular aversion to having you as my friend – that is, if you would wish to be.' *Oh, please,* she was thinking.

Robin Goodfellow stood up straight. The effect was oddly imposing, even though he was hardly taller than her knee. 'I would be proud,' he said, 'and honoured. That, after all, is what I came here for – that and the other thing.'

'What other thing?'

'Nothing we need trouble ourselves about just now. So, tell me – will you or won't you?'

'Will I or won't I what?'

'Accept my friendship in return.'

'Oh – of *course* I will!'

Before she could think more sensibly of it she'd picked him up and pulled him to her, hugging him the way she hugged Mrs Ruggeley. Mrs Ruggeley was her friend, of course, and so was Mudgett in his uncommunicative way, but this was the first time she could recall ever having *made* a friend.

Robin Goodfellow struggled briefly in her grip, and then put his own small arms around her neck.

Now the tears of confusion, which had threatened earlier, came – but as tears of happiness. She found herself sobbing into his felt-covered shoulder, wondering if her nose was running and hoping it wasn't.

When she thought she could keep her voice under control she said: 'And can I come here any time I want to see you?'

His voice in reply sounded muffled, and she realized her grip was forcing him to talk directly into the side of her neck. She half-released him, and he repeated what he'd said.

'You don't have to come all the way up here to the Far-Enough Window to see me – not now, not now we've met each other and introduced ourselves properly again. Now you'll be able to come with me, of course. Besides, now I can be anywhere in your world that you'd like me to be.'

She set him down carefully on the floor. 'You call this *my* world,' she said. 'Where is yours?'

'All around us,' he said expansively, a broad smile spreading across his narrow face. He threw his arms wide. 'Everywhere.'

She laughed. 'Big talk, little friend,' she said. 'But I can't see it anywhere. All I can see is a musty attic filled with decaying rubbish, and you and me in the middle of it.'

'That's because you can't see far enough,' he said swiftly.

' "Far enough"?'

THE FAR-ENOUGH WINDOW

'If you could see far enough you could see all the bits of the world that are normally invisible to you. Just like all the rest of you humans – almost all – you can see only the piece of it that conforms to your own sensibilities. You're like people at a party on board a ship who decide it would be nice to go out for a stroll in the park. You don't know the wild ocean's there, brightly dark under the scimitar moon – so when you go out from the noise of the party what you discover all around you is the park. The ocean's hidden itself, because it knows you didn't want it to be there.'

'But I could see it if I stayed at the party and looked out through a porthole.'

'What porthole? The portholes have all been curtained over by the stewards. Oh, it's a whale of a party you're having, I can tell you, fine Joanna lady – if it weren't that I loved you so dear I'd wish I were there now rather than talking to you in this loft.'

Joanna, suddenly thoughtful, was hardly listening to this last. 'Is that,' she said, pointing along the attic, 'is *that* a porthole? You call it the Far-Enough Window – is it a porthole for seeing . . . far enough?'

He looked up at her, a chuckle beginning to twist the corners of his mouth, and she realized that he'd all along been guiding her conversation to this. 'Surely it'd be a fool who tried to pull the wool over your clear blue eyes, my lovely lady.'

She put her hands on her knees and leaned forward stiffly, peering at the bright crossed circle of the window. 'When I looked through it,' she said, 'I saw the real world – *our* world, I mean. The glass at the bottom made some of the shapes look funny, but it was still the world. I wasn't peeping into a different one.'

'That's because you weren't looking far enough,' said Robin Goodfellow. 'You were seeing quite a long way for a human – '

'A *mere* human,' she said sarcastically. 'Don't forget that.'

' – for a *mere* human, but that was still no distance to speak of, not really. You're like someone who's been given a telescope and used it to stare, not at the stars, but at the lights in the village over there – and you say, "Who wants to see the lights of the village bigger? They're boring enough the size they normally are. This telescope's a useless thing. Pfaugh! Get it away from me!" '

His face was filled with such an intense look of theatrical disgust as he mimed the rejection that she found herself giggling again.

'The distance you looked through the Far-Enough Window,' he said, 'Joanna, my lass, was hardly further than the end of your snub little nose.'

'I didn't know I was trying to look far,' she said. The lines from the Robert Frost poem came to her. 'I was just looking,' she murmured. 'I didn't know it was possible to see out far and in deep.'

'It's always possible,' snapped Robin Goodfellow. 'It's always possible to see further out – and in – than you can.' The disgust on his face now wasn't for histrionic effect. 'I don't blame *you*, my fair one – it's the way they've taught you. "Don't ask for too much from life" – that's the kind of thing you humans say. I've heard it a thousand times a thousand times over. And it's rubbish, lass, rubbish: life is begging to give you more than you could ever dream of, and then a bit more. But you're stopped from realizing it by the folk around you and because everyone's been saying to you since you squirted squalling from your mother's womb that you "mustn't expect too much, dear girl, because you'll only be disappointed when you don't get it".'

The perfect mimicry of Mrs Ruggeley's tones made a coldness in Joanna's heart. The housekeeper was her old friend and Robin Goodfellow was her new one, and the new friend was driving a wedge between her and the old one. What hurt Joanna all the more – hurt her so sharply that it was all she could do to keep herself sitting erect and not doubled over – was that she knew Robin Goodfellow was right. Not that Mrs Ruggeley was a false friend who had lied to her: it was out of love, out of a generosity that made her want to share her discovered wisdom, that the housekeeper had misled her so cruelly. The bars of love that formed the cage imprisoning Joanna had not all been forged by her father: Mrs Ruggeley, too, had had a part in their making.

There were tears in her eyes again – tears of pain, tears of anger, tears of nostalgia for the distant past that had ended only a few seconds ago – but at the same time she felt she could see much more clearly than before.

'How far,' she said, 'would I have to be able to see?'

'Far *enough*,' he whispered. 'Haven't you been listening?' He slipped his hand into hers. 'With those sweet eyes of yours, you should be able to see as far as ever you want to.'

At first Joanna thought Mr Dogg was dead. He lay sprawled out on the dusty floor, his eyes closed and his toothy mouth open, his flanks motionless. But as she ran her fingers through the coarse hairs of his side she could feel that his flesh was warm.

'He's all right,' said Robin Goodfellow, materializing beside her. 'Haven't you been noticing that the clouds are not moving, either?' He pointed out through the murk of one of the turret chamber's tall rectangular windows. 'That tail of cloud that looks like a grandfather's chin is still halfway across the disc of the sun, just as it was an hour ago, when you first came up here.'

Joanna was unsurprised. Stopping time for a while was something she'd often dreamed of being able to do – and, even more so, speeding up time – so it seemed only natural that Robin Goodfellow should number it among his tricks.

'How long can you do this for?' she said.

'Forever and a day,' he said. 'What else would you expect me to reply, gracious lady?' He leaned towards her confidentially. 'To tell you the truth, Joanna,' he whispered, 'that extra day's a real killer in practice, but I add it on just so as not to disappoint folk, and hope I'll never have to actually do it.'

Laughing, she aimed a mock blow at him, and he hopped nimbly away.

'But I want Mr Dogg to be able to . . . see far enough as well,' she said.

Robin Goodfellow looked at her doubtfully. 'Forgive my boyish impertinence,' he said, 'but I don't think you yet quite understand what seeing far enough actually entails. It'll be all right for you, for am I not your liege-servant, sworn to protect you from harm? But the hound already knows the nature of the Farness, so I cannot be liege to him. If he's in the Farness with us, he is his own master, there of his own accord.'

'You talk as if we were actually going there,' said Joanna,

THE FAR-ENOUGH WINDOW

'not just seeing it through the window.'

Robin Goodfellow looked puzzled for an instant; then his face cleared. 'It's as I thought,' he muttered to himself. He gazed into her eyes and said: 'That's what I meant when I said you didn't know what this entailed, Joanna.

'Seeing? Going? What's the difference?'

Four

Far Enough

If you see me with my face all black, don't be frightened. If you see me flapping wings like a bat's, as big as the whole sky, don't be frightened.... Nay, Diamond, if I change into a serpent or a tiger, you must not let go your hold of me, for my hand will never change in yours if you keep a good hold. If you keep a hold, you will know who I am all the time...

— George MacDonald, *At the Back of the North Wind*, 1870

In the end Joanna threw the revived Mr Dogg over her shoulder in a fireman's lift and struggled up the ladder to the loft with him, Robin Goodfellow prancing and dancing around her shouting words of encouragement and helpful instruction, which she ignored. The mongrel seemed to know exactly what she was trying to do, because he made himself as floppy and cooperative as possible, so that all she had to struggle against was his weight and the crampedness of the aperture in the ceiling. She concluded that Robin must have had another silent word with Mr Dogg, explaining everything.

'Well,' she said at last, standing on the attic floor, puffing her cheeks from the exertion, looking down at a tail-wagging Mr Dogg, 'I promised you a very big adventure when we set out, and, as you can see, Mr Dogg, I'm keeping my promise.'

Was there understanding behind those liquid canine eyes? At any other time she'd have ticked herself off for imagining things, for projecting her own wishes onto the animal, but at this moment she wasn't so sure. She patted him on the head, then wondered if this wasn't a rather patronizing gesture towards someone who had all his life seen more of the world than she; patronizing or not, it made his tail beat faster.

Robin Goodfellow had perched himself on her shoulder – she hadn't noticed him arrive. Squinting sideways at him, she half-believed she could see little wings whirring at his back.

'Come to the window,' he said. 'Carry me to the Far-Enough Window, my fine upright wench.'

'I'm not a horse,' she grumbled.

He took her literally. 'I know that,' he said. 'D'you think I'm stupid?'

'Forget it,' she said, crossing to the window. The litter of clothes and bits of broken furniture around her didn't seem like junk any more: it was a landscape.

'Kneel down,' said Robin Goodfellow. 'You're too tall.'

She obeyed, and found Mr Dogg's shoulders on a level with her own, jostling her for space. He had put his paws up on the lower edge of the window's circular frame.

'Give over,' she said crossly.

'Fair shares,' agreed Robin Goodfellow, close by her ear. 'There's plenty of room for both of you.

'Now,' he added once they'd settled down, 'now is the

time for both of you to start looking into the Farness. Both of you together can each look further than one alone, as I'm sure must be obvious. So don't go running one ahead of the other, making a race out of it. Together you can see ... you can see ... can see ... see ...'

What Joanna saw was the grubby frame of the Far-Enough Window, and the smooth, sticky-looking belly of the glass, and the place where the bulge of the flowing glass had pushed out the soft lead, so that the edges of the metal strip were beginning to flake. Then she saw beyond the glass's surface to where tiny bubbles and flaws caught the sunlight and brightened it until they made an unknown constellation flung against a sky of twisted, heavy curves. She flicked her eyes one way, then back again, and the curves moved and breathed.

And still she knew the reason for everything she saw. The glass and the lead were aged, and the flaws had been there from the first. Those anonymous masses in the backdrop were the drive and the herbaceous borders, seen through a lens. It all made for a pretty effect, one that she could stare at perhaps for hours and maybe paint in watercolours afterwards, but ...

The heavy stink of Mr Dogg's breath near her face made her nose wrinkle, but it was also a reassurance. His excited breathing made her realize how much she cared for him, and his loyalty. As if he'd heard her thinking, he casually slurped her cheek with his tongue.

Robin Goodfellow seemed to have gone. Perhaps this was all it was. Pretty shapes and patterns. Like some kind of home-grown Zen teaching: concentrate on the everyday until it becomes marvellous. Parlour-trick mysticism ...

And then, slowly at first but with rapidly increasing speed, she began to see far enough ...

And ...

... she saw on the surface of the glass, undistorted despite its outward curl, her own face. The eyes were the first thing to notice: pale blue-green, like an early-spring sky when the rain has come and gone, and clear, so that you were aware of the distance behind them. The nose – *her* nose – was snub but not wide: tiny; smaller than her thumb's end. Her eyebrows, slightly unkempt, were hardly darker than her hair, which in this light was the colour of acacia honey. Little rusty-coloured freckles ran in an irregular band across the line of her eyes, from the top of one cheek to the top of the other. Her upper lip, perched above the bow of her not-broad mouth, was a little too long. The sides of her face curved in towards the chin, as if seeking to make it end in a point, but then lost courage and instead made a slightly cloven pad. All of the features were in low relief, as if her face were a mask; yet a motile mask: her lips parted of their own accord and her pointy white teeth smiled.

But she immediately saw beyond the mask and ...

And ...

... where are you all where are you I'm lost and I need a home

THE FAR-ENOUGH WINDOW

and . . .

. . . wind rushing at me into me tugging my hair back my ears back, pressing against my eyes blinding me yet enabling me to see and I don't know if I want to see how far *there is, how* far *is too* far*. . .*

. . . forever and a day ahead of me stretching in a corridor with marbled walls until the lines disappear and it's the place where the lines disappear which is where I'm going . . .

. . . I am a person of many colours but they are leaching out of me one by one . . .

. . . being drawn into the corridor that is ever-narrower . . .

. . . my eyes were green-blue but all I can see of them now is pale grey like thumbed newspaper . . .

. . . I cannot tighten my fingers into a grip, I cannot tighten my fingers into a grip, I CANNOT TIGHTEN MY FINGERS INTO A GRIP . . .

. . . I am a person of many colours but they are leaching out of me one by one until I am no colour at all . . .

. . . no colour at all in this *small section of the total world . . .*

'Hello,' said Joanna to a rainbow.

It did not reply, which she thought was extremely rude of it until she remembered how much older it was than her.

She was the iridescent colours on the surface of an oily puddle, coming together to make an elfin-sized self of herself that heaved up out of the muddy water and put its hands on its hips to watch how the world might choose to entertain it.

. . . the flames of the bonfire lick higher and higher as if they want to devour the sky's darkness . . .

. . . and I watch it and I watch it until all changes and I'm no longer a watcher but one of the sparks that climbs and climbs and climbs . . .

. . . no I'm grander than that so I do something much more pretentious dammit than merely climb . . .

. . . I aspire . . .

I once had all the colours of the rainbow in me, but now I have none . . .

She'd once seen a movie – a very old, black-and-white movie – where the camera had been strapped to the front of the engine pulling the London-to-Brighton train. The frames had been sped up – or, more likely, the camera had been slowed down and then the frames shown at normal speed – so that the whole journey, as she'd watched the movie, had seemed to take no more than a few minutes, the wooden sleepers firmly present below and ahead of her yet blurred into invisibility, the signal-boxes and rail-side dwellings and the trees to either side of her whipping past . . .

The few minutes had seemed to last for a year and a half, and all of the time she had *known* she was falling into the flickering screen in front of her: falling in one long, thin, drawn-out scream.

That was the way she felt now.

THE FAR-ENOUGH WINDOW

... I am Joanna I am Joanna I am Joanna I am Joanna I am Joanna I am Joanna I am Joanna I am Joanna I am Joanna I am Joanna I am Joanna I am Joann ...

... I have no name I have no name I have no name I have no name I have no name I have no name I have no name I have no name I have no name I have no name I have no name I have no name ...

... I am Joanna I am Joanna I am Joanna I am Joanna I am Joanna I am Joanna I am Joanna I am Joanna I am Joanna I am Joanna I am Joanna I am Joanna I am Joanna ...

I am *me* ...

I once had none of the colours of the rainbow in me, but now I have them all ...

I am me ...

At the end of the movie, the train had slowed and come to a stop. She felt, she thought, as someone being tortured must feel when the agony has become too great to be sensed any longer: she had entered a painless, timeless, totally tranquil zone.

'Hello there,' said Robin Goodfellow.

He felt me arrive, you know, and he welcomed me. He knew who I was, and he realized how much my essence needed protection from the World outside. It was at his suggestion that we began to construct the seven ReLMS. Only then . . . only then, as we worked, he somehow came to be excluded from them, so that for a long time he's been locked out of Starveling, not knowing how to get in, while me, I've been alone inside Starveling, not knowing how to open up its portals to let him in. I could go outside to join him, I suppose, but then what would happen if neither of us could work out how to open the gates?

Blue. Red. Yellow. Green. Black.
    Crude shapes. Sharp edges.
    No shadows.
    A child's painting of reality.
    Poster colours.
    Bold.
    Straight from the jar.
    A world in slabs of brightness and darkness.

Press your hand down flat on the keys of your electronic keyboard and the cacophony filling the music-room is the colour of the newborn world.

'Can you hear me?' said Robin Goodfellow. 'Are you all right?'

THE FAR-ENOUGH WINDOW

. . . my face is already clean so why do you keep scrubbing it with all these swirling lights?

'I think she's fainted,' said Robin Goodfellow. 'A lot of people do that, the first time they see far enough into the Farness to come here.'

'I saw her eyes flutter,' growled Mr Dogg. 'She's coming round.'

He licked her nose to encourage her back to consciousness, and she lifted an arm blindly to shove him off.

'I told you,' he said.

She heard their voices as if she were alone in the video room and had turned the volume up as high as it would go: she was worried that Mrs Ruggeley might come and hammer on the door, demanding that she 'cut that racket out, do you hear me?' She felt as if she were at the exact acoustic centre of a vast auditorium, seats stretching emptily away from her in every direction as far as she could see. Two mad actors had invaded the stage and were bellowing at her, each new word of theirs superimposed upon the echoes of their last word.

Yet at the same time she could look down on herself lying on a bank of grey grass, spread backwards with her arms and her legs outflung – as if someone had captured her while she was falling endlessly through the air and turned her over and placed her on her back here; her hair was windspread out behind her. Robin Goodfellow was standing at her shoulders, looking down at her anxiously; she could see the expression on his face even though all she could see was the back of his head, with his cap clinging to it. Mr Dogg was standing by her waist, obviously less concerned; his tail was motionless, but aloft. She was wearing her blue-and-brown-and-white-checked gingham dress, which was only right and proper. Her pullover had been lost somewhere along the way. One of her white socks had slid down from her knee to make a grungy crumple around her ankle.

She opened her eyes, and was at once back in her own body.

'You mean,' she said to Robin Goodfellow's upside-down face, 'that *seeing* far enough is the same as *going* far enough?'

He didn't reply.

Her head still felt as if someone else had been shaking it a little too hard, but she pushed herself up onto her elbows and looked around. Mr Dogg put his forepaws heavily on her stomach and leaned forward to nuzzle her chin.

'Thanks,' she said absently, 'I'm sure.'

For a few seconds she didn't notice the most important feature of the place she found herself in.

The grass on which she lay was close-cropped, and there were small black raisin-like droppings clustered here and there. The ground was contoured, its mounding recalling the shapes of her flattened tummy and the upward tilt of her pelvic bones. Beyond the area in which she lay, past the weirdly foreshortened shape of the attentive Mr Dogg, she could see brambly bushes leaning inwards towards the edges of the little clearing, as if they regarded it as their own territory and were waiting until a moment when no one was looking so that they could clandestinely recapture it. Behind the bushes she could see the boles of coniferous trees, and looking upwards she could see their crests zigzagging sharply against the sky. The air was full of small whizzing sounds, as if summer insects were moving too quickly for her to see them.

The sky was grey, but not menacingly so. The sun was a disc of lighter grey – almost white – set crisply in it.

That was when she noticed what was wrong.

Everything was grey.

No, not quite everything. Mr Dogg's head (and since when had *he* learnt to talk?) was still the same uneasy combination of golden-brown and frosted black and tawny white that it had always been, and her dress was checked in the appropriate blue and faded brown. The backs of her arms were pinkly white and the flimsy hairs on them were washed-out gold. But the grass she was lying on was grey, like one of the silvery mosses you can sometimes find in woodland. The bushes tilting into the little clearing had grey leaves and, now she came to look more closely, grey berries. Down beyond her feet, a thinner extension of the clearing laced its grey way across a grey hillside to reach a grey track that ran through the grey cleavage of a grey valley...

And Robin Goodfellow was grey, too, the magnificent peacock's feather in his cap reduced to a fine etching.

'Is this the way the whole of your world is?' she said quietly to him.

He knew what she was talking about. 'Yes,' he said. 'All of it, fine lady. Just at the moment.'

'You mean it isn't always like this?'

Mr Dogg interrupted. 'It's been like this as long as I've known it.'

'No,' said Robin Goodfellow. 'Our aspect of the world has been grey for a long time, but not for ever – only for quite a short time, really. A few tens of your years. Before that it was more gaudily coloured, dearest duchess, than the brightest of your party dresses. There were blues to make your heart sing – blues in every shade of the sea and sky, the blues of jewels and of mountainsides, the blues of jewels and high-tea puddings, the blues of jewels and – '

'There aren't any blues now,' Joanna observed.

'But there *were*. And there *are*, really – it's just that no one has been able to see them for such a long time. They're still *there*: they're just not showing themselves. And that's only the blues! Let me tell you about the pinks and the yellows and the others! Oh, I promise you, sweet maiden, your mouth will start to water when I tell you of the colours of a summer's day!'

'But none of those colours are here right now,' said Joanna, hauling herself up into a sitting position. Robin Goodfellow reached out a hand to pull her to her feet – which was odd when she thought about it, because he was hardly eighteen inches tall and she was five foot seven. From her new, loftier vantage point she could see clearly across the valley and for several miles in either direction along it. 'Don't you think it's a jolly rum coincidence, Mr Goodfellow, that the very day you bring me here to see the glories of your world it just *happens* to be at something less than its best?'

'I'm no fraud,' he piped up at her. 'It's no coincidence. And the colours really *are* there, I promise you! They're just . . . just *lurking* for a while.'

Joanne heaved a sarcastic sigh. 'You expect me to believe you?'

'It's why we – I – why I brought you here, wherever precisely here is,' he said, tugging anxiously at the hem of her dress. 'Listen to me, beautiful lady. Listen to me and I'll tell

THE FAR-ENOUGH WINDOW

you everything in the right order, so you understand. Please!'

'What is there to understand?' she said. 'In the loft you were so full of how we human beings were ignorant, unobservant thickoes who couldn't see far enough to know the true riches of the world – we were stuck in Drabsville, according to you, while you, you little cleverboots, could see all the glamour of the world's full spectrum. But when you try to show it to me it's like a picture in one of Mrs Ruggeley's old family photo albums. "Oh," she says, "the scenery was so beautiful that day we went out on the Ullswater steamer", or "Look, Joanna, look at me in this one – and the scarlet-and-indigo-striped stockings I wore when I was that age and had the legs for them". And I look at the pictures and all I see is bits of grey fading into smudge. *She* sees the cascading colours that were once there; *I* see the monotony that's actually there right now – that's all that's left.

'Well, all I can see of your world is Drabsville personified – and I'm not very much impressed by it, Robin Goodfellow, I can tell you. I think I was better off back where I was – there were more colours in the garden, despite the slush, than I can see anywhere here. You say you're not a fraud – but you are, Mr Goodfellow, you are. You brought me here under false pretences – you promised me splendours and all you can produce is . . . *this*!'

She spat the last word disgustedly and glared down at him.

'Hoity toity bloody woman!' growled Robin Goodfellow; the pitch was about the middle of a tenor's range. 'Stupid bloody human being! You're all so bloody literal! Look at the surface – that's all you can do! Just because you can't actually *see* things, you say they're not there! Have you ever seen an atom, Miss Lardy Dardy Highanmighty? No? Eh? Let me hear you say you have! Hmm? Not a word? Does that mean you don't think atoms exist?'

He leaned across, lifted the flap of one of Mr Dogg's ears, and said in a stage whisper: 'In point of strict fact, they don't, but don't let on, eh, old friend – it'll only distract her into further lunacies and it doesn't actually undermine the logical core of my argument.'

'I will not be *condescended to* by you any longer, Robin Goodfellow!' said Joanna, stamping her foot. The impact made only a dull thunk on the clearing's floor, but Robin Goodfellow leapt back nervously.

'Don't go lashing those great feet of yours around,' he pleaded. 'They're dangerous. There's a difference between having a jolly good stand-up argument, you know, and starting a fight!'

'I wish you'd both shut up,' said Mr Dogg dourly. 'You're like a pair of squabbling infants, if you ask me.' He looked earnestly at Joanna, then at Robin Goodfellow, then at Joanna again. 'Infants.'

'I think you're missing the point here, my cani– ' began Robin Goodfellow.

'No,' said Mr Dogg, 'I think it's you two who're missing the point. We're here: that's fact number one. It doesn't look the way Joanna expected, although it does look the way I've always known it: that's fact number two. You say it really looks different, but not today: that's – your saying of it, I mean – fact number three, but it's a kind of irrelevant fact, as is fact number two, when you come to think of it. The only genuinely important thing is fact number one, that we're here. As far as Joanna is concerned, it's the first time she's ever seen or been in this world, so instead of standing around arguing about it she should be exploring it, and you should be encouraging her to do so rather than bickering about how clever you are. Now I've said my piece, and that's all: it's pretty damn' exhausting, this talking business, when your jaw and your vocal cords and things aren't properly adapted for it.' Mr Dogg stopped speaking and let his head hang forward, his tongue dangling wearily.

'Quite right,' said Robin Goodfellow after an embarrassed pause. 'You should just take things as you find them, young lady, and then you'd – '

'Shut,' said Joanna, 'up.'

Robin Goodfellow gulped and looked away.

'I want to think,' she said. 'Mr Dogg's right – this is a new place for me, and I should be finding the thrillingness in it, not grousing about how it's not very pretty. So be quiet for a while.'

The air smelt the same colour as the sky. There was a slight wind blowing along the valley, making the bushes and trees bob in a formal dance and corkscrewing the smoke rising from the chimney of a little farmhouse about a mile away on the opposite slope. The track in the valley's fold followed a meandering path, as if it were in no particular hurry to get wherever it was going; from time to time it crossed, via little wooden bridges, a stream that meandered along its own, entirely unrelated course. There was a wagon slowly shuffling away from them; it was probably two miles distant, but Joanna's sharp eyes could see that it was drawn either by horses or by something very much like horses – two of them, both coated in a mottling of greys and blacks. The wagon's driver was a shapeless, hunched-up blob.

She shielded her eyes and looked up towards the sky. A

solitary predator bird was coasting on the updraughts. The sun was pale and unenthusiastic, seeming like a thin rubber bag filled with faintly glowing water. Insipid clouds decorated the dome, as if made of tissue paper and stuck there.

All in all, it wasn't the most inspiring of sights ... but it wasn't the house and estate in which she'd been confined ever since she could remember, and the friends standing beside her weren't Mrs Ruggeley or Mudgett. It was *new* to her, and this was sufficient reason to feel her heart beat more impatiently in her chest.

'What are those funny zipping noises?' she asked Robin Goodfellow, waving her hand instinctively as if trying to brush away invisible insects.

'Oh,' he said dismissively, 'just gawkers. Any novelty, and people with nothing better to do gather round to have a rubberneck and gossip about it all.'

Joanna's brow creased. 'Stop speaking in riddles.'

'They're fairies,' said Robin Goodfellow. 'What else did you expect? You're in Fairyland, so obviously there are fairies around.'

'But I can't see them.'

'That's because they're excited. They have only very little minds, d'you see, and when they get excited there isn't room for them to keep it all inside them, so they have to dash around letting the excitement out that way.'

'Like Tink, in *Peter Pan*,' said Joanna.

Robin Goodfellow looked revolted. 'Same general principle,' he said unhappily.

'Can't you ask one of them to slow down?'

'Ask them yourself.' Robin Goodfellow gave one of his eloquent shrugs and turned half-away, indicating that it was really none of his business if Joanna wanted to waste her time on trivia.

'Will they listen to – ? Oh, all right then, I will.'

The fairies must be very small if mere speed could make them invisible. She held out her hand flat, palm-up, and then on second thoughts added the other, cupped against it.

'If you would be so kind,' she addressed the zooming sounds in general, 'I should be very glad if one of you might let me see you.'

There was a whiz past her ear, and she blinked. By the time she opened her eyes again there was a small weight in her hands.

She was astonished: the being sitting there, fanning itself with its gauzy wings, was much bigger than she'd expected – standing up, it (or she, because it was obviously a she) would be about five or six inches tall. She was dressed in – well, Joanna couldn't quite see what it was the fairy was dressed in, beyond the general impression that it was not very much. Perched elegantly on the ball of Joanna's right thumb, with one long, slender leg extended to touch the palm of Joanna's other hand, the fairy looked at her from a perfectly sculpted heart-shaped face.

'You're so *pretty*,' Joanna said. 'Just like in Andrew Lang.'

'Don't tell her that,' said Robin Goodfellow crossly, reappearing beside her. 'She'll be insufferable for weeks.'

In an affronted shimmer of the air the fairy was gone. But a moment later there was another in the cup of Joanna's hands. This one seemed to be a male, although there was nothing masculine about his features to tell her so. He was sitting cross-legged, facing her. There was a grin on his face, as if he were a small boy who had a secret he wasn't going to tell. Despite the wings sprouting from the rear of his shoulders he had a minuscule bow and a quiver to match slung across his back. Before she could take in all the details of his appearance he was gone, to be replaced by a dumpy little fellow, and then . . .

'Told you,' said Robin Goodfellow. 'Very little minds, they have. No concentration-span to speak of.'

'They're *fascinating*,' Joanna breathed, watching the ever-changing display of tiny figures in front of her. 'And so *beautiful.*'

Robin Goodfellow sniffed. 'They're like brightly coloured baubles, and about as much use.'

'But they're not,' Joanna said. 'Brightly coloured, I mean.'

'True,' Robin Goodfellow said as if conceding something. 'Not at the moment, they're not – at least, they don't *look* that way. But in actual fact . . .'

'Oh, you're not starting that again,' rumbled Mr Dogg. 'I'm not sitting around waiting while you two have a long philosophical slanging-match. I'm hungry, and I want to explore.'

Now Joanna thought about it, she was hungry as well. The fairies must have picked up her thought, because after a last one posed briefly for her admiration there were no more. 'There's a farmhouse,' she said, 'on the other side of the valley. Perhaps they would . . .'

But we haven't any money to offer them, she thought. *Perhaps I could give them my Timex watch, or . . .*

'No need for money here,' said Robin Goodfellow. 'We don't use the stuff. If the folk are Finefolk, and friendly, they'll feed us until our stomachs are fit to burst. If not . . .' He shrugged and looked apprehensive. 'I wish I had a clear idea of exactly where it is we've arrived. That's the trouble with the Far-Enough Window, you know: it gets you to and from this side all right, but it lacks *precision*.'

'The Finefolk,' said Joanna. 'That's people like you – and the fairies – isn't it?'

'Oh, we're all fairies,' said Robin Goodfellow, 'but only some of us are Finefolk. The others – the Comelatelies – they're different from us. That's why we needed you to see far enough to be able to come here, my lovely one.'

'What do you mean?'

'Not now. Later. Let's see what we can do about your stomach's needs. If they're Finefolk in the farmhouse . . .'

He set off along the length of the clearing, trudging determinedly and manifestly expecting Joanna and Mr Dogg to follow him. After a moment, they did.

Soon the bushes on either side of them were higher, taller than Joanna, so all she could see of this new world was a strip of grey sky overhead and the trail in front of her as far as the next turning. Mr Dogg trotted along beside her happily enough, every now and again looking up at her as if he might say something amicable but then realized it wasn't worth the strain on his vocal system. She smiled at him, and scratched the flat of his head as she walked. The whizzing and whirring in the air around them continued unabated: she assumed the inquisitive fairies were forming an invisible escort.

About twenty minutes later the bushes came to an end, a few yards from the edge of the track.

Robin Goodfellow halted, and gestured with the flat of his hand that the other two should stay behind him. Joanna gripped the nape of Mr Dogg's neck to restrain him before realizing that of course here, in this world, he was as capable of making judgements as she was. She went down on one knee, and she and Mr Dogg huddled together to look over Robin's shoulders at the rutted, dried-mud surface.

'Now I,' said Robin out of the side of his mouth, 'could whip across this highway to the far side in less than the blink of a gnat's eye – so swift that even a Comelately wouldn't notice my going – but you two lack such an elementary capability, so we'll have to be more circumspect.'

'Couldn't you take us across by magic?' whispered Joanna. This all seemed rather melodramatic to her. She'd seen from the hillside that there was hardly anyone around.

'Of course, but one of the things you'll soon learn about magic,' said Robin Goodfellow contemptuously, 'is that it's never much use when you want it to be. No, we'll have to get to the other side using traditional methods – to wit, walking or running, and hoping that no one pays us any attention. Which isn't too much of a problem for Mr Dogg here, but for you' – he turned around and looked Joanna straight in the eye – 'it's going to be a lot more difficult.'

For a moment she was baffled. And then she understood for the first time that here, in Fairyland, she was as conspicuous as an elephant would be if it were romping around the gardens at home. Where she might go unnoticed in a crowd in her own world – assuming she were ever given the chance – here she was a monstrosity, a freak, a one-of-a-kind whom the indigenes gathered to gawp at. Anyone who saw her crossing ahead of them on the track would yell and run or yell and attack or yell and want a closer look – whatever they did, they'd yell and raise the alarm, which was something Robin Goodfellow clearly dreaded. She looked at her thin arms and her neat hands, and suddenly, for the first

THE FAR-ENOUGH WINDOW

time in her life, felt very clumsy-limbed and lumbering.

'You couldn't wizard me into something else ...' she began. 'Oh, no, silly: magic again.'

He nodded glumly. 'Turning you into something else'd be easy enough, but I'd not be certain I could get you back into being yourself again. Mind you' – he brightened – 'there's nothing particularly special about the form of a young human female. You might like to try being a squab-toad for a while. Or a skylark – lots of fun being a skylark, if you ask me. No responsibility, and excellent scenery.'

'No,' said Joanna. She splayed out her hands and looked at their backs. 'Just ... no.'

His face fell, but he shrugged resignedly. 'All right, all right. The Comelatelies might detect me using magic on that kind of a scale, anyway. We'll just have to employ the orthodox ways.'

'Which are what?'

'Me having a quick spy of the land, my lady fair, and then, assuming the coast's clear, the three of us dashing over as if the hounds of hell were at our backsides.'

'What are you waiting for?'

'Courage,' he said.

'Oh?'

'If one of the Comelatelies is coming along I'd be as good as dead if they spotted me.'

'Oh. But I thought you said – '

He looked exasperated. 'Yes, but I've got to *stop* in the middle of the road *long* enough to *see* if there's anyone *there*, haven't I?'

'The longer you wait for courage to come along, the further away it goes,' observed Mr Dogg hoarsely. 'Old canine

93

saying,' he explained to Joanna.

Robin Goodfellow stared distastefully at the mongrel. 'Right,' he said at length. 'Here goes.'

He seemed to flicker.

'Good,' he said. 'No one about. Come on now.'

Joanna and Mr Dogg sprinted across the track, going as fast as they could without catching their feet in any of its countless interlocking ruts and pits. They arrived on the far side panting, and rolled in a heap with Robin Goodfellow in the shelter of a new patch of grey bushes.

'That wasn't too bad,' said Joanna, sitting up and dusting off the front of her dress. 'You were very quick, Mr Goodfellow, dashing out to the middle of the road to spy out the land for us.'

He stared at her. 'I did more than that,' he said, as if she were being particularly obtuse. 'That would hardly have been a precaution at all. I nipped a couple of miles along the road each way, as well, just to be sure we didn't get any nasty surprises.'

Mr Dogg began to make an odd, half-choking noise, and Joanna looked at him alarmedly until she realized he was laughing.

'Let's go and have a look at that farmhouse,' said Robin.

'Couldn't you just go yourself?' said Joanna. 'I mean if you can go, let me see, eight miles in less than the wink of an – '

'We stick together,' said Robin Goodfellow, 'as much as possible. The Comelatelies are almost as quick as I am, when it comes to the running sort of thing, and if I were caught while you two were still sitting here . . .'

He left her imagination to do the rest.

THE FAR-ENOUGH WINDOW

Climbing the hill wasn't difficult, and soon Joanna found herself humming a snaking little ambling tune that seemed to have no verses or rests, but just went convivially on and on without ever seeming to want to come to a climax or repeating itself. As on the hillside they'd just come down, most of the vegetation consisted of the slightly threatening-seeming bushes, some of them sporting most impressive thorns, but clear bits of ground linked and interlinked between them. There were lots of piles of the raisin-sized droppings everywhere Joanna looked, and she assumed that some grazing animal or other – sheep, perhaps – kept the bushes in check. Although the sun didn't seem to be supplying the world with any heat, she found she was quite warm in just her gingham dress and her white socks and brogues. The grey light, which she'd found so dispiriting when first she'd come into Fairyland, now seemed instead to be relaxing to the vision. She began to think of the strong colours of herself and Mr Dogg as something of a clashing eyesore among all the muted shades of the grass and the bushes.

I must keep remembering that we're the odd ones out in Fairyland, she told herself, *just the same way that Robin Goodfellow's the odd one out in our part of the world.*

As they grew closer to the farmhouse, which at the moment she could see only as the hidden footing of the twisting, braiding column of smoke, Robin Goodfellow's pace eased, and he rounded each new corner between the bushes much more warily. The air was quiet now – Joanna realized their invisible escort of fairies must have abandoned them some little while ago. Mr Dogg had hauled his fleshy tongue into his mouth and was moving along with his jaws clamped firmly shut, making as little noise as possible.

'And you could stop that blasted humming,' hissed Robin Goodfellow.

She'd forgotten she was humming. She ceased, guiltily, mid-note.

A few moments later Robin indicated they should halt. He dropped down onto his knees, and Joanna did likewise. The tip of his peacock-feather was caught by a little eddy of wind, and fluttered upwards against her nose; she drew her head back, stifling any impulse to sneeze.

'It's my estimation – and I've won awards and widespread fame for estimation, so I'd take it seriously if I were you – that the house is just over the side of the next ridge,' he whispered. 'We should be able to see it through that hole in the bumbleberry bushes.' He pointed ahead of them, and Joanna saw a gap about the size of her head. 'But I'm not trusting either of you two strangers to be able to have a peek without getting your elbows jammed in your mouths, so you stay here while I go. Understood?'

'I don't have elbows,' said Mr Dogg.

'And you're being gratuitously horrid anyway,' added Joanna. 'It would be silly for me or Mr Dogg to take a look because we wouldn't know the meaning of anything we saw.'

'Sorry,' muttered Robin Goodfellow. 'It's just my own nerves speaking. Talking of speaking, no more of it – d'you hear?'

They nodded.

Again there was that strange, half-seen flicker, as if he'd abruptly modified his stance.

The expression on his face, though, had changed entirely.

He grinned at them. 'We're all right, my hearties-ho.'

THE FAR-ENOUGH WINDOW

'Can I stand up again?' said Joanna. She'd just discovered she'd plonked her right hand in one of the little mounds of animal droppings.

'No worry at all,' said Robin Goodfellow cheerfully. 'They're friends, up ahead. You'll like them. Your ghost told me as much,' he added enigmatically.

'Friends of yours?' said Joanna suspiciously, wiping the flat of her hand on the grass. 'Isn't that a bit of a strong coincidence? We could be anywhere in Fairyland, for all you know.'

'You'll find that most of the Finefolk are friends of Robin Goodfellow,' he said proudly. 'I get around this corner of the Farness a fair amount, you know, being as nimble as I am. Come on – get a move on. As far as I'm concerned you look just as pretty with a black hand as a white.'

'Then I'll wipe it on your jerkin.'

He scampered on ahead, with Mr Dogg cheerfully cantering along beside him. Giving her filthy hand one last rueful look, Joanna followed more slowly, so that the other two had disappeared by the time she reached the ridge and the hole in the bushes. She had to duck down to squeeze through the opening; as she did so she noticed that the thorny branches retreated from her, leaving about an inch of room on all sides of her body. Even the bushes here must be friends of Robin Goodfellow, she concluded.

The farmhouse was little more than a cottage. Its walls were made of irregular lumps of peat, and the building had a squashed-down look which made it seem more as if it had been moulded by youthfully inept hands. The roof, which could have been of either thatch or dough, was splodged carelessly onto the tops of the walls. There was a stable a little distance away from the house, and from where she was standing Joanna could see that it was empty. Maybe the wagon she'd seen on the road earlier had come from here.

Robin Goodfellow was standing impatiently in the yard, tapping his feet and beckoning crossly to her.

'Hurry up!' he shouted. Hens erupted into motion around him.

'I'm coming,' said Joanna, beginning to pick her way down the slope. There was one minor difficulty that Robin Goodfellow seemed to have overlooked: the farmhouse might be fine for him and even, possibly, for Mr Dogg, but it was built on the same scale as Robin Goodfellow himself, which meant that for Joanna it would make a better sofa than a dwelling-place. Not that she intended to do any dwelling in it, of course, but for the last fifteen minutes she'd been hoping that it would run to something as mundane as a loo.

Robin Goodfellow vanished inside the house's open door as she approached. *Just like him to desert me in my hour of need,* she thought wryly. But then, as she came still closer, she noticed that the door – and the house around it – seemed to be growing bigger, so that by the time she was ready to step over the threshold there was more than enough room to do so.

She stood in a warm kitchen. The floor was tiled and there wasn't a humming freezer in the corner, but apart from that it was astonishingly like the kitchen at home. A woman turned round towards her from tending a cooking pot hanging over an open fire where the cooker should be, and for an instant Joanna thought she was going to see Mrs Ruggeley's familiar smile. The face she actually saw, though it was, like everything else in Fairyland except herself and Mr

Dogg, composed of neutral greys, reminded her of baked apples with cinnamon and currants in their cores.

'Dolly Onskonsider,' said the woman, bustling towards her. 'That's me. You must be the human girl that Robin here's been warning me about. Oh, lorks, I shouldn't be saying words like "warning", should I, because that doesn't make me sound very welcoming, does it, especially since it must have been a terrible trial for you having to put up with him all this while, the rogue he is, though charming with it, that I'll grant you – and oh! – just take a look at that sharny hand of yours. I've got some nice hot water, least it was hot a little while ago when I looked so it should still be at least lukewarm, and we'll get that washed before you sit down and have something nice to fill your – '

'If empty vessels make the most sound, Dolly Onskonsider,' said Robin, 'you must be bigger inside than you are out.'

His eyes twinkled, and there was no malice in his voice. It was disconcerting for Joanna to discover him as large as herself.

'Lorks, to be listening to you you'd think you weren't a guest of mine but someone come tumbling in out of the night and demanding a lodging as if it were their right. Which, come to think of it, Robin Goodfellow, is not so very much different from what you are.' Dolly Onskonsider had grabbed Joanna by the wrist and was dragging her across towards a covered cauldron, but now she stopped and thrust her face close to Robin Goodfellow's. 'Have you, you cocky little runtkin, anything to say about that before I pitch you head-first into the cow-mire?'

'You have such beautiful eyes,' said Robin Goodfellow

earnestly.

Dolly Onskonsider snorted and looked round at Joanna. 'Didn't I say he had more charm than was good for him?' she cried, then continued her plunge towards the cauldron.

A few minutes later, both arms spotlessly clean to the elbows and the front of her dress sopping, Joanna sat uncomfortably on a three-legged stool at the table while Dolly Onskonsider and Robin bantered and taunted at each other. It was obvious theirs was an old friendship, founded on a mutual relish for insult. Mr Dogg lay at her feet, his head between his paws, his stomach rumbling from time to time.

The kitchen seemed to occupy the whole of the ground floor of the little house, and it was as cluttered as it could conceivably be while yet, paradoxically, allowing plenty of room for people to walk around. All sorts of incomprehensible trophies, mementoes and (probably) farming implements dangled from its walls, and hooks in its ceiling beams supported lanterns and a selection of potted plants, all, so far as Joanna could make out, dead. Hens sometimes jerked a few paces in through the open door, looked around, discovered where their pecking had carried them, and flustered out again. Three windows hung lopsided in their frames. Beside the door swayed an overloaded coat-rack. At the far end of the room from the chimney a blackened flight of twisted wooden stairs ascended to the floor above.

Robin Goodfellow stopped suddenly mid-insult and turned to her.

'If it's a jakes, lav, john, head, call it what you will you're after,' he said, 'you'll have a long hunt ahead of you.'

She felt herself blushing.

THE FAR-ENOUGH WINDOW

'Oh, she's modest,' observed Dolly Onskonsider as Robin began to cackle. 'And what a very proper thing it is in a young girl, even if she do have the misfortune to be human, that she has some seemly modesty. But he's right, you know' – this to Joanna – 'we're not very strong on the privy front around here, what with moving house the whole time and there being so many bushes in the vicinity. I'm afraid you'll have to fend for yourself, dearie. Try not to get lost out there.'

She dismissed Joanna with an amiable wave of her hand, and went back to berating Robin.

It wasn't nearly as bad as Joanna had thought it would be. Mr Dogg came with her to act as a guard in case anyone came along – as if anyone would, but she felt glad he was there – and he courteously didn't look in her direction as she widdled behind a clump of shrubbery. Back in the house – which had shrunk as she'd retreated from it and expanded once more as she'd approached – her hands again washed officiously by Dolly Onskonsider, she was able to concentrate anew on feeling hungry.

'Lumpenkulder will be home soon,' said Dolly Onskonsider, 'and we'll have our supper then, don't you worry, you hungry pair. He's gone into market with some pumpkins and to fetch back eggs and cheese and a few whatjacallits if there's any as take his fancy.'

'Was he the man ... the person in the wagon?' asked Joanna.

'Like as not,' said Dolly Onskonsider briskly, the matter obviously being of no importance to her. 'One wagon's much like another, in my opinion, and you could say the same of husbands.'

'Tired of old Lumpenkulder, are we?' said Robin Goodfellow mischievously, and the argument started up again.

Lumpenkulder Onskonsider, when he came – which he did in a storm of stamping feet and flailing arms and huffing cheeks and a jangle of putting the horse away comfortably in its stable for the night – was a bulkier, gruffer, maler version of Dolly, with a redolence of toxic tobacco smoke. He greeted Joanna and Mr Dogg as if he'd expected them to be waiting there for him – which perhaps, Joanna suddenly wondered, he had – and obviously knew Robin Goodfellow well. He threw his furs in the direction of the coat-rack and embraced Robin, biffing him roundly on the back with his square, strong hands.

'Your supper's on the table, light of my life,' said Dolly Onskonsider and, when Joanna turned to look, there it was: five big wooden bowls with a steaming mash of mushrooms and onions and various other vegetables in them. In front of each of the bowls was a stool, and Mr Dogg was already sitting at his, his tongue lolling eagerly.

'Wait a minute, Mr Dogg,' said Joanna under her breath. 'They might say grace, or something, in Fairyland.'

They didn't.

Joanna found the vegetable stew remarkably filling – far more so than she'd anticipated – and by the time her bowl was half-empty her appetite had left her, though she carried on eating both to be polite and because the food was delicious, even if the flavours were very subtle. She wondered if tastes were like sights here: very pleasant if you were prepared to appreciate their subtleties, but basically done in shades of grey.

THE FAR-ENOUGH WINDOW

Earlier she'd found it impossible to think while Robin Goodfellow and Dolly Onskonsider had been railing at each other – their shouting had tensed her – but Lumpenkulder's badinage was of a gentler sort and the fellowship between the three Finefolk more obvious. In fact, she suddenly noticed, this meal was offering her the first time for thought since she'd arrived in Fairyland. And she was starved of contemplation. At home there was always plenty of time to think things through – far too much time, in fact, so that you ended up thinking them through until you were sick of them. But here in Fairyland events seemed to come with jagged edges, so that you could never properly relax in case another one suddenly charged at you and knocked you sideways.

From what little Robin Goodfellow had told her, it seemed plain that something pretty dreadful had happened to Fairyland, and that it was associated with or probably even caused by the arrival of the entities Robin referred to as the Comelatelies. It was often difficult to read Robin's animated facial contortions and rapid gesticulations correctly – he was like an actor constantly dropping out of one rôle and into another. But of this Joanna was certain: the mortal terror he felt towards the Comelatelies was not simulated. And the effect the Comelatelies – or *something* – had had on this world was like a sort of Thinning, a sort of diluting. The colours had paled and paled until they were just different greys, and the air had a slight mustiness that was not born of age but, instead, a mixture of all the scents it should have held, but hardly a trace of any of them.

The meal she was just finishing tasted very nice, but there wasn't a strong flavour of any kind in it. And, now she thought about it, although the dishes had steamed, they hadn't given off any detectable odour of onions, or mushrooms, or courgettes, or whatever those odd little yellow-green vegetables were.

But if all the sensual information – it was a clumsy phrase dredged out of an old lesson with one of her tutors, but it expressed what she was getting at ... if all the sensual information were being thinned out of the world, where was it going? She didn't think it could be being siphoned off into her own world, because she hadn't noticed things becoming more colourful there – although if it had been happening gradually, of course, she might not have noticed. It could, though, be leaching into different worlds of what Robin Goodfellow called the Farness. He had hinted that there might be hundreds or thousands of these other worlds (or different aspects of a single world, but it was easier to think of them as separate worlds), and quite what they might contain was well beyond Joanna's conception. If there were indeed lots of them, then all of them – including her own – could be accepting a tiny modicum of Fairyland's sensual information without anyone there being any the wiser.

Really, though, it didn't matter where the stuff was going *to* – it was the fact that it was going *from* Fairyland that was important. Again her thoughts reverted to that sense of *Thinning*: what kind of creatures could these dire Comelatelies be that their presence so diluted a world?

Her speculations might be more fruitful if she had more solid grounds on which to base them but, as it now forcefully struck her, she was desperately short of explanations. On more than one occasion, Robin Goodfellow had made a great song and dance about how he was going to tell her everything. But each time something had happened to forestall him before he had properly got started, or his attention had drifted on to something else, so that she'd been left stranded or, not at first realizing that the path they were taking was a destinationless diversion, had followed him into irrelevance. But it was certainly time for him to be pinned down and forced to give her an account of what was *really* going on.

If only she could trust him to stick to the subject. She had the feeling that, even literally pinned down, he might let his freewheeling garrulousness drag him off in all the wrong directions.

Still, it was worth a try.

'Ahem,' she said pointedly, rapping the table with the handle of her wooden spoon.

The three Finefolk paid her no attention at all.

'Hey!' she said more loudly.

Still they kept on yattering.

Mr Dogg let out a howl that could probably have been heard all the way to the Lampeter Wing.

There was a shocked silence as the echoes faded away.

'Ahem,' said Joanna into it. 'Thank you, Mr Dogg. There's a question or two I'd like to as– '

'What did you make that racket for?' Dolly Onskonsider asked Mr Dogg. Her face held a look of polite enquiry.

'Bloody canines,' said Robin Goodfellow. 'Can't take 'em anywhere.'

'Is there something ailing you, my friend?' said Lumpenkulder Onskonsider.

'We were just having a good conversation,' Robin groused.

'He was trying,' said Joanna determinedly, 'to create a

little bit of silence so that I could – '

'Well, if it was silence you were after creating you were going the wrong way about it,' said Dolly Onskonsider kindly to the mongrel. 'I've never heard such a din.'

'Please be quiet,' Joanna insisted. 'I want to ask you all a question.'

'She's right, you know,' said Lumpenkulder Onskonsider. 'Here have us three been, gabbling away like there was no tomorrow, and our friends from across the Farness, whom we should be treating as our honoured guests, haven't been able to get a word in edge– '

'*Please*,' said Joanna.

'Oh. Sorry.'

She took a deep breath. 'There's a lot I don't yet understand about the Far-Enough Window, and about Fairyland, and about you people, and about all sorts of other things, but there's one thing I'd like to know the answer to right now. And it's this . . .'

'You've only got to ask for us to answer, dearie,' said Dolly Onskonsider.

'Shush!' said her husband, who seemed to be getting the hang of things.

'Who – or what – exactly *are* the Comelatelies?'

The three faces in front of her looked pained – in Dolly Onskonsider's case so much so that Joanna worried the woman might be about to burst into tears.

'They're the same as the Oldcomers,' said Robin Goodfellow after a few moments. He spoke as if the words tasted rancid.

'That's not helpful,' said Joanna deliberately. 'It doesn't make me any wiser than I was already. Try again, Mr

THE FAR-ENOUGH WINDOW

Goodfellow, until you get it right.'

Robin made a bitter little noise between his teeth and looked at the Onskonsiders as if for protection from this unreasonable interloper and her even more unreasonable interrogation. But the other two just looked back at him.

'It's a perfectly sensible question,' said Lumpenkulder Onskonsider. 'And if anyone's going to tell her the answer, Robin Goodfellow, then it really ought to be you. You were the one as brought her through the Far-Enough Window.'

'Hmmf,' said Robin, but he seemed to agree. He stared at the spoon he was twirling in his fingers. 'If you'd serve us all up a mug or two of mead,' he said to Dolly, 'just to make my tongue flex the better . . .'

Mugs appeared instantly in front of each of them. Robin looked disconcerted by the speed of Dolly's magic. Magic wasn't supposed to be useful.

'Talk,' Dolly said grimly.

'Well . . .' said Robin Goodfellow, and then he seemed to decide that there was no point in further prevarication. He leaned forward, put his elbows on the table, and looked straight at Joanna.

'The Comelatelies are the same as the Oldcomers,' he began, 'because they're the folk who used to live through all of Fairyland. They were a proud folk, and a cruel one: they were harsh in their ways to each other and delightingly harsher in their ways to whichever mortals they could entice into this world from yours. Your ancestors, Joanna my lovely, knew well enough to be afeared when the Finefolk – or the Little People, as they ignorantly called them – were said to be at large. It was the Oldcomers who devised the Wild Hunt, when every spirit of the sky and earth rode astride the heavens to seize and slay one fleeing unfortunate after another. It was the Oldcomers who disguised themselves as benefactors to go among you humans, offering riches or power or seductions for a price that seemed to be nothing when the contract was struck but proved to be immense when the time for payment fell due.'

I've heard Daddy say that about building contractors, Joanna thought irrelevantly.

'It was the Oldcomers who gave you your legends of the Devil, because they often affected horns and cloven hooves. And it was they who made promises, then broke them, or stole away human children for sacrifice and left in their place their own cruel offspring, so that human mothers found themselves rearing blood-hungry sneak-killing witch-monsters. Oh, the painful tricks the Oldcomers played upon your stodgy world of mortals! – and not only on you, but on other creations among the Farness.

'They had to be stopped, but there was no one to stop them – or, at least, we thought there was not.'

'Where were you Finefolk all this time?' interposed Mr Dogg.

'We were like the colours are today in this world,' said Dolly Onskonsider absently. 'We were there, all right, but you couldn't see us.'

Robin Goodfellow was staring balefully at Dolly and Mr Dogg. 'It's no wonder the girl complains about no one ever giving her a straight answer.'

Dolly looked at him askance. 'Sorry,' she said unconvincingly.

'What was I saying?' said Robin. 'Ah, yes, we thought – all of us throughout the Farness thought – there was no one could do anything about the Oldcomers. And so things went on, and we suffered, and . . . my mug's empty.'

Dolly folded her arms and Robin Goodfellow's mug was suddenly overflowing with sticky sweet mead. Reminded, Joanna took a sip of her own: it tasted like watered-down honey.

'Harrumph, yes,' said Robin. 'But we'd got it all wrong, d'you see. Everyone, from humans out to the furthest reaches of the Farness, thought that the Oldcomers were the rulers of the roost, that they were the wellspring from which everyone else in the Farness derived. Everyone believed they gave the orders and the world had to obey, because that was the way the world was made. But that wasn't the right of it – not at all. The ones everyone else tended to overlook, the stolid, clayey, matter-ridden, plodding denizens of the mortal area of the Farness – you and your kind, my adorable lady, in fact – were the ones who had the making or altering of it all.'

'Us thickoes, you mean,' said Joanna acerbically. 'Underestimated, as usual.'

'You thickoes, indeed,' said Robin Goodfellow congenially, 'because you hadn't the first clue yourselves that this was the case. You more than anyone else thought you were at the mercy of the Oldcomers. When they tweaked, you winced and yelped: you accepted it as the natural order of things. But then you changed, and your changing sapped the power out of the Oldcomers.'

'What do you mean?' said Joanna. 'How did we do that?'

'You started to ignore them. And the more you humans ignored them the less they were able to interfere with your lives, so the greater the impunity with which you could ignore them. And so on it went, in ever-diminishing circles, until the

Oldcomers were – quite literally – merely shadows of their older selves, confined in a shadow-world. This world, in fact – looking much as it has come to look again today.'

'We *thinned* them!' said Joanna triumphantly. 'We thinned Fairyland.'

'Yes you did,' said Robin Goodfellow simply. 'And you've done it again. Only now the effect of your Thinning has been to allow the Oldcomers – or Comelatelies, depending on how you look at it, sweet Joanna – back in.'

Five

In the Hall of the Fairy King

He was so tiny that no human eye could see him.
– Hans Christian Andersen (trans by H.W. Dulcken), 'The Rose-Elf', 1839

The others got to sleep that night easily enough – the whole upper floor of the house, which somehow was vastly bigger than the lower floor, shook from their snoring – but Joanna's mind was too much of a ferment for her to be anything other than wide awake. Even Mr Dogg – the traitor! – had snuggled down willingly enough, and now slumbered raucously across her feet. She was too hot under the furs the Onskonsiders had given her, or a few moments later she was too cold. The bed was too soft, or not soft enough. The furs itched her skin even through the voluminous silk nightie that Dolly had lent her. She wasn't properly tired, or she was far *too* tired . . .

She suspected there was a lot of truth in the latter: she'd reached that state of exhaustion where she no longer had the

strength to quieten her mind.

Robin Goodfellow had refused to say anything more on the subject of the Comelatelies beyond repeated confirmation that it was through the second Thinning of Fairyland by humans, even though humans were confined on the other side of the Far-Enough Window, that the Comelatelies had been allowed to return. The Onskonsiders hadn't been much help either. After some further conversation, they'd dragged out musical instruments from concealments around the kitchen and insisted that everyone contribute to an impromptu ceilidh. Joanna had picked out the melody line of 'Yellow Submarine' on a three-stringed instrument she hadn't recognized, and the tune had fascinated them. But of the Comelatelies there had been no further discussion – and now, lying in the dark, listening to everyone else's snores but her own, Joanna realized that for yet a further time Robin Goodfellow had failed to answer one of her questions even though having started out to do so.

Nevertheless, she could put together a lot of the pieces herself, she felt sure. She knew that she was intelligent, and that her education had trained her in the use of her intellect. What she could not confidently deduce she could guess, and if enough of the guesses, when put together, formed something that seemed to make sense – why, then she could deduce that her guesses had probably been accurate.

She recognized who the Oldcomers had been, of course. Robin Goodfellow had given far more than a sufficiency of clues to guide her to their identification. They were the fairies and elves of the earliest legends: the Siddhe, trickster spirits who made mortals' lives a misery. In the Middle Ages they'd been as real and as sadistic as all the other creatures who had plagued the people's lives: demons and warlocks and werewolves (and real wolves, for that matter), and ghosts and vampires and succubi and every manner of other. There had been little to choose between them and the Devil – although perhaps their evil, while no less dark, had been of a more mischievous nature. They were the fairies – or faeries – who had lured Thomas the Rhymer into their demesne, so that he was released from their deceit only by the courage of his beloved Janet. Renowned for their cruelty and their general malice towards mortals, they had been a far cry from the elves who had helped the shoemaker, or the fairies who had visited that Cottingley garden.

Joanna sat bolt upright in bed for a moment, then subsided back onto the scratchy pillow. She remembered having seen photographs of the Cottingley fairies, with their childish smiles and their air-light grace. These were the fairies – not the same individuals, of course, but manifestly the same species – whom she'd held in her palms the day before. They were the fairies who had been ushered in by the Victorian age to replace in people's imaginations the harsh beings who had terrorized earlier generations. They had dominated fairytales for a hundred years or more before fashion had swung against them and storytellers had begun to flesh their tales once more with the fairies of old.

She remembered Mrs Ruggeley reading *Peter and Wendy* to her when she'd been very small, and how she'd had to clap her hands to show she believed in fairies . . .

And there was the key to it. From what Robin Goodfellow had said, the Finefolk of his type had, for upwards of a century, populated Fairyland – in other words, for the very period during which they had accorded with human beings' pictures of them. As Robin had said, the Oldcomers had dwindled when humans stopped believing in their existence – Fairyland had been thinned. But this power of human belief over Fairyland was not merely a negative one: it had also 'thicked' the new version of Fairyland that was populated by impish, playful little beings like Robin Goodfellow himself.

Except that Robin Goodfellow, in earlier visions of Fairyland, had not necessarily been this cheery little chap: his other names, apart from Puck, had included Hobgoblin. Shakespeare had chosen to concentrate on his less atrocious aspects, but even Shakespeare had recognized him as a spirit whom it would be mighty unwise to cross. So were there two Robin Goodfellows?

Or were there two aspects of the *same* Robin Goodfellow?

'We were like the colours are today in this world,' Dolly Onskonsider had said. 'We were there, all right, but you couldn't see us.' Could it be that what she was really saying was that they – all of the Finefolk whom she'd encountered – had always been there because they were the *other selves* of the Oldcomers? They had been there, latent, beneath the grim visages of the malicious beings of old, ready to be conjured out into the open by the force of human credence? In which case, the recrudescent Comelatelies weren't really invaders at all: they were merely the long-submerged aspects of the Finefolk coming once again to the surface.

Was this why Robin Goodfellow and the Onskonsiders were so terrified of the Comelatelies? Not that these powerful beings would literally kill them, but that they would – like some infectious disease – contaminate them so that their repressed evil characters would regain dominance, with the inevitable destruction, at least for the time being, of their current personalities?

The more she thought about it, the more Joanna liked the theory – or disliked it, in a way, because it made it very difficult for her to trust her new companions. Whatever their intentions, they might turn into enemies when she was least expecting it. She contemplated waking Mr Dogg to warn him of this eventuality but, propping herself up on her elbows to take a look at his log-like form, dismissed the possibility.

For hours longer she lay sleepless, the fears and fancies dancing in an endless chain through her mind.

Dawn came finally, although the rest of the little household slept on, unaffected by the chilly grey daylight trickling in through the crooked windows.

Joanna slid her legs carefully out from under Mr Dogg and sat on the edge of her bed, flexing her numbed feet and stretching in a series of yawns. Oddly enough, she felt less sleepy now than when she had gone to bed, however many hours ago that had been. Maybe this was another of the magical characteristics of Fairyland – or maybe it was just an illusion, and she'd find herself falling asleep in the middle of the afternoon.

She was certainly thirsty. Probably an after-effect of the sticky mead.

Joanna tiptoed down the rickety stairs to the kitchen, watching the wall as she went for any sign of some join that might explain how the cottage's upper floor could be so big. There was none, of course. There hadn't been any tangible explanation, either, for the way the house grew larger as you approached it.

THE FAR-ENOUGH WINDOW

Nor were there taps in the kitchen. For a moment she was confounded: how could she have forgotten something so obvious? Then she saw a pail in the corner which, on investigation, proved to contain fresh cold milk. She drank from the wooden mug that had held her mead last night, wincing at the slight cloying tang this gave the watery milk.

She pottered out of the front door, which opened with a prolonged scrape, and blinked.

Suddenly the meaning was clear of Dolly's remark that the Onskonsiders frequently moved house. She'd meant it literally. They must shift it every night to somewhere new as a protection against the Comelatelies. The scene in front of Joanna's eyes was nothing like the bushy valley where she'd arrived with Robin Goodfellow and Mr Dogg the day before. Instead, the house stood thirty or forty yards from the shore of a broad, waveless lake that stretched to the horizon. She took a few steps towards the shingle, her mouth open. Then she turned and looked behind her, and saw that the farmhouse squatted in front of the foothills of a major mountain range, whose peaks were far lost in cloud overhead. The slopes were impossibly steep – the sort she might have scrawled in infancy when Mrs Ruggeley asked her to draw a mountain. Yet they were slopes rather than cliffs: grass and bushes and trees ran well up them, and here and there Joanna could see little white blotches which she assumed were sheep. As far as she could see to left and right the mountains extended in an unnaturally even line, as if someone had set a boundary beyond which they could not advance.

It was far colder than it had been last night, yet this couldn't be because of the wind off the lake, because there wasn't any. If Fairyland were a world like her own, then the house seemed to have been transported halfway to the poles. She glanced at the sun, but it was still too low to the horizon for her to verify this guess.

Joanna hurried behind a bush to relieve her bladder – the reason for coming outside in the first place – washing herself clean afterwards with a bunch of grass in a little stream. Then she crunched down the shingle to the edge of the water. It wasn't quite as still as she'd imagined. Little wavelets patted the wet stones of the lake's rim.

'Hey there!'

She looked up, assuming that one of the others in the house must have woken at last.

'No – over here!'

Turning in the direction of the voice, she saw a young man smiling at her. He was about her own height, and slender. He was leaning against a brine-seared tree-stump that must have been swept ashore in some long-ago storm.

He had pale brown skin and dark eyes, and was dressed in vest and trousers of a purple so deep that it was almost black. His hair was a very dark brown, and curly.

It took her a moment or two to register his strangeness.

Colours!

Unlike anyone else she had so far seen in Fairyland except herself and Mr Dogg, this person was in colours. He must be another traveller from the mortal world like herself!

'Have you been here long?' she said, walking towards him.

'I only got here a few seconds ago.' Joanna liked the sound of his voice: rich, and yet not deep. 'I was watching the water when you came out of the bushes.'

She felt blood rising to her face. 'I didn't mean that,' she said, forcing herself not to stammer. 'I meant how long had you been here' – she waved an arm at the lake and the sky beyond – 'here in Fairyland.'

'Oh, is that what it's called?'

'Well, that's one of its names. I think it has lots of names.' She was near enough almost to touch him now, and wondered if she dared do so. He seemed somehow much more *substantial* than the Finefolk: it would be reassuring to feel the firm flesh of his forearm against her fingertips – something to ameliorate the faint feeling of homesickness that was beginning to affect her. 'How did you get here?'

'I walked along the shore,' he said, turning half away from her and gesturing behind him. 'Look, you can see my footprints.'

Her eyes followed a line of pits and kicked-up heaps through the shingle.

'Where did you come from?' she said. 'I don't recognize your accent.'

'I don't recognize yours, either,' he said with a laugh. 'I've got a camp about ten minutes' walk along the beach. Would you like to see it?'

Joanna looked back at the house.

'I wouldn't worry about them,' he said. She reckoned that he must be at most about two years older than herself. It was rather odd being in the company of someone her own age – especially since he was a male. The only other male she'd ever seen outside videotapes was Mudgett, who for one reason or other didn't really count. 'They'll still be sleeping for a while, I expect.'

'I shouldn't want them to wake and start flapping because I'm gone,' Joanna said, biting her lower lip.

'It's not very far,' he said. 'Just come and have a quick look – just a quick look can't hurt anyone, can it? – and you'll be back again in no time, far too soon for anyone to become concerned.' Ringlets of his hair fell onto his brow. His eyes regarded her merrily.

She shrugged, and began to follow the marks he had made along the shore. He fell in beside her, whistling under his breath.

'What's your name? Mine's Joanna.'

He broke off his whistling. 'That's a very pretty name – for a very pretty person.'

She glanced back the way they had come and saw that the Onskonsiders' little farmhouse was already tiny. Surely she couldn't have walked this far already? Of course, it was very difficult to know exactly where you were with a house that seemed ready to change size at any time.

'Are there many others like us already here in this world?' she said.

He didn't reply for a moment. Then: 'There's no one at all like us, here or in any other world. We're unique, both of us: unique. Everyone's unique. Nobody's like anybody else. Wouldn't life be boring if it were otherwise?'

Joanna grinned at him, and he grinned back. 'That wasn't what I meant, and you know it,' she said.

'How do you know I knew it?'

'Oh, shut up!' she cried, giggling, and before she thought she playfully pushed his bare shoulder. He staggered, but caught his balance almost immediately.

The contact had been so brief that she'd hardly had time to appreciate it. She'd expected some kind of mysterious pulse to pass between them – his maleness to her femaleness

THE FAR-ENOUGH WINDOW

– but there had been nothing: just the smooth feeling of clean skin with lithe muscles beneath it. She wished she could think of another excuse to touch him – just to find out properly what it was like.

'We'll be there soon,' he said. 'It's just round the next head.'

A light breeze had sprung up, and it pressed Joanna's night-dress to her. She suddenly realized she'd become astonishingly cold without noticing it. The sun didn't seem to be supplying the day with any heat at all.

'I wonder where in the world we are?' she said.

'A long way from home, Joanna?' He cocked his head at her.

'A very long way,' she agreed, wrapping her arms about herself for warmth. Hard on the heels of discovering how cold she was came the realization that she wasn't wearing very much – certainly far less than she should in the company of a member of the opposite sex. 'What did you say your name was?'

'Oh, look, here we are.' As they came around the little outcrop he pulled one of her hands away from her body. His grip was dry and firm.

She stopped dead in her tracks.

He hadn't said there would be others in his camp.

There had to be sixty or seventy tents here, making a riot of colour in the greyness of the bay. Cooking fires smoked here and there. From the topmost points of several of the tents long pennants fluttered, one or two with grotesque insignia on them.

Moving nimbly among the tents were people like the young man who'd brought her here.

He tugged her insistently forwards.

'Let me go!' she hissed.

He laughed, and for the first time she heard in his laughter a trace of malice. 'No, not so easy as all that. I went to a deal of effort to entice you here, so I'm not just letting you go!'

His face was changing, too. There were no details she could pick on as definitely altering – nothing that would have shown in a drawing or a photograph – but overall the balance of features had shifted, so that what had been open and ingenuous was now secretive and sly.

Staring at him, pulling backwards on their joined hands, she began to scream, but a sudden puff of wind over the lake reached inside her mouth and plucked the scream away.

'You came of your own free will,' he said. 'So you must remain our guest for as long as we wish the pleasure of your company.'

The breeze had apparently stolen not just her nascent scream. Her powers of speech seemed to have deserted her entirely. She kicked out at his shin, but he evaded her deftly, grinning that new, spiteful grin of his.

'Besides,' he said, 'you've given me your name.'

She had – that was the worst of it. And he hadn't given her his. Every question she'd asked him, he'd avoided – and with such ease that she could hardly bear to think of it. She'd been so fascinated by his presence that she'd hardly listened to his various answers. Robin Goodfellow irritated her hugely with his habit of failing to give full explanations before drifting off down another line of reasoning, but this had been on a different scale.

He wasn't a man: he was an illusion of a man. In just the

same way, his companions in the camp towards which he was rapidly dragging her must be mere simulations of people. And, now that she looked at them more closely, she could see behind their faces, delineated by the chance falling of shadows as they went hither and thither among the tents, features that were entirely non-human: there a glimpse of stubby horns on a forehead; here scaly cheeks and narrow eyes. Some of the 'people' didn't walk at all: in place of legs they had curtains of sparks and cobweb-thin trailers, on which they seemed to float.

Staring abruptly at him, Joanna discovered that her companion floated like this – though she could have sworn he had boasted supple, agile legs earlier. And he had left footmarks on the beach – unless those footmarks had been as illusory as everything else about him.

These must be Comelatelies. The cruel fairies, the malignant ones: the Siddhe.

'You will enjoy yourself here,' said the youth confidently. His voice had changed, too: it had become harsh and choppy. It reminded her of wind flipping over the pages of an open book. 'This is a royal court, and guests are gifted all the finenesses that they might expect. Our banquets are legendary – and justly so, I can tell you. You will be given splendid robes to replace that skimpy gown of yours, and servants will attend your every whim. You will – '

'It's not a skimpy gown!' she said hotly. At last she had her voice again. 'It's Dolly Onskonsider's spare nightie, which she was kind enough to lend me!'

He was pulling her between the flapping tents now. Some of the Siddhe paused to look at her, their smiles derisive, but most paid her no attention, instead concentrating on their morning tasks.

Joanna wondered how far away she was from the Onskonsiders' cottage. It seemed to have taken her only a few minutes to reach this camp of unfriendly strangers, but how could she be sure it hadn't been much longer? Or had the sensation of walking along the shingly beach been just another illusion? Perhaps her abductor had flown her here, or magicked her. She cursed herself as a ninny for ever having agreed to go with him, leaving the others ignorant of her whereabouts. Perhaps they were waking up now, not at first worried by the fact that she wasn't immediately in evidence – though curious, maybe, with their curiosity only later turning to panic...

Get a grip on yourself, Joanna! she thought grimly. *If you lose your head now, then everything will certainly be lost. There must be some way out of this predicament – there* must! *If I left footmarks then Robin Goodfellow and the rest will be able to follow them and rescue me. Cling to that notion, Joanna! Any minute now Robin and the Onskonsiders, with Mr Dogg barking in support, will come running round that rocky outcrop and ...*

What could they do? There were only four of them, while this encampment contained perhaps as many as five hundred of the Comelatelies. Magic? Robin Goodfellow had informed her that magic never did exactly what you wanted when you needed it to – and, even if he'd been misleading her, there still wasn't a chance that three little Finefolk's magical power could match itself against such a mass of the Siddhe. Even with a dog on their side.

So just keep calm, Joanna. Go along with the deceiver quietly, and do everything you're asked to do – within reason. Pretend you've decided to cooperate: that he's broken your will already. This'll be a

THE FAR-ENOUGH WINDOW

waiting game: sooner or later an opportunity will present itself...

One of the tents was significantly larger and grander than the others, and it was towards this that they had been making their way. Despite the fact that the wind was fickle and not strong, the tent's huge pennant jutted out flat, as if whipped taut by a gale. The device on the banner was a pair of crossed, vicious-looking whips – not a reassuring sight. The tent itself was black, with gold trimmings along every loose edge. The flaps of its door had been tied open, but all Joanna could see within was baleful darkness.

'Can you tell me your name *now?*' she hissed at her captor.

He turned his face towards her, and she began to see its true nature. Gone was the pale brown skin and in its place were purplish, iridescent lizard scales. His eyes were yellow, and narrow slits. He had no real nose, only a slight bulge with nostrils set slantwise beneath it.

'Yes,' he clacked. 'You may know my name. I'm Peaseblossom, at your service. And the one to whom you'll shortly be presented is none other than Oberon, the most mighty Great High King of all the levels of the Farness: our monarch, of whom even you must have heard.'

Joanna recovered herself. *Peaseblossom! But Peaseblossom was a cute little female fairy in Shakespeare, surely? Not this... thing!* 'Indeed,' she said as coolly as she could, 'I have heard of great Oberon, and of his fair queen, Titania.'

'I wouldn't talk too much about Titania, if I were you,' clattered Peaseblossom quietly as they drew near the gaping door of the royal tent. 'She's a bit of a sore point around here.'

The response was so incongruous that Joanna, despite her fear, had to stifle a giggle.

'Now be quiet,' continued Peaseblossom, 'for you are about to be received by King Oberon.'

There were no guards at the tent's door, yet Peaseblossom halted as if he had been challenged, and waited expectantly, his grip on Joanna's hand never weakening. At last he nodded slightly, acknowledging an indiscernible permission to enter, and led her within.

Although only darkness lay outside, the interior of the tent was brightly lit. Garishly coloured cloths were laid out on the ground, and four or five fires smouldered on tripods, giving off an aromatic smoke. Two servants, both looking very much like female versions of Peaseblossom, moved swiftly and silently about unknown tasks, pausing every so often to turn towards the throne at the tent's centre and briefly bow their dark-scaled heads.

On that throne sat a being – she perceived him instantly as a man, though mortal man he most assuredly was not – of such latent power that the breath was pressed out of her. The throne was of carved bone, its details picked out in golden paint, and Oberon sat tensed in it, as if ready at any second to explode into some hideous flurry of mayhem. Standing up, he would have been perhaps a head and a half taller than Peaseblossom, but she sensed that, though he was by no means fat, he bore at least three times the mass of her captor. His thick, potent body seemed to radiate a dark energy.

He turned his great, scaled head towards them.

'You have brought the mortal,' he said. Joanna had difficulty making out the words: Oberon's voice was deeper than any man's, and his enunciation was thickly guttural. 'You have done well, Peaseblossom.'

Peaseblossom bowed from the waist. 'It has been my

honour to serve. The task was not an arduous one.'

Indeed it wasn't! thought Joanna angrily. *I came along with you so easily you'd think I hadn't got a brain-cell in my head! You picked an easy prey, my friend.*

'Nevertheless,' boomed Oberon, 'you have served me willingly and will not go unrewarded. But that is for the future, Peaseblossom. For the present you must leave her alone with me.'

'But, my lord,' Peaseblossom began, 'she may be dangerous. No mortal is to be trusted! She came with me so easily that there must surely be a possibility of subterfuge. Let me remain here to defend you should she – '

'I have spoken, Peaseblossom,' rumbled the monarch. 'Do not undo any of the credit you have earned yourself through making this capture.'

Looking at the king's vibrant figure, Joanna couldn't imagine herself being able to inflict the slightest harm on him, even if she had the foolhardiness to try. Oberon could flatten her with a casual blow from the back of one of those scaled, ridged hands that clutched the throne's armrests.

'Besides,' the king added, 'I have my handservants to protect me, should the mortal choose to attack.'

Joanna glanced at the two females and shuddered. They had drawn back their thin lips to reveal jagged rows of filthy but obviously razor-sharp teeth, between which darted green-black forked tongues. They hissed at her briefly, warning her.

'I wish you no harm, sire,' said Joanna, curtseying.

'All mortals lie,' said Oberon, his voice seeming to emanate from the ground she stood on. 'But I believe the fact is you could do me no injury. Now' – he swung his head – 'begone, Peaseblossom. Did you not hear my command?'

The slighter Comelately bowed hastily and fled through the tent's door.

Oberon stared at Joanna and rumbled deep in his fleshy throat. He was jacketed in cloth of gold, and on the boles of his legs were trousers sewn of gold-embroidered canvas. His feet were bare: they were scaled like the rest of his visible body, and the toes ended in curved talons. His eyes, like Peaseblossom's, were narrow yellow slits, with an upright line of blackness at their centres.

'Be seated, mortal,' he said finally. He flicked a horned finger and a servant came forward to deposit a low stool in front of the throne.

Tremulously Joanna advanced and, with a little dip of respect, sat on it. She tucked loose strands of hair behind her ears and looked up into the forbidding face of the Comelately monarch.

Again there was a long silence while he stared at her, his fingers moving restlessly on the throne's arms. Joanna wondered if he was waiting for her to say something, but she didn't dare speak a word. She wrapped her arms around her knees to keep her hands from shaking. Although it was certainly warm – too warm – here in Oberon's tent, she wished fervently that she were dressed in something less flimsy than Dolly Onskonsider's spare nightie. Despite the circumstances, the warmth and her long-delayed exhaustion conspired to make her eyelids heavy.

When at last Oberon burst into speech, she almost fell over forwards onto her face.

'I forget how ugly you humans are,' he boomed reflectively. 'It is a pity I was given no say in the creation of you.'

THE FAR-ENOUGH WINDOW

She bit back any response. *Remember, Joanna, you must subject yourself entirely to the Comelatelies, as if you had not an ounce of rebellion in you. Your spirit has already been broken: don't forget that. Bear any insults that are tossed your way – you'll be able to laugh at them later, when you're free once more and this great reptile is thrashing around in frustration because he's been thwarted by one of those 'ugly humans'. For the moment, though, let yourself be downtrodden . . . all you have to do is wait.*

'I didn't ask that you be brought into this world,' Oberon said. 'It was done to spite me by the parasites that infested this land of ours in my temporary absence. They knew it would hurt me, because I was cruelly spurned by someone who resembled a mortal much like you when I was . . . otherwise . . . Ach, I have stayed my hand from destroying them far too long.'

Still Joanna said nothing. With the king's eyes on her, she nodded tightly, as if to show there could be no possible disagreement with what he'd said. She'd already let him get away with claiming that he might have played a part in the creation of the human race, whereas she knew as a fact that matters had been almost exactly the opposite way around.

'I could have you destroyed, here and now, as a ghastly example to them of the folly of going against my wishes,' said Oberon. 'I could have you roasted alive on a spit, or nailed to a tree. I could have you slowly flayed alive. Your screams of anguish would fill every reach of the Farness.'

Joanna controlled herself with difficulty. *He's only saying these things,* she persuaded herself. *He probably couldn't actually do them. Act complaisant!*

'But that would be to torment the poor dumb animal for the sins of its master,' ruminated Oberon, 'and I am not a cruel monarch. Besides, your ugliness is almost quaint. I have decided to keep you close by me as my plaything.'

As a pet? thought Joanna in dismay. *All those years of expensive tutoring to end up as a reptile's pet? No – No, Joanna: it's the best thing you could have dreamt of. After a while, no one pays too close attention to the antics of a pet. Think of Mr Dogg . . . think of Mr Dogg. Oh, Mr Dogg, I hope you're safe!*

'In the mean time,' he continued, 'I will send Peaseblossom with a party of others to try to trace the place where you spent the night. The parasites that brought you here cannot be too far from there. Peaseblossom will seize them, and tonight we shall enjoy their torment while we feast upon our suppers.'

The house! thought Joanna exultantly. *Peaseblossom was blind to the house! Some trick of the Onskonsiders' must keep it invisible to the eyes of the Comelatelies!*

Still she kept her face calm.

'You are house-trained, I suppose?'

She nodded.

'Can you speak? You have said nothing since you came before me.'

'I did not wish to commit any disrespect,' said Joanna. 'I waited until Your Majesty bade me break my silence.'

Oberon growled. 'Do you have nothing you wish to say before my handservants take you away to bathe and feed you?'

'Just one thing, Your Majesty.' *It's all right to show just a trace of vestigial independent thought. If you're one hundred per cent bovine he might become suspicious.* 'These ones you hate so much and describe as parasites,' she said nervously. 'Without wishing to correct you in your wisdom, may I say that they call themselves Finefolk.'

A terrible smile split Oberon's face.

'We are *all* Finefolk here in Fairyland,' he said. 'Whatever they may have told you. Only *you* are not of the Finefolk. You are too different from us for us to hate.'

The rear of Oberon's great tent was divided by partitions into a number of small chambers, and it was in one of these that the two grim handservants settled Joanna.

First, though, they bathed her, stripping her of Dolly Onskonsider's spare nightie and rubbing her all over with lukewarm water and some kind of soapy stone. To begin with she found the experience shaming, but their scaly hands were much smoother and gentler than they looked, and soon she found herself relaxing under their attentions. Afterwards they clothed her in a one-piece robe of cool white cotton, belted with a braided rope of green-gold. Then they showed her into the room that would be hers, at least in the short term, with its pallet of cushions and rugs in one corner.

Close by, another room held a simple privy. She was given a plateful of fruit and little savoury sausages to eat, and then they left her alone. Throughout this time they had said not a word to her, and she not a word to them.

She didn't know what she was supposed to do next – stay confined in her allotted small chamber or wander around the rest of the tent, as an animal pet would be expected to do. She decided that circumspection was the better part of valour, and stayed where she was.

She wanted to be on her own, anyway, to try to sort out the confusion of her thoughts. She had determined that she would remain totally submissive until she saw an opportunity to escape or her friends somehow managed to rescue her: the decision having been made, it was as if the problem of her capture had been coped with – because anyway there was nothing else she could do about it for the time being – and it no longer troubled her. What was confusing her, though, was her own response to Oberon – to the Comelatelies in general, but in particular to him. His appearance had at first revolted her: his bunched, too-powerful body, his scales and his talons and his slatted eyes. His evident capacity for brutality horrified her, and of course he had stated as his aim the extirpation of her new friends and all of their kind – including those somewhat twee, innocently mischievous creatures she had cupped in her hands. From his brief fits of monologue, it seemed plain that he wasn't any too bright: the combination of innate brutality and unremitting stupidity would make him capable of cruelties far in excess of anything a more intelligent being could perpetrate. He would not have the wit to empathize with his victims – she had read enough of war and warriors, of tyrants and conquerors, to know the full scale of the misery and suffering the unimaginative could inflict. Moreover, he was imprisoning her – and dealing her the finest humiliating insult by merely tolerating her as a household pet.

She had every reason to loathe and dread him; yet that was not the response his presence, or the thought of him, kindled in her body. Instead, repelled as she was by every characteristic of his she knew, she found his presence vaguely attractive: all other things being equal, she would rather be in his company than elsewhere. Was this the famous allure of the traditional fairy-folk, or was it something different?

Peaseblossom had lured her, all right, but he had relied upon illusion to make himself attractive to her. There was no pretence about the crude reality of Oberon: was his allure more subtle, based not among the overt senses?

She wished she knew, because the resonance he sparked in her inevitably coloured her perception of what he was and stood for. It was hard for her to regard him emotionally as The Vile Foe when she did not find him vile in person. If, though, he were merely exercising some form of control over her discernment of him, then it would be possible for her to hate him as she felt was her duty.

Unless, of course, Oberon were right and Finefolk and humans were simply too different to be able to hate each other. Yet surely that should mean she should be immune to the glamour of him?

Joanna found she couldn't keep herself still: as soon as she settled herself down on the cushions that formed her bed she was standing up again, pacing to and fro. The chamber allocated to her was four paces long and three paces wide: an extremely small universe. She ate most of the fruit and savouries not because she was hungry, not even because she tasted them – she didn't – but automatically: eating was something for her hands and her mouth to *do*. She wondered what would happen if she shouted for one of the handservants: would they come and obediently take her for a walk around the Comelately encampment? Oberon hadn't been specific about their relationship to her: were they, within limits, at her command, or would they simply tend her as his pet?

At last she could stand her own fidgeting no longer. She cast aside caution with the flap of her chamber's door, and ventured into the next room. It was empty except for a bed like her own, and she continued through it.

At last she came to a place where a black-robed handservant – Joanna couldn't be sure if it was one of those who had bathed her – was weaving fine scarlet cloth, using her long, slender fingers for a loom. Joanna watched, fascinated, for a few seconds before the woman – hard not to think of them as women, despite the scales and gashlike eyes – realized she was there. When she did, the handservant leapt to her feet, the cloth and the fibre vanishing instantly in some direction Joanna couldn't follow, and retreated with a hiss towards the corner, holding up her scaly hands as if in defence.

'It's only me,' said Joanna, turning her own hands palms-outward. 'I won't hurt you.'

The handservant relaxed slightly, but only slightly.

'I was just looking for some company, for something to do,' Joanna said. *Remember that you must behave subserviently at all times. Lull them out of any suspicion they might have. Be docile.* 'If you'd rather, I'll go back to my own chamber. It's just I've been getting very bored there, and I'd like to – '

'Monster,' said the handservant hoarsely.

'I'm not a monster.' *Bear all their insults. Their insults don't matter. It's not as if you care what they think.* 'I'm just me.'

'Oberon fears you,' said the handservant. 'Even great Oberon. Mustardseed fears everyone. Mustardseed fears Oberon. Mustardseed fears anyone Oberon fears. Mustardseed fears monster.'

'But I'm *not* a monster. I may seem strange to your eyes, but where I come from there are lots of us who look like this.' *Only, of course, I never see them, except their flickering representations on my video screen.* 'You look strange to me, too, but I don't think you're a monster. You're just . . . different.' *Mustardseed. Another fairy whom Shakespeare portrayed. Where's Moth? Where's Cobweb? And where is Titania? Yes, that's the really big question: where is Titania?*

'Monster,' repeated Mustardseed.

Joanna kept all sign of irritation from her face. Oberon had seemed to be of fairly low intelligence, and this handservant seemed to be little more than moronic. Were all the Comelatelies so stupid? If so, it was surprising that they posed much of a threat to Robin Goodfellow and his kind – even with the force of human belief behind them. Yet Peaseblossom had possessed at least a degree of wile . . .

'Please don't be frightened of me. I would never harm you.' And did the handservant's bizarre claim that the powerful Oberon feared Joanna bear any relation to the truth, or was it just the misconception of a profoundly stupid observer? 'Here, take my hand.'

Joanna reached out and at last, with much trepidation, Mustardseed brought her own hand to touch it.

'Friends,' said Joanna.

The handservant was obviously too confused to respond, although she gripped Joanna's fingers with a little more confidence.

'I would like to see the rest of the encampment,' said Joanna coaxingly. 'Would I be permitted to do this? Would you be permitted to accompany me?'

The handservant hesitated.

'Oberon didn't tell me, one way or the other,' said Joanna.

'I think you can come outside me with me,' said

Mustardseed slowly. 'But' – she flashed her evil teeth – 'no escaping, mind. You are Oberon's possession now. Mustardseed will die to stop the loss of Oberon's possession.' Another flash of the teeth.

'You make yourself abundantly clear,' murmured Joanna. 'Lead on.'

They perched on a hillock a little upslope from where the Comelately encampment spread. Their tour of it had taken only a little while, since one part of it was very much like another – and very much like, Joanna guessed, any soldiers' encampment anywhere, though perhaps more abandoned in its colouring. And an encampment of soldiers this certainly was: there were no children among its population – and no old people either, although Joanna was uncertain that the Siddhe ever aged. Of all the individuals there, the only one to show any sign of advancing maturity was Oberon himself.

Mustardseed had grown much more relaxed in her company, although any sudden move Joanna made could set the handservant hissing with fear. Before leaving Oberon's tent Mustardseed had made a few passes in the air with her hands, and now she and Joanna were linked at the wrists by an invisible bond. The effect, Joanna had decided, was rather like being attached by a pair of handcuffs, except that the two cuffs were separated by several feet, and the chain between them was not only invisible but immaterial. Several times other occupants of the camp had walked between herself and Mustardseed without showing any signs of impediment.

Distanced from the camp's clamour by a few tens of yards, bathing in noonday sunshine, Joanna felt sleep once more handservant.

'Time had no dawn. There has always been time.'

'But you, yourself – you haven't always been as you are now, have you?'

'I have been Mustardseed forever.'

'Yes, but – '

'You are right. For a long time I did not look like this. I resembled – I was – one of the parasite Finefolk. I was no larger than your forehead, and my thoughts were also small. I had wings, and I was as ugly as a mayfly.'

So I was right about that, thought Joanna gleefully. *The Comelatelies are a different phase of the Finefolk.* 'But now your thoughts are bigger?' *They must have been infinitesimally small to be any smaller than they are now.*

'My thoughts are as big as bountiful Oberon allows them to be.' The handservant bowed her head in a curiously human gesture of shamefacedness. 'It is my sin that often I wish Oberon would permit my thoughts to be larger. But he is wiser than I am.'

Even the crudities of Mustardseed's speech could not hide the irony of the last remark. *Oberon may not realize it, but his throne is far from secure if even an airhead like this resents him. What plots might someone like Peaseblossom be capable of hatching?*

'Are you happy as Oberon's handservant?'

'What Finefolk could not be blissfully happy to serve so close to the great lord?'

Joanna admired the way her question had been avoided.

'Do you have no aspirations to do something . . . greater?'

Abruptly Mustardseed raised her head to look Joanna directly in the eye. 'This is something that I would rather you did not ask me.' She held her gaze, and in the end it was beginning to creep over her. The sun had crept only halfway up the sky and would soon begin to descend again, so her guess that the Onskonsiders had moved their home closer to one pole of a globular world seemed to have been correct. The day was far from hot, yet the warmth on her skin was sufficient to be soporific.

'Talk to me,' said Joanna. 'Tell me something of yourself to keep me from falling asleep.'

'Mustardseed has little to tell that could interest a mortal monster.'

'I'm *not* a monster! How many times do I have to tell you that?'

'You are Joanna, at whose name even Oberon himself must tremble.'

Joanna laughed bitterly. 'What makes you think that?'

'It is forbidden to talk of the thoughts that drive Oberon.'

'Why?'

A long pause. 'Because it is forbidden.'

'Then ... then tell me about yourself, as I asked you. Where do you come from? Where were you born? Do you have a ... a mate?'

'These are mortal questions.' Mustardseed's voice, though harsh, was no longer unfriendly. 'They make very little sense. I was not born anywhere, for birth is a mortal thing.'

'Do your people not have children?' That might explain their absence in the encampment.

'We have children, but they have always been and will always be children.'

'Always?'

'Always.'

'From the dawn of time?' Joanna leant towards the

THE FAR-ENOUGH WINDOW

Joanna who looked away.

Beneath them the activity around the cooking fires was increasing. Clearly it was nearly time for a meal.

'You must be hungry,' said Joanna. 'I have had plenty to eat, but you . . .'

'Mustardseed is hungry, but it is causing her no pain. She is glad to attend you.'

'Oh, don't be silly,' said Joanna, pulling herself to her feet and brushing grey grass from her bottom. 'You're not my slave – not even my servant. I asked you to be my friend.'

'Mustardseed did not answer you.'

Joanna looked askance at her. The handservant was correct – although Joanna had taken the touching of hands as a symbol of agreement. 'I would still like you to be my friend,' she said. 'So I ask you again: will you?'

After another perceptible pause Mustardseed nodded slowly. 'Mustardseed is Joanna's friend,' she said gravely.

'For as long as Joanna is Mustardseed's friend,' the Comelately added, turning to lead the way back down the hillside to the fairy encampment.

Mustardseed seemed to have no other duties. After she had eaten a meal of a sort of spicy vegetable stew that Joanna had tried a spoonful of and liked but been too full for, she was happy enough to spend the rest of the afternoon in the company of Oberon's pet. Of the king himself there was no sign. On one occasion Joanna caught a glimpse into the tent's major chamber and saw the throne empty and the fires cold. With Mustardseed she took another listless walk around the encampment, surprised by how little interest in her the other Comelatelies took, but any suggestion that the two of them might stroll a little further from it in search of new scenery was greeted with distress by the handservant.

Joanna took the chance to observe as much as she could, hoping that some of it might be useful to her later, when some prospect for escape opened up. But there were no guard positions to note or caches of weapons to remember: the Comelatelies seemed to see no need for either guards or weapons, and that was in some ways much more chilling than if the place had been armed to the teeth.

After only a short while they wended back to Oberon's tent and settled in for the afternoon, keeping a desultory conversation running as Mustardseed resumed the weaving that Joanna had earlier interrupted.

The process was a fascinating one, because it seemed to be entirely impossible and yet was taking place directly before Joanna's eyes. Mustardseed performed the various operations without any attempt at subterfuge – even, on request, for a while in slow motion. Yet, while Joanna could see that each step in the procedure was mundane enough, the totality was beyond her comprehension. The skeins of scarlet and purple and green fibre came from somewhere about Mustardseed's person – some pocket somewhere in her simple black robe – yet Mustardseed was incapable of leading Joanna's eyes to exactly where that was.

The handservant's fingers were plain enough – Joanna rubbed her own hands over their surprisingly soft scaliness – yet when they began dancing with the threads they became a loom, pinning each strand momentarily in its perfectly precise position for the continuance of the weaving. The cloth that was produced with such speed vanished to wherever it was that the original fibres had come from.

Joanna had asked Mustardseed to describe to her what was going on, in hope of understanding it that way, but all the Comelately had said was: 'If Mustardseed talk the weaving then Mustardseed become unable to weave the weaving.'

The cloth so produced was not in plain colour, but had regular decorations upon it. Everything moved with too much speed for Joanna to make these out, but she had the slightly uncanny sense that they were some form of writing. Perhaps, like herself, Mustardseed was a diarist.

Except that Joanna's diary had been written for only a single day – and that page had been written not by herself but by her ghost.

Home and Mrs Ruggeley and Mudgett and Knolly Mutton seemed a very long way away, and a lifetime ago.

Although Mustardseed was not forthcoming about the intricacies of hand-weaving she told Joanna, in dribs and drabs, a great deal about other things – perhaps rather more than she realized.

Oberon was not just the king, but the Great High King, and always had been. His reign was eternal, by definition, in both past and future. He held the power of life and death over his subjects – although this was largely academic, since it was virtually impossible to kill one of the Finefolk, the nearest they knew to death being the total submergence of one of their characteristics beneath another. This was the form of death that Robin Goodfellow and the Onskonsiders so feared. Yet the Great High King could (and on occasion did) order the execution of other forms of being – mortals who strayed inadvertently into Fairyland, discovered too much to be allowed to return yet refused to subjugate themselves to his rule (*How lucky I chose from the outset to project total submission,* thought Joanna), or beings from other reaches of the Farness who disputed Oberon's reign within his own realm.

And some of the punishments that the Great High King, in his wrath, inflicted on his own subjects were such as to make death seem the preferable option. As he had half-threatened Joanna, he was not reluctant to have those who displeased him flayed or roasted alive, though they would survive the torment and, over years or decades, recover. On occasion the punishment would be grimmer yet: a torment might be set to continue for eternity, and none had the power to call it off save Oberon himself, who never did.

Or, at least, not the Oberon who ruled the Comelatelies. In his other aspect, the one that human belief had forced him into for some decades, he had been a much more merciful ruler, and those condemned for eternity had soon been granted remission.

He was not like that now: he was stern to the point of cruelty – and yet Joanna received the strong impression from Mustardseed that he was not an unfair despot. Most of his subjects loved him not just because it was forbidden to do otherwise, not just because loving him was the natural order of things, but because they regarded him as worthy of their love. Joanna related this to her own ambivalence towards him, and wondered if perhaps this was part of the same thing – but she found it impossible to ask Mustardseed if this might be the case. Perhaps, had the maidservant been possessed of greater verbal fluency, Joanna might have attempted it, but the prospect of trying to explain, in three or four different ways until she found one that Mustardseed understood, how

THE FAR-ENOUGH WINDOW

Oberon made something respond inside her was too appalling to consider.

The Great High King's subjects might be almost without exception devoted to him, but he took no chances. At last Joanna began to realize what Mustardseed had been hinting at when she had talked of wishing Oberon would allow her thoughts to be greater. To some extent throughout his realm, but certainly within his own immediate vicinity, the Great High King exerted a sort of mental thrall on his subjects. While he could not control their thoughts entirely – for that would have meant he had to think all those thoughts himself – he could *limit* them. It was very hard for Mustardseed to think thoughts that did not correlate in some way with her duties as Oberon's handservant. She was able to communicate with Joanna even as much as this only because one of her duties had become to look after Oberon's pet, and that meant satisfying in some measure the pet's curiosity. The thoughts of a Comelately further up in the court's hierarchy, like Peaseblossom, were significantly less limited in the terrain over which they could range.

A trusted agent in the field required a certain independence of mind in order to be able to cope with unexpected eventualities – but even so was strictly circumscribed. The Comelatelies honoured to be in the court of the Great High King were all, to one degree or another, like Joanna, his playthings.

Again she recalled the mysterious attraction the monarch had seemed to exercise over her, and wondered. Was she, though as a member of a different species less susceptible to his imposed allure, his mental control, nevertheless to a certain extent sensitive to it? She found this explanation less disturbing to entertain than any other.

At one time when Mustardseed fell silent to concentrate on weaving a new and yet more elaborate pattern, Joanna realized that Oberon's direct governance of his courtiers' thoughts was in several ways a weakness. It meant that Joanna, through her very presence at his court, was a very great danger. For, if she could without intent extend the range of ideas of a simple-witted soul like Mustardseed into even mild resentfulness, what new notions might she not spark off in a mind of higher calibre, like Peaseblossom's, if she were in his company for long? She didn't know but, more significantly, neither did Oberon. Of course, he would have been vulnerable had he let himself be surrounded by those in whom he could place no trust. But, in a way, he was even more so now because, at any moment, one of those in whom he justifiably placed his complete reliance might suddenly, unpredictably, turn for a moment against him.

Furthermore, he would have no conception of how he might deal with those who were impervious to his mental sway. He would be unprepared for . . .

Perhaps Mustardseed had been right when she'd said Oberon feared her: the mortal; Joanna.

A thought suddenly dazzled her. *Does Oberon realize at all that I am not under his control?* Except to Mustardseed, who hardly counted, she had given every impression since coming to the camp of being completely cowed. She had acted the part of a submissive ninny. To be fair, she thought with a new flare of anger towards herself, she had *been* a total ninny to be fooled by Peaseblossom at the outset, but since then she had been playing a rôle. Had Oberon been taken in by that rôle only because it conformed to his expectation?

THE FAR-ENOUGH WINDOW

The idea that she might be *dangerous* – the first time in her life it had ever occurred to her to be any such thing – started a fire of delight inside her. She grinned savagely, then recomposed her face before addressing Mustardseed again.

'Will the camp move tomorrow?'

'The camp never moves. Sometimes the world moves around it, but the camp itself never moves.'

'Are you always in attendance on the Great High King? Have you always been? Will you always be?'

'For as long as Mustardseed is allowed to remember. For now. For perhaps all the rest of the nows there will be. Oberon has not opened the book of the future to me.'

'Do you think Oberon will want me to be with him forever?'

'It is forbidden for Mustardseed to contemplate the thoughts of the Great High King.'

'Do you love him?'

There was no answer.

'Do you love anyone else?'

'Mustardseed loves Joanna. Mustardseed has discovered she is allowed to love Joanna.'

Joanna felt her face warm. 'Joanna' – she gulped, realizing it wasn't entirely untrue – 'Joanna loves Mustardseed. Mustardseed is Joanna's friend. But do you love anyone else apart from me?'

Again there was no answer – not for a long while. Joanna was about to try a different tack when the handservant abruptly said: 'Mustardseed loves Oberon. Mustardseed *has* loved Robin Goodfellow.'

Joanna was dumbfounded. This might be another chink in the Great High King's armour.

Mustardseed made a grating noise that might have been a sigh. 'So many *have* loved Robin Goodfellow, and he has loved so many. Mustardseed is but one among them. Yet . . .'

There was a world of yearning in that 'yet'.

'Then do you – ?' Joanna began, but there was a sudden din outside and the doorflap to the chamber in which they sat was thrown back. Mustardseed's weaving disappeared as she started to her feet.

'Come with us, monster,' said a handservant – certainly one of those who had tended Joanna earlier. Her hours with Mustardseed had made her better able to tell these folk apart. 'The Great High King desires your presence.'

Outside the tent there was a crash of trumpets.

Joanna was jostled and bustled by the two handservants through crowds of the Comelatelies down to the lakeshore. The sun was nearly setting, and the textures of greys that its light created in the sky would have captivated her at any other time. But now she had eyes only for the procession that was advancing along the shore towards the encampment. Perhaps a dozen of the Comelatelies, both male and female, rode tall upon what Joanna at first thought were magnificent white horses and then realized with a shock of breath were unicorns, tossing their long silvery manes, the horns of their foreheads gleaming. Hemmed in by the unicorns was a small party trudging along on foot – and her heart sank. Even before she could make out their details she knew that these must be her friends – Robin Goodfellow, Dolly Onskonsider, Lumpenkulder Onskonsider and Mr Dogg. Apart from Mr Dogg, they seemed sad, resigned and grey.

THE FAR-ENOUGH WINDOW

Oberon stood with his back towards her, his great legs apart, his fists clenched on his hips. Even from behind she could sense his triumph.

Leading the procession was Peaseblossom, bearing upright a long lance with a pennant flying from its tip. On either side of him were two splendidly dressed Comelatelies with, wound about their necks, curiously curved brazen instruments. As Joanna watched they put these to their lips and again there was the noise of trumpets.

As the troop came closer, Oberon turned towards Joanna.

'My enemies make a sorry spectacle, do they not?'

'Assuredly so,' she said. 'They are so small, and you are so great.' For now, outside their house, the Onskonsiders were no taller than Robin Goodfellow, and he was hardly as tall as the knees of the unicorns around him.

Oberon seemed slightly dissatisfied with this answer, for he stared at her a long moment before turning back to contemplate his captives.

'Come stand beside me, Joanna,' he said.

She hurried to obey. No more than a couple of feet from him, again she felt that tingling.

'What do you think I should do with them, Joanna?' said the Great High King almost conversationally.

'It is a sign of true strength to show mercy,' she ventured.

'Many mortal kings have said that and died not long after.'

'Many mortal kings have said the opposite and died not long after just the same,' she said, 'and have been cursed in every generation since.'

The Great High King threw back his head and laughed. 'A plaything with a sharp wit! But, as I cannot die, it makes little difference what I say!'

'Though it may make a great difference to what others say of you,' said Joanna. *You must not push this too far. You're totally docile, remember. You may have a quick tongue, but you're still just the Great High King's pet, completely under his sway.*

He swivelled his head and looked down upon her. 'What difference does it make what anyone else says of Oberon?'

'None,' she admitted.

Peaseblossom was almost up to them.

'Sire, we have them! We found them not far from where I discovered the mortal girl, as you predicted. They were too stupid to conceal themselves from us properly.'

Too stupid . . .? Staring at Robin Goodfellow, Joanna saw him suddenly wink at her. Then his face resumed its look of abject disconsolation.

'Thus are downtrodden all foes of the Great High King of all the Farness, Oberon!' yelled Peaseblossom. Joanna could hear, lurking within the guttural bray, the pleasant, light tones with which he'd wooed her attentions this morning. So that young man hadn't been entirely an adopted persona? It was hard, looking at Peaseblossom's strained face, yellow saliva dripping from his jag-toothed mouth, to imagine the modestly handsome features of the other, but presumably they, too, must lie hidden there somewhere. But which was the mask? The guise Peaseblossom had worn when talking with her by the lakeshore, or this grim, vindictive countenance? Which disguised which?

'Take them to my tent, where I will decide their fate,' rumbled Oberon. He himself turned and, crushing shingle beneath his taloned feet, marched perfunctorily away towards the encampment. The Comelatelies who had straggled down to the shore behind him waited until he had passed them, then slowly followed in his steps.

Joanna, left there, stared up at Peaseblossom.

'I've never seen a unicorn before,' she said shyly. 'Will it let me touch his horn?'

'Inquisitive monster,' said Peaseblossom.

Joanna reached out an arm. Immediately she was seized from either side by the two handservants.

'No, let her touch him,' said Peaseblossom dismissively. 'It is a request of no importance.'

The handservants released their grip and she reached out again. The beast regarded her placidly through an eye that was huge yet, size apart, more resembled a human eye than a horse's – and was not at all like the slits of the Comelatelies.

She touched the horn. A sharp ridge – so sharp that she was fearful of cutting her finger – ran in a helix all the way up it from base to needle-like tip. Taking a half-step closer, she ran her hand with more confidence along the touch-warm bone. The animal continued to eye her, unfrightened by her attention. She imagined that she was standing beside Rapscallion: although he was black and the unicorn was white, they had the same full, fusty smell. She put the flat of her knuckles on the beast's broad forehead and rubbed it: the white hairs were like silk. The unicorn lifted his head against her touch and moved it from side to side, rubbing her in response. He made a low *harrumph* noise with his thick lips. The steadiness of his gaze upon her would have been unnerving except that there was a total absence of malice or fear in it.

'Hrimfaxi seems to like you,' observed Peaseblossom coldly.

'I never thought he would do otherwise,' murmured Joanna, regarding the soft eye that was upon her.

'We have delayed obeying our lord's command long enough,' said Peaseblossom abruptly. He beckoned behind him to the two trumpeters. 'Sound the triumph once more, and then let us take these scum to the tent of the Great High King.'

This close, the sudden blast from the two brassy instruments was deafening, and Joanna staggered away, hands over her ears, to be caught by the handservants. She looked back and saw Peaseblossom leering maliciously at her discomfiture. But she also saw Hrimfaxi continuing to regard her in that gentle, inquiring, friendly way. Peaseblossom was not, perhaps, as clever as he thought. Some kind of a bond had been forged between her and the beast.

Remember to submit in all things, she reminded herself.

'Thank you for letting me touch your unicorn, Peaseblossom,' she called after the troop. 'It was kind of you.'

He didn't turn his head.

Robin Goodfellow seemed small when standing beside Joanna. In front of Oberon he was minuscule. The Great High King loured impassively down on the tiny figure, observing him but rarely moving. Robin, for his part, had chosen to adopt the rôle of Perry Mason or Henry Drummond – she had watched *Inherit the Wind* several times, and assumed that Robin must have done likewise. He strutted before the throne, tugging from time to time on a waistcoat that he did not wear. Behind him the Onskonsiders sat on the floor, looking around them with bright interest. Mr

THE FAR-ENOUGH WINDOW

Dogg, the only one of the quartet not to be in shades of grey, sat or stood or fidgeted or scratched at fleas: he was playing, Joanna realized, the rôle of a dumb animal.

She was part of a crowd that ringed the main chamber of the Great High King's tent. Still she had the two fierce handservants in attendance, one on each side; Mustardseed, who had trailed around behind them earlier, was nowhere to be seen. Men and women of Peaseblossom's troop were stationed here and there around the interior of the circle, as if to hold back the press of Comelatelies.

'. . . so I must ask you, mighty lord,' Robin Goodfellow was saying, 'if, though your reign is indeed extensive, you indeed have jurisdiction over these poor innocents who cower behind me. Look at them, if you will: two cravens and a beast who is all lick and tailwag. Are they subject to your rule, or are they as the animals of the wilds, free of all legislation? This is not a mere intellectual debate, may I remind you, but a matter of gravest concern, for the precedent you set will . . .'

Joanna grinned secretly at Robin's impersonation. If only there were a jury he could flamboyantly address. Every eye was on him as he strode backwards and forwards beneath the Great High King's gaze.

She glanced at the Onskonsiders. Mr Dogg, having gone to sniff suspiciously at the nearest guard, was ambling back to join them. He lurched slightly in his stride and . . .

. . . his muzzle passed clear through Lumpenkulder Onskonsider's shoulder.

Joanna blinked. She was certain no one else had seen: the Comelatelies, Oberon included, seemed without exception to be hypnotically fascinated by Robin Goodfellow's performance.

As if sensing her consternation, Dolly Onskonsider looked over towards her and smiled in a distracted way.

'... and to exact punishment upon those who are not truly his lieges is surely, great monarch, the symptom of a tyrant – an accusation that has never, to my knowledge, been levelled against you except by insidious rebels against your rule. For has it not been said that ...'

Joanna was bewildered by Robin Goodfellow's strategy. Surely this barrage of words, of pseudo-legalisms, was pointless? All it could do was irritate the Great High King so that, when finally he pronounced his judgement, it would be all the more dire because of his anger. Yet she remembered the confident wink Robin had given her down by the shore ... and there was the way that Lumpenkulder Onskonsider's shoulder had just now seemed so insubstantial.

And the way that her friends had been 'too stupid' to hide themselves. Too stupid? Robin Goodfellow? It was hardly to be believed. Had they *wanted* to be seized?

Were they here to rescue her? She had thought they might find a way. But, if they had, it was difficult to discern. It looked much more as if Robin were blathering them all to a cruel doom.

'... and some of you may say that I've talked enough.' Robin Goodfellow pulled himself up to his full diminutive height and sucked on an imaginary cigar. 'And, though it may come as a surprise to this court to hear it, I must admit that I agree with them. Enough of talking, say I! 'Tis time to rush to judgement. The defence is ready to rest, your honour. The territory of justice is prepared for you to enter it: it is a measure of your greatness that even angels fear to tread there. I am, oh mighty lord and monarch, your humble servant, Robin Goodfellow.'

He bowed deeply, the peacock-feather of his hat flopping over to touch the ground in front of his nose, and vanished.

There was a moment's stunned silence, then the yelling began.

The Onskonsiders had disappeared in the same instant. Of the original quartet before Oberon, only Mr Dogg remained. He circled around where the Onskonsiders had been, sniffing the lavish cloths of the tent's floor and whining miserably.

Oberon pounded the armrest of his throne.

'We have been deceived!' he bellowed. 'Tricked! Made fools!'

Joanna was as stunned as all the rest. She stared at Mr Dogg, still acting in character as a confused brute. He sat down and began to howl woefully.

'Bring Peaseblossom to me,' roared Oberon. 'Bring the wretch here! He is the author of this folly!' His courtiers milled about chaotically, urgent to be seen obeying his command.

Buffeted by them, Joanna tried to hold her position. 'Mr Dogg!' she called softly. 'Over here, Mr Dogg!'

What she'd witnessed was magic – of that there could be no doubt. And it had been much-needed magic: whatever sentence Oberon might have pronounced on Robin and the others, they could hardly have hoped for a kindly fate. Yet Robin had told her, had he not, that in Fairyland – at least for the thinned Finefolk – magic never worked reliably when you really wanted it to. He and the Onskonsiders would hardly have allowed themselves to be brought into the court of the

Great High King relying solely on magic to bail them out. And she still couldn't dream of what they had come here *for*. Their abrupt disappearance seemed to rule out any motive of rescuing her.

But Mr Dogg was still here. Perhaps he knew. She called him again, and this time he stopped howling and glanced towards her. He seemed to be smiling.

Then her arm was grabbed.

'Joanna must come away,' said a hoarse voice. 'Joanna in danger!'

She turned and saw Mustardseed's anxious face.

'Folk might hurt Joanna, thinking to please Oberon,' the handservant gasped. 'Come away.'

Joanna allowed herself to be dragged through the mêlée. Looking back over her shoulder, she saw Mr Dogg shrug and make to follow her – then her view was obscured by a jostle of limbs and torsos.

'To my room,' Mustardseed said. 'Joanna must hurry. Mustardseed and Joanna will be safe there for a while. Mustardseed is Joanna's friend. Mustardseed help Joanna.'

Somehow they hauled themselves clear of the crowd, and slipped through various corridors and partitions of cloth to reach the chamber where Joanna had first discovered the handservant, weaving. The commotion was terrifyingly loud in their ears, but at least they could no longer see the angry eyes and faces.

'Joanna must leave here,' said Mustardseed hastily. 'The Great High King would protect you if he could, but he cannot be everywhere. Those under his command might kill Joanna first, before he could stay their hands...'

'Escape?' Joanna said. 'Does Oberon know of this?'

THE FAR-ENOUGH WINDOW

A look of complete confusion knotted the handservant's scaly face. Then it cleared. 'The Great High King would approve of Mustardseed's actions if he knew of them,' she said defiantly. 'The Great High King is afeared of Joanna, but she is also his, and he guards jealously the safety of his possessions.'

Someone must have knocked over one of the fires in the main chamber, for a threatening orange glow began to billow against the wall of Mustardseed's room.

'But how can I escape?' said Joanna. 'Your people would never let me go, and they're everywhere!'

'Call the unicorn!'

'Hrimfaxi?' Joanna was about to add 'but we've only just met' when she realized how foolish that might sound. 'But I don't know where he is! I don't know how to call him! What makes you think he'll come?'

'He'll come, all right,' said a grating voice behind her. She turned and saw that Mr Dogg had crept in. 'Why do you think Robin Goodfellow made his own ghost bring him to meet you?'

'But I – ' *But surely that's the wrong way around,* she thought. *Hrimfaxi is Peaseblossom's steed, and it was he who brought Robin here. But I would never have met the unicorn if Robin and the others hadn't been . . .*

'And you don't have to do anything to call him except *want* him to come,' Mr Dogg continued. 'That's the way it is with unicorns – haven't you read the books?'

'Haven't I – ? Oh, you mean because I'm a – ' She flushed.

'A rare item in Fairyland,' said Mr Dogg sardonically, 'where everyone else has been alive for all eternity. Now that Hrimfaxi and you have touched, he'll be able to find you wherever you are in the Farness.'

'Hurry!' said Mustardseed. 'Joanna must *hurry!*'

Joanna dropped down beside Mr Dogg. Her mind was in too much of a confusion for her to be able to concentrate on wanting Hrimfaxi to come to her. She clutched the mongrel to her, finding comfort in the familiar smell of him, the prickliness of his hairs against her face.

'Help me, Mr Dogg!'

'You must help *yourself*,' he said hoarsely. 'This is something only *you* can do. I'm male, and anyway I've . . . had my moments.'

The orange glow on the wall was brighter now, its edges limned with the darkness of smoke.

'Joanna must fall into herself,' said Mustardseed, snatching Joanna's hand. 'Fall into herself and find her core.'

The words didn't mean much to her, but they served to shock Joanna into an unnatural calmness.

In that calmness she remembered the unicorn's gentle gaze on her, and the silky touch of his forehead on the back of her knuckles. She felt his strength, and suddenly a wave of the affection he must hold towards her swept over her, drenching her in the knowledge that their spirits were inextricably bonded. She smelt his warm scent filling her nostrils, and knew the tranquillity of his presence . . .

He was there like smoke in their chamber, insubstantial and yet undoubtedly *there*. Only his eyes and his horn were clearly delineated: the rest of him was hazy, misty. Yet she knew without question that Hrimfaxi himself was with her.

Seize my horn, said his soft voice in her head.

She reached out with her free hand. Mustardseed was still holding her other and now tried to pull herself away, but

THE FAR-ENOUGH WINDOW

Joanna, with sudden determination, clutched the handservant's fingers grimly. Mr Dogg slipped himself quickly into the nook of her arms and pressed himself against her chest.

Fly, Hrimfaxi! thought Joanna, knowing at last just exactly what she must do. *Fly!*

Six

Forgotten Fears

So, resolutely turning her back upon the house, she set out once more down the path, determined to keep straight on till she got to the hill. For a few minutes all went on well, and she was just saying 'I really *shall* do it this time – ' when the path gave a sudden twist and shook itself (as she described it afterwards), and the next moment she found herself actually walking in at the door.

'Oh, it's too bad!' she cried. 'I never saw such a house for getting in the way! Never!'

– Lewis Carroll, *Through the Looking Glass, and What Alice Found There*, 1872

Joanna was always afterwards unable to pin down in her mind exactly what took place next: it was as if, every time she tried to place them under the glass of memory, the events moved away in the moment before she brought the glass into focus. But what it *felt* as if had happened was this:

The smoky unicorn snorted and reared up on his hindlegs, his forehooves clawing at the air. Joanna was astride his broad, aethereal back, with Mustardseed clinging on tight behind her and Mr Dogg draped inelegantly across the mist of Hrimfaxi's shoulderblades in front of her. She clutched the tresses of the unicorn's feathery mane in her hands.

Then, beneath her, Hrimfaxi faded into substantiality. Out of the corners of her eyes she could see the walls of Mustardseed's room, one of them now beginning to char and smoulder, fade into a thin fog.

And then the unicorn leapt; cold, empty air was whipping her hair back in a tangle behind her, pulling her lips back from her teeth, pressing against her eyes so that they filled instantly with tears . . .

They were in the midst of a starfield, one starfield among many, the brilliant points of light clustering here and there, or cast like tiny grains of diamond across the black velvet of eternity. The pulse of Hrimfaxi's mighty strides beat up through her, making her whole body ache. Colossal bulbous billows of gas, glowing in softly radiant colours, puffed towards them, then retreated as Hrimfaxi galloped at full tilt by them, his neck outstretched, his mane lashing, his horn like an arrow fleeing to the furthest corner of the universe. The clouds of bright stars shifted and turned from the speed of Hrimfaxi's flight among them: spirals unfolded and dissipated, unknotting themselves into nothingness; pools of light erupted silently into fountains of brilliance; scintillant shards of ice melted and flowed. Bright stars in reds and whites and golds and blues and oranges whipped past Joanna's face as she leant forward into the terrifying gale of Hrimfaxi's swiftness. She lost all notion that Mustardseed and Mr Dogg were with her: there were only herself and the unicorn and the infinite fields of stars and the waves of the sea that is everness . . .

THE FAR-ENOUGH WINDOW

And through the dreadful stillness she heard, faint at first, the notes of a song, a song that was beyond ears, the song that all the universe is, the song that she and Hrimfaxi were minute parts of, consonances that filled out the everlasting chorus of the starfields . . .

She was everywhere at once, and she was also a woman clad in a belted white robe and seated astride a vibrantly alive creature that plunged ever onwards through the lit blackness. She herself was the light of the stars: she saw herself with their remote, flaringly chill eyes. She was a part of the great, the infinite song, and yet she was its entirety. For it, too, was only a part of her. She was a rain of starlight on the bleak, still waters of an unseen lake. She was silence and the shout of a million throats. She was living and yet she was somewhere far beyond all life. She was the soul's night that never ends, and the luminosity of a newborn smile. She was tinier than a lepton and huger than the colour violet. She was nameless, and the One Who Has All Names. She was the gods – she was none less than Qinmeartha, the Insane God – and she was the humblest, most tenuous of all their creations. She felt herself spread out thinly so that there was a taint of her in everything that there ever was and ever would be, from the brightness of spun platinum to the sere voracity of a hole that swallowed space. She was too vast, too vastly isolated from the rest of herself, to sustain thought, yet her thoughts were the song that was all things . . .

And still a core of her remained. A core that was herself, Joanna, whom she could both see and be as she clung to Hrimfaxi's mane and was preternaturally aware of the softness of its frondy hairs against her fingers and palms.

She was the Farness.

The Farness was her.
She was *in* the Farness.
The Farness was *in* her.
Forever.
Never to leave...

They were in a place where white desert stretched out on every side of them. She knew they had been there a long time – hours or years, she was uncertain of the precise duration, although she knew near enough – perhaps ever since they had left the smoke-smelling prison of the court of the Great High King. The sky was entirely black above them – not a star to be seen – and she sensed they were on some world far beyond all stars. Yet the white sand of the ground glowed with a soft milkiness sufficiently bright that she could see her companions and her surroundings perfectly.

'The surface of the moon,' she breathed. Her bottom was a mass of aches from the ride: she shuddered to think how bruised it must look.

Mr Dogg, coming up behind where she sat cross-legged on the sand, gave a little growl of disgust. 'I love you dearly, Joanna, but sometimes your persistent failure of imagination appals me. Always so *parochial*! Hasn't it yet begun to get through to you who you are – who you can become?'

'I seem to be the same person I always was,' said Joanna crossly, pinching her leg just above the knee to see if her flesh felt any different from usual. 'I live in the big house with you and Mrs Ruggeley and Mudgett and Knolly Mutton and ...'

'But *you're – not – there – now!*' snarled Mr Dogg. He trotted away across the sands, clearly too angry to talk with her any more.

She watched his retreating tail sadly. Why was he suddenly being so horrible to her? Mr Dogg, her only friend from home – her lifeline.

Hrimfaxi was standing about twenty yards away, his head bowed as if he were grazing. His great flanks still heaved from the exertions of the wild gallop. Mustardseed stood at his neck.

The handservant felt Joanna's gaze on her and looked up. 'I didn't want to come with you, you know,' she said, 'and the anguish of being torn away was like the flesh being ripped off my bones, but I thank you, Joanna. Thank you for giving me my larger thoughts back.' Mustardseed gave a slightly pained smile. 'Thank you,' she repeated.

'Where are we?' said Joanna.

Mustardseed shrugged. 'Hrimfaxi has brought us out of Fairyland and into the further realms of the Farness. We are beyond anywhere that even the Great High King can reach us. Great High King!' she snorted. 'His dominion is one of the grains of sand in this desert, and who could tell which one?'

Joanna looked around her, felt the desert floor beneath her outspread palms. The desert ran away from her all the way to the black horizon in every direction, and she sensed that the horizon was almost infinitely distant. She could cup a million grains of the desert's white sand in her hands . . .

'Are these all realms like Fairyland?' she asked numbly.

'No,' said Mustardseed. 'Only one. The rest are merely chalky sand.'

The thought of Fairyland's vast loneliness made Joanna's

spine cold, and she shifted uneasily, as if she could warm it.

The desert, she began to realize, was not featureless, despite the near-uniformity of the light. It rolled in low hills and shallow valleys, some only a few yards across and others many miles. She did not at the time wonder why she could see clear across great mountain ridges to the horizon beyond them. Her sight was caught by one particular structure, the only feature that disturbed the smooth line where the white sands met the blackness of the sky: a mountain that jutted steeply out of the desert, its pitted sides nearly cliffs, its top a jagged plateau like the crown of a carious tooth.

'What's that?' she said, pointing.

Mustardseed turned to look. 'I don't know.'

It's where we're going, said Hrimfaxi's quiet voice. Joanna could see Mustardseed hearing it as well. *It's the reason I brought you here. It is the route we must take if we are to go back to where we came from.*

'To Fairyland?' said Joanna, aghast. 'But surely that's the last place we want to – '

Of course we must return there, said Hrimfaxi mildly. *Otherwise there would have been no reason in our leaving.*

'I thought we left so that we – I – could escape from being slain by the Comelatelies?' Joanna nodded guiltily towards Mustardseed. 'Present company excepted, of course.'

Robin Goodfellow's still there. Dolly Onskonsider's still there – and Lumpenkulder. They caused themselves great pain to conjure their ghosts out of themselves, so they could lead me to you. They haven't escaped from Fairyland. There was a definite note of reproof in Hrimfaxi's thought. *Your friends,* he added.

Joanna's hand flew to her mouth. 'How selfish of me to have forgotten – even for a moment! Yes, you're right – of course we must go back! If there's any chance we can help them we must do so! What are we waiting for?' She threw herself to her feet in a cloud of white sand, which settled only slowly around her bare feet. 'Come on, Mr Dogg! Come on, Mustardseed! Let's get going!' She shook sand out of the creases of her robe. 'May we ride upon you once more, Hrimfaxi, or are you weary from your flight here?'

I cannot be weary when you and I are touching, Joanna. She imagined she felt Hrimfaxi smile. *It's a matter of fact – not just a compliment.*

'Then let's be on our way,' she cried, running towards him. She put her arm around his great, strong neck, and felt the might of him throb against her skin.

'Do *we* get a vote on this?' said Mr Dogg.

Joanna looked around the nakedness of the white desert. 'You can stay here if you'd like,' she offered.

'No,' he muttered after a moment. 'I just wanted to make a point, that's all.'

Only Mustardseed seemed reluctant to set off for the distant crag. She stood as if she were alone, her narrow eyes drinking in the barren white and the impenetrable darkness. 'I have so many thoughts to explore,' she whispered. Her voice was no longer harsh and clangorous – had not been since first she'd spoken to Joanna here. Her whisper was like soft dust moving over polished stone. 'To think, I never knew there were half so many there.'

'Come on, Mustardseed,' said Joanna from her seat on Hrimfaxi's back. 'We can't leave here without you. Remember, Mustardseed is Joanna's friend so long as Joanna is Mustardseed's friend – and I'm still your friend.'

The handservant shook her head once, twice, as if trying

to jerk dreams out of it. 'Yes,' she said. 'Of course I'll come with you. I was just enjoying the sensation of being me, that's all.'

She moved quickly across the sand and leapt easily up behind Joanna.

The unicorn set off across the desert at an easy canter, his big muscles moving smoothly. She put the flat of her hand on the base of his neck and felt the flow of his power. She felt Mustardseed remove one hand from her waist; glancing back, she saw the handservant balancing easily as she surveyed their surroundings.

'See anything?'

'No,' said Mustardseed. 'Just desert. But oh what a *freedom* it is to be able to see just desert.'

Joanna pondered for a few moments. 'Why did you join Oberon's court, if you hated being there so much?'

'I didn't. Hate being there so much, I mean. I was perfectly content, until you appeared. Oberon allowed me just enough range of thought to perform all the functions he required of me – nothing like enough to become unhappy with my lot.'

'But you must have known from before – '

'Known what I was letting myself in for, you mean? Listen, after the Oldcomers had been thinned from existence, leaving us to be merry peris and leaping leprechauns, most of us didn't have enough of a mind to remember our names, let alone what it had been like to serve the Great High King in the before-times.' Mustardseed smiled suddenly. 'Don't mistake me, when I was a little fairy with gossamer wings I was still in the service of Oberon, but he too was different. He was languid and youthful and very, very beautiful.' She sighed.

'We all loved our king in a way that was not entirely pure, except that he was devoted to his queen, Titania. So most of us fell in love with Robin Goodfellow instead: he might not be half so handsome, but he had a *much* better sense of humour. And Robin loved us all back, as much as his cynicism would allow . . . and I thought he probably loved me most of all. Likely all the other fairies thought the same. Then, when the little Finefolk were thinned in their turn, we all changed – all except Robin Goodfellow and a few others – and I found myself once more the handservant of a ruthless monarch.'

She smiled tightly.

Joanna remembered a question that had been troubling her earlier.

'What happened to Titania?' she said.

'Oh, she was beautiful – almost as beautiful as you are when you let yourself be, Joanna.' Mustardseed chuckled. 'How odd. I've only just realized. Back in the court of the Great High King I thought you were hideously ugly. Now, here, although you haven't changed, this same pair of eyes sees you as beautiful. As you are. And growing more so.'

Joanna discovered that the same transformation of perception had occurred in her, too. She saw the exquisite sheen of Mustardseed's scales, the grace of her flattened nose-that-was-not-really-a-nose, the glow of her yellow gaze. She said as much, and the handservant smiled broadly. The teeth – yes, well, everyone had imperfections. And often it was the imperfections that created their beauty. Mrs Ruggeley was, a mass of imperfections, beautiful.

'About Titania – ' Joanna prompted.

'She was beautiful, as I've said. She had long hair that

reached to her ankles and was the colour of weeping willows. Her face was a pale acorn. Her eyes – ah, her brown eyes danced and shone to the tune of a pond's ripples. I think we all loved her as much as we did Oberon – and, truth be said, with considerably more chance of requital, for she did not in full match his besotment. But towards the time of the Thinning of the little ones, Titania's face became clouded with presentiment. She knew what was coming, and she had no wish to be part of it. She tried to tell Oberon of this, for she loved him enough for that, but he was living all his life in the middle of a midsummer day and would not let her put clouds in its sky. He waved her away, with her troublesome frets, and when next he looked for her he found she was gone.'

'Gone? Gone where?'

'If anyone of us had known,' Mustardseed said darkly, 'you can be sure Oberon would have known as well. But nobody did. And when the change in him came – as it came in all of us – he vowed vengeance on the one whom he decreed had betrayed him. Which, had he thought about it, was himself.'

'She just . . . vanished?' Joanna said.

'Gone from Fairyland. Seemingly gone from all the realms of the Farness where Finefolk minds could reach. She no longer wished to be Oberon's queen. Disappeared – as if she had never existed outside our memories of her.'

Mustardseed held up both hands as if to show they were empty, and Joanna thought she might fall – but the handservant's balance was perfect.

'And no one knows?'

'Oh,' said Mustardseed, 'assuredly there must be some

who know. This steed of ours, for example.' She heeled Hrimfaxi's flank with insouciant roughness. 'Unicorns can see further into the Farness than any Finefolk can, although often they are not free to tell of what they see there. Ask him, if you like.'

Joanna reached out her thoughts towards Hrimfaxi, and felt his warm response. But almost at once his mind recoiled a little.

Don't ask me your question, Joanna. I cannot lie to you, and I could not refuse to answer you – yet it would hurt me greatly if I answered you truthfully. So please, Joanna, please do not ask.

'You see?' said Mustardseed.

Joanna fondled the back of Hrimfaxi's head. 'Don't worry, friend,' she breathed. 'I'll not hurt you. Only my curiosity wanted to know.'

All this time they had been approaching the great structure that rose into the black sky of this silent world. Such was its vastness that now, although it towered over them, they seemed to have come no closer to its sides.

'What *is* that place?' said Joanna.

Hrimfaxi seemed reluctant for a moment to answer this question as well. Then he said: *It is the Lair of Forgotten Fears – the first of two gateways through which you must pass if you are to reach Fairyland once more.*

Joanna turned to look at Mustardseed, but the handservant merely shrugged, seemingly as baffled by this response as she was herself.

When you awake, Joanna, in the middle of the night with ice clutching your heart and a scream frozen on your lips, and you know that you have dreamt of horrors and worse but cannot remember anything of them – those are the worst nightmares of all, the ones too dreadful to recall. Or the things that used to terrify you as a child – the tap of a branch on a curtained windowpane, the pummel of thunder on the roof – which now you can vaguely recollect seemed frightening, though the fear itself has been drained out of them by time.

Joanna thought she wouldn't mention that she still found thunderstorms ... well, *terrifying* was probably too strong a word to put on it, but ...

And then there are the terrors that used to make your ancestors quake – the werewolves and the selkies, the kelpies and the frost giants – but now are remembered only as folktales ...

'The Oldcomers – the Comelatelies – they were among those,' said Joanna.

Yes, you're correct: and the Siddhe also. But the Siddhe were returned to Fairyland – returned there by human mortals like yourself. Cast even further than Fairyland. And where did you think they'd been all those years?

'Repressed,' said Joanna. 'I thought they were the repressed selves of the Finefolk – their dark aspects.' She glanced back once more at Mustardseed, who was looking horrified.

True enough: that is what happened in the realm of the Farness called Fairyland. But this is not Fairyland: you are no longer there, but here. In the reality of the Farness as a whole what happened was that the Siddhe, the fear of them forgotten, were brought here – leaving their other selves to rule Fairyland until their time, too, would come.

'Then the little ones are here now, in their place?' Joanna grappled with the concept that two quite different explanations for one thing might both be true at once.

Who has ever feared the little Finefolk? said Hrimfaxi. *No, you won't find them here – they're in a realm far from here, waiting in their own lair until some change of fortune will return them to what they regard as their own kingdom. Only the creatures of nightmare come to this place: the forgotten fears, the ones that no one any longer has a use for – at least for the time being.*

Joanna wrinkled her face. 'Are other ... people in the Farness tormented by nightmares as well? Not just we humans?'

Ask Mustardseed.

Once again Joanna swivelled in her seat. One look at Mustardseed's expression was enough. There was no need to ask her.

'This,' said Joanna carefully to the unicorn, 'must be a very terrifying place that you are taking us to.'

Yes – I did not tell you about it earlier, in case you would refuse to come. But we have to go through this portal if we are ever to rediscover Fairyland. So I allowed my silence to deceive you.

Joanna felt a rush of hot anger. 'I thought you were my true friend!' she said. 'Didn't you trust me to do what is right, no matter how terrifying it might be?'

Hrimfaxi's thoughts were silent.

'Some friend!' muttered Joanna.

'Er, Joanna,' said Mr Dogg from below, 'don't whatever you do *alienate* him, will you?'

Still they drew closer to the vast column, so that now it seemed to be extending colossal rust-streaked wings to enfold them. They must still be two or three miles from its almost sheer walls, but already it was evident that the edifice was – even if based upon a natural formation – artificial, with tall thin windows like knife-slashes arranged symmetrically along its frontage and a great double door, perhaps a hundred yards tall, piercing it at the base. Joanna craned her neck trying to see the structure's top, far above them, but its sides – like railway lines – seemed to narrow forever towards somewhere that was lost in distance. Its mere vastness was not its most intimidating quality: rather, it was the overwhelming sense of massiveness the pile projected. She felt that they were travelling towards it less because of Hrimfaxi's pounding hooves than because it was sucking them in by sheer gravity.

She could find no words to express the depths of her demoralization. The others, too – even the unicorn – were silent. If the outer face of the structure exerted this grip upon them, what hope had they against the horrors within?

The building grew until there was nothing else left of the world. Mustardseed's grip around Joanna's waist was like iron. Mr Dogg kept so close to Hrimfaxi's side that he was in constant danger of being trampled underfoot.

The desert beneath them was still white, but Joanna had the fancy that it was no longer composed of sand but instead of powdered bone. The stuff absorbed the sound of Hrimfaxi's gallop: all she could hear of their passage was a long, low shushing sound. No echoes: instead the face of the edifice seemed to emanate chill.

And suddenly Joanna giggled.

The sound jerked all of them out of the depression that had been swallowing them.

'Something funny?' said Mr Dogg. 'Or are you just lapsing into maidenly hysteria?'

'I just thought,' said Joanna, 'I just thought that if you put a lightning-storm in the sky behind this place and set loose a flock of bats to swoop around it, you'd have the perfect setting for a Dracula movie.'

'Dracula was a vampire,' observed Mr Dogg. 'That's not so hilarious. Vampires are forgotten fears, too, aren't they? And if this vampire's on the same scale as his castle . . .'

'Yes, only – ' She let it be. But she could feel Hrimfaxi sharing her amusement.

Now they were entering their final approach towards the colossal doors, and the unicorn began to slow his pace.

The doors will open for us, he said. *This is a place never barred: all are welcome to enter.*

'And to leave?' breathed Mustardseed, close behind Joanna's ear.

That is a different matter, replied Hrimfaxi with finality.

Just as the unicorn had predicted, the doors began to creak open, their screech coming almost as a relief after the deadened sound of the past few miles. Inside, Joanna could see a red glow like the heart of a furnace. She braced herself for a waft of heat that didn't come.

Now Hrimfaxi's hoofbeats began to echo. Mr Dogg barked a challenge at the front of the construction, and seemed vaguely cheered when it seemed to bark back. Thank goodness for something so prosaic as an echo, at last! The doors opened further, their hinges giving a curiously deep squeal, like a bassoon inexpertly blown.

'We're going to be all right,' said Joanna over her shoulder to Mustardseed. 'I can feel it.'

There was no reply from the handservant, only a further tightening of her grip around Joanna's waist.

And then they were between the doors, and seemed to

travel for far too long the distance through the structure's wall towards the fiery glow within. The deep, wrathful red was marbled with flickering streaks of living orange-yellow and puffs of a pale, alien blue. They seemed to be galloping voluntarily into the heart of a pyre, and yet still they felt no heat.

It must be illusion, Joanna told herself fiercely. *All the worst horrors are merely illusion. Nightmares drift away, given time; they're less substantial than air ... Oh. This is the place to which nightmares drift away, Hrimfaxi said. Maybe here they're a bit more subst– I wish I hadn't started this train of thought.*

Suddenly they were through the incandescent husk. The sensation was like puncturing the skin of a soap-bubble, and Hrimfaxi lost his footing entirely, tumbling forwards so that Joanna and Mustardseed fell from his back. Mr Dogg dancing clear of their limbs, the three of them rolled over and over on the dusty floor of what seemed to be a huge cathedral. Joanna's head cracked back against something that seemed like stone, and for some moments all she could see was the wet, soapy-tasting sound of someone busily scraping her face with a hard-bristled brush.

When she returned to the present it was to discover Mr Dogg's face close above hers, watching her anxiously.

'You all right?'

'A bit groggy, that's all.' She shoved herself up onto her elbows. 'And a bit wobbly as well. How are the others?'

'They're OK, though your Siddhe friend seems too terrified to move. It took us a lot of persuasion to get her to uncurl from a foetal ball.' He sniffed Joanna as if to check she really was in full working order. 'Do the Siddhe have foetuses, being immortal and all? Don't know. Still, that was the kind of ball she was – '

'Mr Dogg, she's not *my* Siddhe friend - she's *our* Siddhe friend. Remember that. Besides, I'm not sure that, strictly speaking, she's a Siddhe any longer. As far as I can gather from what Hrimfaxi was saying, the Comelatelies are only Comelatelies when they're actually in Fairyland.' She rubbed the back of her head cautiously. 'When this starts hurting, it's going to hurt a *lot.*' Her fingers came away with a few small streaks of blood on them.

Mr Dogg moved round behind her for a look, his paws clicking on the stone. 'Very punk,' he commented.

'What *is* this place?' she said, looking around her. They seemed to be inside a truly colossal space, but the sound-dampening gloom was such that it was impossible to tell for sure. She had the impression that there was a roof vastly far above them. Of the doors and fiery skin through which they had penetrated there was not a sign, and Joanna had the uncanny sense that they, too, were now hugely far away. She had the image of the four companions as minute playing pieces on the board of a giant's game.

Hrimfaxi came hulking out of the dimness, the clopping of his hooves sounding reassuringly normal.

Let my soulstuff heal your hurt, he said without preamble.

'It hasn't started hur– '

But it will, unless . . .

He came close to her and lowered his head so that the spear of his horn was pointing directly towards her heart. She reached out and clasped the bony shaft, and at once felt warmth seeping through her. She held on until the warmth was covering the back of her scalp, and then Hrimfaxi retreated a pace.

The wound will take longer to heal, he said, *but it will give you no pain.*

Whatever his soulstuff had done, it had also filled her with a strange, bubbly sensation – a feeling of eruptive vigour. She sprang to her feet, startling Mr Dogg, and tried to make out any details of their surroundings through the murk, which seemed to blow smokily around them. The place smelled smoky, too: perhaps the illusion of embers at the doors had not been entirely misleading.

'Have you ever been here before?' she said to Hrimfaxi.

He shook his mane. *No.*

'Where's Mustardseed?'

Over here.

She and Mr Dogg followed him as he led them a few tens of yards across the featureless floor to where the handservant lay curled against something that Joanna finally identified as the end of a wooden pew. She had thought in that first blinding moment of their entrance that the place was like a great cathedral, and it seemed she'd been right.

You've made *it into a cathedral,* Hrimfaxi corrected.

She stared at him. 'How do you mean?'

Many of the things we see in the Farness, Joanna, are too remote from anything we've ever experienced for us to be able to see them as they truly are – if they can even be said to have a true form. So our minds reinterpret what we see and sense . . . but your *mind – these realms of the Farness have never been exposed to a raw mortal mind before, only to the refined, sophisticated consciousnesses of their higher denizens. Your primitiveness has given you great potential power, Joanna. You seem to have the power to mould the reality of the Farness. That is why I say you made the Lair into a cathedral. It was you, I conjecture, who also created the sere white desert outside here.*

THE FAR-ENOUGH WINDOW

Your ability may be of great use to us as we travel through this portal.

Joanna continued to stare at him incredulously. 'You mean, I'm a sort of god here? I don't believe you!'

No, because a god would be aware of what he or she was creating. You obviously aren't – you have no control, and I would think you probably cannot *have any control over this. Yet, as I say, your ability may nevertheless be of great assistance to us. But leave that aside: first you are needed to console our friend, Mustardseed.*

'Yes – yes of course.' Joanna hoped none of the others had realized that for a few moments she had completely forgotten about the handservant's existence. 'Have you given her some of your – of your "soulstuff"?'

She will not receive it.

Joanna went down to her knees beside Mustardseed and cradled the Comelately's head in her arms. 'Come on, dear,' she said, feeling inadequate. She'd never really had to comfort anyone before – just Mr Dogg and Knolly Mutton, and she suspected they'd have got along just as well without her ministrations. 'Look on the bright side. Things aren't so bad.'

Mustardseed didn't respond. She seemed almost catatonic.

'Every cloud has a silver lining,' Joanna tried. 'It never rains but it – No, hang on, try again. I'm sure it'll all turn out for the best. There's bound to be light at the end of the tunnel.'

Mustardseed stirred slightly, snuggling her head further into the crook of Joanna's shoulder.

'She's probably trying to block her ears,' snapped Mr Dogg. 'Really, you're *hopeless*. Look – *this* is how it's done.'

He planted his forepaws firmly in the middle of

Mustardseed's chest and started industriously to lick her face. After a few moments the handservant's features puckered, and she put out an arm to fend him off.

'See?' said Mr Dogg. 'Told you – works a treat. Works even better, come to that, if you've just had a bowlful of dog biscuits, but – '

Joanna pushed him away herself, feeling miffed. 'Are you better?' she said to Mustardseed. 'Probably you just needed a good sleep.'

'Where – ? How did we get here?' said the handservant, gasping the words. 'Where did the jaws go?'

'The jaws?' said Joanna. 'What are you talking about?'

She must have glimpsed this place just before you did, said Hrimfaxi. *You must have blinked just as we came through the barrier, Joanna. Long enough for Mustardseed to see her own vision of what the Lair looks like before you remodelled it to match your own conceptions.*

Joanna absorbed this. 'Jaws,' she repeated to Mustardseed. 'What exactly did you see?'

'I . . . I don't want to . . .'

'Of course not, dear Mustardseed. Of course you mustn't talk about it, or even think about it, if it distresses you so much. We'll just wait here until you're feeling a bit steadier, and then we must set off to . . .' She looked up at Hrimfaxi and Mr Dogg. 'Does anyone have any clear idea of where it is we're setting off for?'

Fairyland.

Joanna looked scathingly at the unicorn. 'That may be true,' she said. 'But it's not very helpful as a route-plan.'

'If you ask me.' Mr Dogg coughed. 'If you ask me, I think this place is going to decide itself where we're going next. I don't think we actually have much choice in the matter.'

He turned his head meaningfully and indicated a direction seemingly at random. 'Breathe deep,' he said. 'Perhaps you'll be able to smell it.'

Standing up, leaving Mustardseed sitting where she was with her back propped against the end of the pew, Joanna sucked air in through her nostrils. Aside from the individual animal smells of Mr Dogg and Hrimfaxi, there was just the fusty scent of disuse and antiquity. She was half-opening her mouth to say as much to Mr Dogg when she caught the faintest whiff of something else. The odour was intimately familiar, but for the moment she couldn't identify it. She screwed up her eyes, trying to locate the smell in her mental library.

'It's – ' she began tentatively.

'Blood,' Mr Dogg concluded. 'Human blood.'

She felt the colour drain from her face.

'Blood?' But she knew she didn't need to ask for confirmation. That was the word on the spine of the book she'd just put her finger on.

'I smell it too,' said Mustardseed.

Joanna looked at Hrimfaxi's eyes and they were sad. *I fear what we may discover,* he confessed.

'It's only blood,' she said, trying to sound braver than she felt. 'I've smelt it often enough before. It doesn't necessarily mean that ... well, that there's anyone being killed, or anything. In fact, it probably doesn't. There's probably a perfectly healthy explanation for this.' She put her hands together and made confident washing movements with them. 'Probably.'

'We'd better go and see,' said Mr Dogg doubtfully.

Mustardseed used the pew to pull herself to her feet. She swayed dizzily for a moment, clutching at Joanna's shoulder for support.

Hrimfaxi turned in the direction from which Mr Dogg had indicated the smell came, and began to trot slowly towards it. The others followed him, Mustardseed relinquishing her hold on Joanna after a few paces. The ends of pews appeared either side of them as they walked: they must be moving up the aisle of the cathedral towards the altar. After a little while their surroundings began to brighten slowly, as if the murkiness were being drawn off into vents far overhead. Joanna found she could see further and further along the pews, which extended emptily on each side as far as her eyes could discern. She hoped they *stayed* empty: the prospect of discovering a silent worshipper sitting in one of them made her breath catch in her throat.

She glanced at Mustardseed to see how the handservant was bearing up. Well, by the look of her. The handservant flashed her a watery grin.

It didn't occur to Joanna to speak. There was too much of a weight of accumulated years of silence in here.

No – not quite silence. Despite the steady clop of Hrimfaxi's hooves and the skitter of Mr Dogg's claws, she could hear from somewhere a steady, rhythmic ticking noise.

The gloomy air ahead of them lethargically began to take on an orange cast – she was reminded of the flames she had seen through the wall of Oberon's tent, and of the inferno into which they'd seemed to plunge as they entered this place. But this wasn't the glow of fire: the colours – for there were reds and yellows and blues in the mix as well – hung steadily and still, almost like draped flags.

THE FAR-ENOUGH WINDOW

If this is a cathedral, Joanna thought, *and we're approaching the altar, then that would be the stained-glass window behind it...*

A couple of minutes later her supposition was proved justified. The altar the companions approached was a simple and singularly unimposing affair – merely a block of some pink-grey marble, unpolished, with a white cloth spread across it. But the window behind it was enormous, perhaps a hundred and fifty feet high and almost as wide before it curved inwards at the top in the form of a gothic arch. The scene depicted was of the crucifixion: a monstrous and almost monstrously beautiful naked Christ hung beneath a nailed parchment bearing the letters INRI. The crown of thorns had been rammed firmly onto the Saviour's forehead, so that blood ran down either side of his face, and the gash in his side likewise poured blood. Around the nails driven through his wrists and ankles the blood had dried into black scabs. Gelatinous tears oozed from the Saviour's eyes, though the eyes themselves were an image of tranquility and peace, as if he had come to some kind of accommodation with the pain.

But this was no mere tableau. Christ's chest rose and fell irregularly with his tormented breathing. A slight wind was blowing his sweat-soaked black hair back from his swarthy face. The scene stank of the blood that gushed from the fearful wound in his side.

All was silence save the dripping of this blood to the stone floor behind the altar, where it pooled.

And all of a sudden Joanna remembered where she had seen this image before. She had been very young – perhaps three or four, certainly no older – and Mrs Ruggeley had been reading her to sleep from a book of Bible stories. With the typical misjudgment of the childless, Mrs Ruggeley had made the last story before the lights were switched out that of the Passion, with Christ nailed to the cross until he cried out, in his anguish, 'My God, why hast though forsaken me?' The book had been illustrated in graphic colour, and Mrs Ruggeley had held it so that Joanna, incapable of comprehending the lines of print, had been able to look at the pictures. The scene of the crucifixion had been depicted in particularly loving detail, the bright, cheaply printed colours gleaming from the page.

That night Joanna had woken screaming into the chill loneliness. Mrs Ruggeley had rushed to comfort her, but the child had been unable to explain what it was that had so terrified her. 'Just a bad dream,' Mrs Ruggeley had said comfortingly as she led the little girl to her own fruity-smelling bed for the rest of the night.

But now Joanna was able to recall well enough what the nightmare had been. She had stood, full-grown, among the other women and the disciples at the base of the cross upon which the Saviour's pain-contorted body dangled. Christ's side had not long been pierced by the one merciful man among the brutal Roman troops whose task it was to put the criminals to death. Blood was gushing from the wound, running down the Saviour's leg, and then splashing to the ground.

Not to the ground. The women were huddled directly beneath the cross, and the blood had been falling on Joanna's head and shoulders. As the youngest person there she was not allowed to draw the attention of the others to this, nor to shove them aside so that she could escape from the sticky flood descending on her. She had been forced to stay there, tolerating the horror.

She could recall her loathing, her fear, yet . . .

That was all she was doing now: recalling them. She wasn't actually *experiencing* them. The child-Joanna who had sprung from sleep with her eyes bulging and her lips stretched across her teeth was a creature of the past.

'I know what's happening,' she whispered to the others. They were looking at her with a mixture of consternation and dread. 'I know.'

She felt herself being pulled, her feet sliding without resistance across the smooth, cold floor towards the moving glass. There was a slight tug on her midriff as she passed directly through the solid-seeming marble altar.

And then once more, just as in the nightmare, she was at the base of a cross that seemed to loom forever into the sky. She glanced up, but all she could see, grotesquely foreshortened, were the Saviour's crossed feet and the crude iron nail punched through them and into the splintering wood, Christ's feet and the spate of blood descending towards her.

The blood poured into her upturned face, its splashing din filling her ears as it drenched the white robe over her shoulders and torso. She could taste its saltiness, its iron, its mellow wholeness, even though she kept her lips tight shut. Gobbets clung to the rat-tails of her hair, gumming them to her cheeks. More blood filled her nostrils and, frustrated by the rigid line of her mouth, washed down over her chin and neck, down, down beneath her robe to soak her belly and her legs.

She lowered her gaze and saw, through a curtain of red, her friends staring at her in misery.

'It's all right!' she called, her voice half-choked by the sticky flood. 'It's nothing, really. Just blood. It's *yucky*, but all it is is blood. I won't *drown* or anything.'

The flow abruptly stopped, and she staggered from the suddenness of her reprieve.

Her robe was dry, unstained, pristine, white. She extended her arms in front of her, and saw the pattern of fine golden hairs and tiny freckles on their backs. She turned them over and saw her palms, the creases pink, cleaner than they could possibly be after all that she had gone through since last she'd washed them. A few strands of hair dropped in front of her face and she absent-mindedly crammed them back behind her ears.

She turned and looked upwards. She was too close to the great window to see the scene properly, but she was able to tell that it no longer lived: it was merely a construction of stained glass and strips of lead.

The unicorn clipped around the altar to reach her.

What's happened? What have you done?

'Grown up,' she said. 'Learned a little. The terrors of this place can't hurt us, because they're all *old* terrors.'

She stroked his forehead.

'Well,' she qualified, 'they can't hurt *me*, anyway. Or Mr Dogg. I'm not so sure about you and Mustardseed, who're immortal. Mortality's the big advantage Mr Dogg and I have, you see: we change and develop as we grow older, so that things that frightened us long ago don't do so any longer.'

Mustardseed, who had approached behind Hrimfaxi, touched her on the elbow. 'Why did you stand there under the window?' she said. 'You looked so . . . so glorious, Joanna. Glorifying.'

'I was washing in blood.'

'We saw you bathing in that shaft of red light that was falling through the glass, yes,' Mustardseed said impatiently. 'But that was no cause to worry us so much.'

Hrimfaxi shifted beneath Joanna's hand, and he gazed at her. She could feel him pulling the memories of the experiences of the past few minutes from her mind and passing them to Mustardseed and Mr Dogg.

'Blimey,' said Mr Dogg. 'So *that* was what was going on. You must have been – '

'But I *wasn't* frightened!' exclaimed Joanna. 'Don't you see? I was a bit revolted – that's all. Disgusted, nauseated, call it what you will – but I wasn't the least bit *frightened.*'

There was a shuddering creak from overhead, and all four jerked their faces towards it.

Another groan, as of a great weight straining against insufficient supports to be allowed to plummet groundwards.

'You've broken the window,' growled Mr Dogg, turning. 'Quick – run!'

Joanna stood rooted to the spot as a network of cracks suddenly sprang into being across the stained-glass image. It was so beautiful, this suddenly modified depiction, as if the reticular lines were somehow dragging her perception of it into a further, hitherto unconceived dimension. The window portrayed the light of the world, but behind it, giving it light, there was a greater light, now poised to reveal itself in its full lambent glory . . .

'Come *on*!' screamed Mustardseed, yanking her arm.

Snapping out of her daydream, Joanna gave a little shriek and scrambled behind the handservant towards the front rows of the cathedral's pews. Behind them the crackings of the glass sounded like fusillades of shots. The floor was shaking to a series of profounder thuds.

Joanna and Mustardseed threw themselves over the back of the frontmost pew and into the sheltering darkness beyond it just as the enormous stained-glass construction, with a final convulsive scream of tortured matter, erupted in a cloud of singing coloured shards. The air above where they cowered filled with speeding, sharp-edged death. The noise was like a million cats declaring war.

It seemed to last for hours.

'What was that you were saying about the terrors of this place not being able to do us any damage?' said Mustardseed when at last peace came.

Joanna made no reply, but cautiously rose to her feet. The air was filled with suspended glass-dust, so that everything sparkled with an unnatural hyperreality. On the far side of the aisle she could see Mr Dogg's muzzle poking inquisitively out, testing the air. Hrimfaxi, with his greater speed, had run far further than the others but had been unable to find adequate protection for his great white form, and there were bright red streaks along his flanks as he staggered down the central passage towards her.

'You're hurt!' she cried.

Not badly. My wounds will soon heal.

And indeed, even as she watched, the angry weals were fading.

She heard a rapid intake of breath behind her.

Mustardseed, standing, was facing towards where the stained-glass window had been. Her reptilian mouth had fallen open; her eyes were as wide as Joanna had ever seen them.

Joanna looked, too – looked at the light that had been behind the window.

They were beings, seemingly living creatures. Stretching from the floor to far overhead, they were like pillars formed purely of light, and they shuffled and moved among each other like any human crowd. Others were bulbous incandescences, slowly sinking towards the ground. As soon as she set eyes on them Joanna knew, without benefit of her senses, that they were staring at her. Not at her three companions: just at her. And their stare was not friendly.

Who are they? she thought to Hrimfaxi.

I don't know, he responded unhappily, coming level with her. *Like everything else here, they're products of your mind, Joanna. I've never seen anything like them before.*

But she had – she *must* have, for wasn't this place composed of her own forgotten memories? She racked her brains trying to recall where she'd encountered them, but still there was not the slightest resonance of familiarity.

Think, Joanna! said Hrimfaxi, his thoughts beginning to sound anxious. *You triumphed over the fear of Christ's blood because you were able to focus on when you had felt it before – only that way were you able to withstand it and defeat it. You were right – the things here cannot directly harm us because they're your discarded fears, and can be* remembered *into impotence. But if you cannot remember them . . .*

'I'm trying,' she wailed.

'Try harder,' suggested Mr Dogg helpfully.

'Shut up! How can I think if you keep – ?'

'Can't you hear them?' said Mustardseed, clearly unaware of the others' conversation. 'Can't you hear their power?'

Joanna seized on the clue. She could hear nothing at all,

and then – yes, there was something. A steady whining growl, almost beneath the limit of hearing.

Throw your mind back as far as you can, Joanna, said Hrimfaxi urgently.

Silence! she thought furiously at him. The growl – the sound of a car on a wet road at night . . . Fifteen or more years since last she'd heard it . . .

Yes, yes, far back . . . Back when Mummy had still been there with them, her softness and the warmth of her embracing arms the core of a tiny Joanna's universe. And one night Joanna had woken to find herself not in her own puke-redolent cot but lying on her back amid blankets in a strange box, with the batter of a giant's roar coming up from beneath her. And she'd looked up to a shiny blackness, where pillars and globules of light moved backwards and forwards in a terrifyingly hostile – because inexplicable – formal dance. How she'd screamed and screamed, until the roar had abated and slowly died, until the strange figures of light had swept away from the blackness, which was no longer black but a dirty orange . . .

And her mother's voice, appearing out of nowhere. 'They do choose their moments, don't they, Aubrey? Bloody babies – remind me never to have another one.'

Her father's laughter as her mother's arms had come from somewhere to lift her up. Joanna's nappy was a heavy warmth, dragging her down, but that didn't seem to matter as Mummy's face had appeared, smiling wearily, to kiss away the fears . . .

'They must have been headlights on the car's rear window,' gasped Joanna now, extrapolating from ignorance into possibly false comprehension, staring at the vastly huger columns and balls of light. 'We must have been on a big road, with lots of other cars behind us. And the rain on the window turned the beams into pillars! Bright raindrops, coursing down the glass. I – I thought they were monsters, come to watch me and – and prey on me because I was so small and I didn't know where I was and Mummy and Daddy were nowhere to be seen . . .'

'They're so fine,' said Mustardseed in a low voice. 'So cruel but . . . so fine.'

'They're not cruel,' said Joanna, jumping into motion. 'They're not anything except beautiful. They're just light – no more than pretty arrays of distorted light.' She stepped out into the cathedral's aisle. 'Look, Mustardseed – look, all of you – they can't harm us. It's you who've given them their evil stare.'

She walked assuredly towards the altar once more, crunching broken glass beneath her feet. The lights began to cluster ahead of her, as if grouping for defence. She didn't break her stride until she reached the altar; she paused for a brief moment, decided she didn't have the confidence to believe she'd be able to go right through it a second time, then walked around it, her hands outstretched towards the lights.

'Don't be frightened of me,' she heard herself saying to them, as if they were nervous infants. 'It's only me. Joanna. I'm not a frightening person. I won't hurt you.'

And, in less than the space of a single instant, the lights were gone.

'Oh.' Her hands dropped to her sides. She felt disappointed, let down. Daddy hadn't come for Christmas, again.

Ahead of her, where the lights had stood, there was a grey tunnel, winding out of sight.

Claustrophobia hit her before they had gone more than a few hundred yards down the tunnel. She and Mustardseed were seated on Hrimfaxi's back, as before, with Mr Dogg once again loping along beside. The tunnel had seemed generously wide at first, but after the first bend it had started to narrow. Now she felt as if it weren't large enough to allow her to breathe.

'I can't – I can't – '

Yes you can, came Hrimfaxi's firm thought. She wished she were so certain.

They rounded another corner and were immediately plunged into bedlam. A thousand thick, clammy tendrils sprang from the sides of the tunnel to grope at them. Each of the tendrils ended in a circular mouth, ringed with hungry teeth. The mouths were chattering to each other even as they bit at Joanna and her companions.

'Oh, I'd like a munchy of your smooth creamy flesh . . .'

'Come closer, come closer, come closer . . .'

'Such a *pretty* face, my dear. You look delicious – really quite good enough to eat . . .'

'Tender to the tooth, tender to the palate, tender to the tummy-tum-tum . . .'

'*Lampreys!*' Joanna screamed. 'I saw some lampreys in a natural-history movie – Disney, I think – see Lenny Lamprey as he makes his new home – that kind of thing – only lampreys – I was about ten – I dreamt of . . .'

Hrimfaxi lowered his shoulders and charged on through

the lampreys, raking his horn from side to side, ripping their pallid flesh.

All at once the lampreys were gone and the tunnel was clear again.

But only for a few seconds. Now there were pirates – pirates big, pirates small, pirates handsome, pirates grotesque, pirates young, pirates old, and all of them eyepatched and parroted and with a hook in the place of at least one hand. In their other hands they clutched icily sharp sabres, which they brandished at Joanna's eyes. 'Boil her in oil!' they chanted.

'It's a bit much, if you ask me, thinking I'd still be afraid of *pirates*!' she blurted angrily. 'I'm not a *complete* child.'

The pirates looked vaguely guilty and disappeared.

So did the tunnel. So did everyone else. Joanna was alone, perched unsteadily on a loo. She knew, as a matter of complete, certain, strict, no-arguments-countenanced cast-iron fact, that a witch lived somewhere within the inexplicable intricacies of the loo's workings. The witch was released when you pulled the handle and the waters churned. What you had to do was wash your hands *first* (whatever Mrs Ruggeley might say to the contrary), then press the handle down and hold it there – because the witch wasn't freed until the waters started thundering and that didn't happen until you let go of the handle – so you stood there with your body tensed, like an athlete on the blocks, until just the very right moment appeared. Then you let go of the handle and you sped to the lavatory door and were through it and slamming it behind you before your feet properly had a chance to touch the ground and certainly before the wicked witch had time to get even the tip of her pointy black hat above the level of the seat . . .

'I gave up believing in *this* one before I even *started* having bad dreams about *pirates*,' said Joanna with heavy irony to the air in general.

She was back astride Hrimfaxi, with Mustardseed pinned to her.

'I've had such *mediocre* fears,' she confessed sadly to the unicorn.

They only seem that way to you because they're yours, said the unicorn faintly.

Now the tunnel – which was certainly beginning to narrow quite rapidly, so that Mr Dogg was having to race ahead of Hrimfaxi rather than run alongside him – was awash with toothless, gibbering creatures whose eyes were blue flames and who moaned with the wordless sound of the wind in an old chimney. Their bodies seemed made of grubby tissue paper, disintegrating at their lower edges. They fumbled for Joanna with a sort of wayward purposefulness.

'The Ghost of Christmas Yet to Come,' she said contemptuously. 'Always the most dreadful of the three. I must have been nine.'

The creatures melted into emptiness. As did the lurching *Tyrannosaurus rex*, in its turn. And the hag from the gingerbread house, and the lynch mob, and the parasitic worms that lived in one's tummy, and the marching army of carnivorous phalluses (Joanna was excruciatingly embarrassed about these, but her friends seemed not to recognize them as anything particularly special), and the cake that dripped with concentrated sulphuric acid (Mrs Ruggeley had one day made a joke about having your cake and being eaten by it, and the notion had resurfaced in the seven-year-old Joanna's dreams), and a long period of falling helplessly through a pitch blackness that stank of mildew, and the giant slugs that crawled up your legs while you slept and might go *in there*, and spiders that scuttled and toothed lizards that flew, and figures of Joanna herself with various different terrible (differently terrible and terribly different) mutilations and mutations, and...

All of them – well, almost all of them – she managed to face off with some measure of equanimity, although many of the apparitions manifestly terrified one or other of her companions. Mustardseed, in particular, began to look at her betweentimes with an expression of almost reverent awe, as if she had discovered herself in company with a heroine out of an old battling myth.

'It's a lack of imagination that makes her so strong,' Joanna heard Mr Dogg confide to the handservant.

Her temper flared, although she kept her exterior calm. Mr Dogg couldn't have got it more wrong. It wasn't a *lack* of imagination that was enabling her to dismiss each new assault but a *power* of imagination: she was imagining herself to be facing them off bravely, casting herself into a courageous rôle, and the reality was obediently trailing along behind.

By now the tunnel had narrowed so much that they were having to move in single file, with Joanna in the lead, then Mustardseed and Mr Dogg and finally Hrimfaxi, who was easing himself along backwards in case the constriction grew so tight on him that he got stuck. Progress was slow. The tunnel walls were spongy and covered in rough hairs, like the fibres of a doormat teased out individually to make a shaggy fleece. Joanna had to push herself forward almost as if she were swimming, and could only occasionally catch glimpses of her friends behind her. The tunnel seemed to be pressing in on each of them equally now, even though they were all different sizes. Her robe was tangling up and hindering her, so she shucked it off and let it lose itself behind her, even though the coarse fibres hurt her skin.

It was the hot pain of the abrasion that brought the forgotten nightmare suddenly back into focus.

It had been a recurring dream and, through its appearance every few months, had done much to shape her childhood. In the dream she had been staying in a house with half a dozen or more other children – an experience she had known only vicariously through *The Sound of Music* and *The Goonies* and *Oliver Twist* and who knew what else.

The other children had belonged to the house, or it had belonged to them; Joanna was a guest, a tolerated interloper. She was aware that adults were in supervision somewhere, and that she'd seen them reassuringly often; but in the dream they were always somewhere else just now.

All the children had decided to play some sort of hide-and-seek game, and during it Joanna became aware that there was something not quite *right* about the house: nothing overtly menacing, probably nothing dangerous, but something unseen that was silently pursuing her. Her search for a hiding-place had taken her up into the house's attic, where there was no real lighting except for whatever sunlight penetrated the cracks in the roof.

The place was a repository for old rugs and rolls of carpet, and it smelled of dust and ancient, gracefully decaying wool and sacking. Whatever the thing that was following her was, it was somewhere behind her, perhaps even on the flight of stairs leading up to the attic. It seemingly wasn't trying to catch her: it was just waiting. Yet there was no possibility of retreat: she could just about tolerate the something's existence, but she most certainly wasn't going to risk coming face-to-face with it . . . if it had a face.

She noticed for the first time that one wall of the attic was formed of two masses of coarse carpeting — except that it wasn't for the first time, because it was at this point in the dream that she suddenly realized she'd been here before, countless times, and knew exactly what would happen next. The line between those two bulks of matting was a way of escape from the attic. She had no idea what lay on the other side, but that didn't matter: the important thing was that it was not-attic.

She moved quite calmly towards the slit and probed at it with her fingers. Then there was a rush of awareness that the something on the stairs had tired of merely waiting, and was slowly coming up towards her. With the awareness came the knowledge that again she had known this was going to happen, that she remembered it from last time – whenever last time had been. She wasn't terrified, hardly even scared, but she knew she wanted to leave the attic as quickly as possible, so she forced her head and shoulders in between the two volumes of carpeting (the gap had moved from vertical to horizontal without her noticing), and began to drag the rest of herself in, straining with her arms against firm but not overwhelming resistance. Now she was right inside the carpets, and was being pressed lung-flatteningly between them, so that breathing was an impossibility. The swimming movements of her arms took on a real urgency as she struggled further into the warm, dark pressure and . . .

And that was when she always woke up, still for long

seconds suffocated by the dream before she could drag a breath and lie shaking in the darkness, reaching out for Knolly Mutton and his comforting familiarity.

When she was twelve or thirteen Mrs Ruggeley had given her a book on reproduction and childbirth and told her to read it, and Joanna had concluded that her recurring dream must be some kind of deep memory of her own birth trauma. Explained, rightly or wrongly, in this mundane way the dream never returned, and she had forgotten all about it until . . .

'The dream!' she whispered with the last puff of breath in her lungs. 'There was *birth* on the other side of the carpets!'

Seven

Was or Might Have Been

It was a large lovely garden, with soft green grass. Here and there over the grass stood beautiful flowers like stars, and there were twelve peach-trees that in the spring-time, broke out into delicate blossoms of pink and pearl and in the autumn, bore rich fruit. The birds sat on the trees and sang so sweetly that the children used to stop their games in order to listen to them. 'How happy we are here!' they cried to each other.

– Oscar Wilde, 'The Selfish Giant', 1888

She was falling into brilliant sunlight.

She landed on a grassy bank and, eyes shut against the painful brightness, rolled over several times, her limbs flailing. A succession of thumps nearby told her that her companions had likewise escaped from the confines of the tunnel. A final, much larger thrash, accompanied by a whinny of pain, signified Hrimfaxi emerging.

She lay on her back in the warm sunshine, arms and legs

spread, eyes still closed, hearing the sounds of a summer's day – the trees swishing easily, a stream burbling somewhere in the distance, insects zipping on their inscrutable ways or hovering interestedly over a clover head. This was like when she had first come through the Far-Enough Window, but she felt less of an outsider. The grass was welcomingly long, its stalks coolly tickling her sides.

Good heavens! She wasn't wearing anything except a watch and a thin gold chain and a key! She'd struggled out of her robe back when they'd been groping through the final compressions of the tunnel.

She relaxed a little – though only a little. Who would there be to see her? Mustardseed, who was old enough to be at least her big sister and possibly her mother – although in point of fact, come to think of it, Mustardseed was old enough to be her mother a million times over. Hrimfaxi, who had wandered through the deepmost recesses of her mind, so that mere physical nakedness seemed as nothing. Mr Dogg, who'd watched her dress and undress a thousand times before, or who had poked his head over the edge of the bath to watch her splashing. Yes, but Mr Dogg hadn't been able to talk in those days, and somehow that made a difference. Quite a big difference, now that Joanna had noticed it. Besides, a stranger might stumble along and see her here, spread shameless to the sun.

She wished she'd clung onto her robe. But if she'd done so she might not have been able to . . .

She felt a shadow pass over her body, and opened her eyes.

'Here,' said Mustardseed, standing above her. 'Your robe. It wrapped itself around my face and I couldn't get rid of it.'

The Comelately dropped it in a bundle on Joanna's tummy. Mustardseed tugged at her own robe. 'Though it's warm enough here that we could probably go without.'

A cottonwool cloud, drifting aimlessly in a pure azure sky, seemed to give Mustardseed a hairstyle like Harpo Marx's. Joanna giggled, then decided to not even try to explain what she found so funny.

'Where do you think we are?' she said to Mustardseed, still not moving, wondering why she didn't need to cover herself.

'I think we're in Fairyland,' said Mustardseed.

'So soon? Hrimfaxi said – How *is* Hrimfaxi? I heard him cry out.'

She sat up, gathering the cloth of the robe to her.

'He broke a leg falling, but' – Mustardseed held up a hand – 'don't worry. He'll be all right. He's a unicorn. They heal quickly.'

Joanna peered across an undulating surface of grass. The unicorn was lying on his side, his head towards her. He was breathing slowly and steadily, waiting for his bones to knit together. Mr Dogg was standing beside him: she could see the tops of the mongrel's ears and the flat of his head. The grass was greener than any grass she had ever seen – she remembered the pictures she'd painted with poster colours when she'd been very little and 'grass' had been just a uniform splodge direct from the pot. In the distance were trees for which she'd used a dirty brush.

'This can't be Fairyland,' she said. 'Hrimfaxi told us we'd have to pass through more than one portal like the Lair of Forgotten Fears before we regained Fairyland.' She fumbled her upper half into the robe. 'Unless he was wrong, of course,' she added, 'although I get the impression unicorns aren't often wrong.'

'Hardly ever,' Mustardseed agreed.

Joanna, fully clad, waded through the grass to where Mr Dogg was attending Hrimfaxi. The unicorn was still on his side, but now he seemed to be resting rather than suffering. He raised his head to look at her.

The pain is almost gone now, he said. *I'll soon be on my feet.*

Joanna knelt down and, wary of the horn, nuzzled his forehead with her own. 'There's no hurry,' she murmured. 'We seem to be perfectly safe here.' Time enough later to ask him if he knew exactly where 'here' was.

'I'm starving,' announced Mr Dogg.

Joanna, too, for the first time since they'd left Oberon's encampment – however long ago that might have been – realized that she was aching with hunger. Perhaps, wherever they'd been in the Farness, hunger was a sensation that didn't have any meaning – in the same way that the colours leaf-green and lobster-pink have no real meaning to a blind person. Or maybe it had just been that the unremitting apprehension of their journey across the desert and through the Lair of Forgotten Fears had driven all consciousness of bodily needs from her mind.

'What is there to eat?' she said dully.

'Plenty,' said Mustardseed from behind her. 'If this isn't Fairyland, it's somewhere very like it – like the Fairyland in which we were all little Finefolk with hardly a thought in our heads. Every meadow held succulent grains or ripe fat vegetables a-plenty; every tree was burdened low with fruits and nuts. We couldn't starve there, and I'll warrant the same is true here – isn't that right, Hrimfaxi?'

The unicorn shifted his gaze to the Comelately. *This is . . .*

this is Fairyland, in a way. You'll find what you need.

'Good,' said Mustardseed. 'Then I'll go gathering.' She lifted up the front of her robe to show that it would make a fine collecting basket. 'You three wait here.'

'Fruit and vegetables,' said Mr Dogg in disgust. 'Ha!'

'And perhaps a fish will leap from the stream for me,' said Mustardseed. 'Who knows? Do you want to come and see?'

'Right-o.' Mr Dogg wagged his tail.

The two vanished through the grass, leaving Joanna alone with Hrimfaxi. He moved his head and laid it in her lap, careful not to hurt her with his horn.

I lied to them, he said, his thought barely more than a whisper. *I lied to all of you.*

'I know. How badly are you really hurt?'

The leg? Oh – the fracture is healed already, and the pain is on the run. I broke a couple of ribs as well, but they're mended. No, the injury I've suffered isn't as straightforward as a cracked limb – and it can't be healed so easily, either.

'What's the matter?' She felt the tears on her cheeks before she noticed she was crying. 'Is there anything I can do to help?'

I couldn't have lived so long as I have if it hadn't been for your presence – you've given me so much already, dear Joanna. But now it's nothing you can heal.

'Then what is it?' She wrapped her arms around his great neck. 'Tell me.' Her mind was awhirl with notions brought from her own world: cancer, perhaps, or a brain tumour, or bovine spongiform encephalitis, or . . .

We unicorns are creatures of the present, Hrimfaxi began. *We have some notion of the future, and hazy memories of the past, but really we're designed to live from one moment to the next, always within and a part of the current moment. We can travel through the realms of the Farness, but we're not intended to live anywhere but in the present.*

She was confused.

The place where the Lair of Forgotten Fears has chosen to debouch us isn't the present, said the unicorn wearily. *As you and Mustardseed both guessed, it's Fairyland – but it's not the Fairyland of the present.*

'Is it,' she said shyly, 'is it the Fairyland of the past?' Mustardseed had said it seemed like that, and now Joanna realized that not all the hummings and buzzings in the summery air around her were insects: some of them must be little fairies, like the ones she'd conjured into her hands when Robin Goodfellow had first ushered her through the Far-Enough Window.

Not really. He moved his head again. *Not exactly. It's Fairyland as it* might have been *in the past. A possible past – one of countless other possible pasts, just as from any particular moment there are countless possible futures.*

It took a few moments before Joanna could wrestle her mind around what he was trying to say. 'As if only *now* is real?' she said. 'A focusing down, a crystallization, of all the possible pasts there might have been, in preparation for all the possible futures that might be to come?'

Yes. Only the present is truly real. The past and the future are just an array of possibilities, with some more likely than others. Some creatures can make their homes in one or more of those possibilities, and perhaps never even notice that the place they're inhabiting isn't real. But not unicorns. No, alas, not unicorns. As I said to you, we unicorns are tied always to the present – we can live only in a state of reality.

'You're dying,' she breathed.

Fading slowly from existence, he said. *It hurts a lot less than dying.*

He strained his neck backwards so that one of his fist-sized eyes could look directly into her face.

'We could try to get back into the Lair of Forgotten Fears,' said Joanna impulsively. 'It's not the ideal place to live out the rest of our lives, but perhaps we could go through it again in the opposite . . . direction until we found the chalky desert, and from there we could – '

No. Look around you, Joanna. Where's the way back into the Lair of Forgotten Fears?

He was right. There was only the hillside with, at its base, a plain of natural fields criss-crossed by streams and patched with copses.

'It must be here somewhere!' she wailed hopelessly.

But it wasn't. There was nothing remotely resembling the huge edifice through whose complexities they'd moved. She strained her eyes to see if perhaps, further up the hill, there might be caves or rock formations which could be the gateway back into the Lair, but there was nothing. Her shoulders shaking with a sob, she let her head fall and hugged him tightly.

There isn't any way back, he said quietly, as if she were the one who was dying. *There never really is. The present always heads for the future, not towards the past.*

'But – ' She remembered herself saying, 'Unicorns aren't often wrong', and Mustardseed agreeing: 'Hardly ever.'

There's nothing you can do, Joanna, except be with me. Your closeness makes all pains and regrets seem very, very distant. I'm lucky to have had the time with you that I have: it would be gluttonous to resent not being able to have more of it.

'There must be something!'

There isn't. But listen to me – you must listen to me if you and the others are ever going to be able to return to Fairyland. The real Fairyland – the Fairyland of now. And you will be able to do that, if only you can find the right portal to reach there. It would have been so much easier if I could have been there to guide you, but . . . but if you listen hard to what I tell you, and remember it all, then in a way I'll be guiding you just as much as if I were at your shoulder.

She could hardly see his face for her tears now. 'I'm listening.'

There was the faintest trace of wistfulness in his thoughts, but otherwise he seemed to have reached a state in which he was utterly unconcerned about his own imminent demise. *The world – the universe – in which we currently find ourselves is made up in its entirety of possibilities, likelihoods, might-bes . . . They may seem real to you, Joanna – and certainly they're solid and tangible enough to present genuine dangers to you: you could break your neck here just as easily as you could anywhere else. But they're not. Nothing here is set: everything is in a flux, hovering between one thing and another, and yet a third thing. But the tendency of all likelihoods is towards reality – towards their own reification. Some are better candidates than others: you and Mr Dogg and Mustardseed are the best candidates for reification of all, because of course you have already achieved realness and are now separated from it only by a flimsy barrier of time. Other strong probabilities will tend to gather themselves around you, to gravitate towards you – you'll soon begin to have visible proof of this, I'm sure.*

'What sort of – ?' she began.

Hush, Joanna. I don't have very much time left. She saw how already he was losing definition, his flanks beginning to take on the appearance of arbitrary collections of curves rather than solid bulks of flesh. *Listen, I tell you. Though you will naturally pull to yourselves pockets of higher likelihood, that alone won't be enough for you to be able to burst back into the real Fairyland. You must go questing to find, somewhere in this universe of potentials, the site where reality is being able to take the firmest of holds. That will be the portal you seek.*

'How will we know it?'

You'll have no trouble recognizing it when you find it. That's the only description I know. It may be very nearby. It may have drawn us to itself.

He lay silent in her arms, his weight a fraction of what it had been only minutes before. She sensed his tranquility – also the strong current of life, of soulstuff, that still ran through him, even though she could now see the flattened grass mistily through his outflung mane.

'Why did you bring us here, Hrimfaxi?' she said softly. 'You could have left us in the Court of the Great High King, and you'd have been safe. Doubtless we'd have been safe, too, in the end – certainly Mustardseed and Mr Dogg would have been. Yet you must have known that aiding me would be at the cost of your life.'

I had no choice in the matter. He breathed a weak sigh, making a sort of empty, disused sound. *It's not just that you were – are – a virgin and I'm a unicorn, though that in itself would have been enough to make me act as I did. It was the fact that, although you thought we were fleeing from your danger, we weren't running away from anything at all: we were running* to *somewhere. Here.*

I said to you a while ago that the only point of leaving Fairyland was to return to it; what I didn't try to explain, then, was that our real destination was Fairyland as approached from this world of past might-bes. Only if you have done this will you be able to reclaim the Fairyland-that-ought-to-be from the Fairyland-that-had-become. Only in this way can events fall into their proper order so that the equation is made complete.

The soulstuff in Hrimfaxi might still flow strongly, but the body was fast disappearing. She was kneeling in the grass with only the wispy ghost of a unicorn in front of her.

'But why, Hrimfaxi?' she cried. '*Why?*'

All will become obvious in its correct time.

She had to strain to catch the thought. His body was now delineated only by memories and crushed grass. His eyes had slowly glazed and faded, and then been gone. His horn alone remained solid, seeming if anything to grow heavier as it sagged towards the ground. And then it fell free, thumping her thigh as it rolled away.

'Hrimfaxi!' she screamed.

The chord of his life that she had sensed to the last now seemed to circle her, an eddy of indistinguishable music that, with a final swirl, evaporated towards the sky.

Only herself and the horn were left among the lightly waving grass, and now the tears invaded her in earnest.

'What's up?' said Mr Dogg, a timeless time later. 'Hrimfaxi slunk off to find himself a tree?'

'Shush,' said Mustardseed. Then, to Joanna: 'He's gone, hasn't he? He's died.'

Joanna couldn't speak.

'Snuffed it?' said Mr Dogg incredulously. 'Leaving us here all on our own? Well, that's a fine how d'you do, I must say. I thought unicorns were supposed to be immortal, and all?'

Now Joanna was able to find some words. 'He hasn't so much died,' she said, 'as stopped existing.'

'Doesn't seem much difference to me,' said Mr Dogg, investigating the bent stems where the unicorn had lain. 'Hmm, although there's no smell left behind him, which there should have been. He wasn't without his rustic odours, our Hrimfaxi, as I'm sure you must have noticed.'

'How can you be so cold-blooded about this?' Joanna blurted, punching out at him. 'He was our friend! He saved our lives! Don't you *miss* him?'

'Not a lot. When you're a dog, you learn that the only friends who ever stick around for very long are humans – and only a few humans at that. And *they're* very unpredictable. You get used to the fact that everybody else is here a bit, then gone.' He looked at her earnestly. 'There'll be another unicorn along some time, and if there isn't – well, there won't be. That's all there is to it.'

Joanna began to feel irrationally furious with the mongrel. It made a change from feeling guilty. She'd caught herself sitting here wishing that it could have been Rapscallion's life that had been taken away from her, not Hrimfaxi's, and that was just the same as wishing for Rapscallion's death, wasn't it?

'Stop arguing,' said Mustardseed. 'We've eating to do.' She let go of the front of her robe and a tumble of various half-recognizable fruits fell out onto the grass, followed by a flopping trout-like fish. 'And some planning. There's something a bit wrong about this place. It took a while for me to realize it, but now I'm certain – it's not really Fairyland, you know, even though it looks like the Fairyland I used to be a part of. But it's somewhere else, and I don't like it. I'd rather be back in the tunnel, dodging your nightmares. I want to put a long distance between me and here just as soon as possible – but not before we've eaten.'

Joanna had thought her hunger had been driven out by her grief, but as soon as she dutifully took one of the firm, green lemon-apple fruits in her hand it returned with a vengeance. Offering up a prayer that anything Mustardseed reckoned was edible wouldn't be too poisonous to a human being, she bit into the fruit's juicy flesh.

A few minutes later she wiped the last of the sweetness from her lips and explained to the other two what Hrimfaxi had told her.

'That's what I thought,' said Mustardseed. 'There's something not properly *real* about the place. Not real grass. Not real air. Not real sunshine.' She rubbed at the purplish scales of her arm as if trying to wipe the reflected gleams of fake sunlight away.

'Seems OK to me,' said Mr Dogg, his voice smelling of raw fish. 'I thought I saw some rabbits back there. I've never caught a rabbit in my life, and this feels the sort of place where an old dog might just strike lucky for the first time.'

'Or maybe it's a place where the rabbits chase the dogs and kill them,' said Joanna.

Mr Dogg looked shocked. 'Do you mean that?'

'We don't know anything much about this place at all,' said Joanna. 'That's the point I was trying to make.'

'That fish tasted real enough to me. And it's filled a real hole that was in my belly. Not that fish is a proper food for a dog, o' course. If some of my old friends could see me now they'd – '

'And the fruit tasted real enough, too,' said Mustardseed

thoughtfully. 'But . . . but there was something else about it that seemed to be . . . seemed *missing*, somehow.'

Joanna knew what she meant. The fruit hadn't tasted remotely like oranges – in fact, it hadn't tasted like anything she'd ever eaten before – but the difference was as if she'd taken a gulp of pure orange juice poured from a carton while thinking she was going to drink juice freshly crushed. All the same substances were in the orange juice, and the taste was really exactly the same – but you *knew* the difference.

She tried to explain something of this to Mr Dogg, who remained sceptical.

'I don't care what either of you two think,' said Mustardseed suddenly. 'I'm going to try to get away from this creepy world, and the best way I know of doing that is to follow Hrimfaxi's advice. I say we – '

'And just what would you be thinking was so terribly wrong with this place?' said a new voice. 'This seems a pretty enough hillside to me, and you a pair of pretty enough young ladies to be sitting picnicking on it.'

'Robin!' cried Joanna, throwing her arms wide. 'Oh, Robin!'

Perched on a little knoll, Robin Goodfellow was abruptly uneasy. 'Can't say as I've ever had the pleasure, beautiful miss,' he said. 'Mind you' – he looked fixedly at a point some way to the right – 'someone in my line of business has to meet a lot of young ladies during the course of the years, and even one as lovely as you is likely to get forgotten in among all the – Oh! I say!' He leapt backwards and looked frightened. 'I should have noticed! You're a mortal!' He looked to Mustardseed. 'Is she safe?'

'As safe as ever I was, Robin Goodfellow,' said Joanna,

nonplussed – and offended. 'Don't you recognize me?'

'No . . . no.' Anxiously. '*Should* I?'

Mustardseed was starting to laugh, and Mr Dogg let out a gleeful little yip. Joanna couldn't for the life of her see what was supposed to be so funny.

'I haven't been in the world of mortals for a *very* long time,' said Robin Goodfellow. 'It's easy enough for a chap to misremember, you know. I hardly ever forget a face, particularly when it's a face as beautiful as yours, my lady, but then I mightn't have been concentrating too hard on your face – not when your legs are as long and as fine and as smooth as yours are.'

He seemed to think he had delivered her an ultimately suitable compliment, because he paused with a winning smile on his face.

Joanna swiftly tucked away the offending legs beneath her. Now she felt nakeder than she had when spread out under the sunshine.

'You started everything,' she said hotly. 'You brought me here to Fairyland through the Far-Enough Window because you said that I, and only I, could help you regain it from the Comelatelies. Now you *pretend* that you – '

'The "Comelatelies"?' mused Robin Goodfellow, crestfallen that his compliment had failed him. 'I never did hear of those.' He rubbed his chin, and the peacock feather curving behind his head twitched in crazed syncopation.

'Don't you realize,' Mustardseed burst in, 'he's never met you before, Joanna?'

'I'm relieved to hear you say that, ma'am,' said Robin Goodfellow earnestly. 'I was beginning to worry about my memory, that I should forget those le–'

Of course! Joanna slapped the heel of her palm against her forehead and began to giggle with Mustardseed. Robin Goodfellow had never met her before because they were now in a version of Fairyland – a might-have-been Fairyland – that hadn't yet seen Robin come through the Far-Enough Window to meet first her ghost and then herself. How stupid of her not to realize! And yet, seeing an old friend once more ...

'Perhaps we should explain,' she said.

Robin Goodfellow was disbelieving at first: had it not been that there were three of them, all with very much the same story to tell (although Mustardseed's story started later, of course), it was unlikely that he would have credited them at all. As far as he was concerned, Fairyland was in the midst of an Arcadian age that showed no signs of ending. The notion that the Siddhe would return to claim the territory that had once been theirs, would become the Comelatelies who had learned to tyrannize this realm of the Farness, was inconceivable to him. But what stuck in his craw the most was the idea of the Far-Enough Window.

'Yes,' he said, time and time again, 'there are ways that lead between here and the world of the mortals, but I've never heard of one like this.'

And Joanna would repeat to him how he had first met with her ghost and then with her, herself, and taught her how, by squinting in exactly the direction she'd never thought of squinting in before, she could see far enough to enter Fairyland.

'And what of Dolly Onskonsider?' she said. 'And

THE FAR-ENOUGH WINDOW

Lumpenkulder? I can't have found their names just floating around. I *know* them. I know them as friends of yours – and of mine.'

That was probably what convinced Robin Goodfellow. 'I know the Onskonsiders,' he said huffily, 'and worthy Finefolk they are too. They ... You know' – turning to Mustardseed – 'this is really fascinating. I've never known anything like it before! This wench – sorry, this extremely cultivated lady – has done what no Finefolk has ever done. She's – '

'Finefolk have done this,' Mustardseed said coldly. 'I did it. Hrimfaxi did it, though he died in the doing. Not just my mortal friend and her dog.'

'Yes, but to come into the past . . .'

'Not the past,' said Mustardseed. 'Haven't you been listening, Robin Goodfellow? The past is a place that no longer exists. It's a collection of likelihoods that might, if they're lucky, come to be the present. At the moment, sitting here in front of us now, you're nothing more than a figment, Robin Goodfellow. Although,' she added not quite under her breath, 'an extremely becoming figment.'

'And you say I was – will be – your friend?' said Robin Goodfellow, turning abruptly to Joanna.

'You said you were. That was why I followed you through the Far-Enough Window – because I thought you were a friend.'

'I wish,' said Robin, fretting at the front of his cap, 'I wish I knew a little more about this Far-Enough Window – I wish I knew *anything* about it.'

'But you *will* know,' said Joanna. 'When the time comes. You'll know because I'll have told you about it.' She smoothed her gown over her knees, thinking that, even if the sunlight *were* only an imitation of the real thing, it shone on the white cloth very pleasingly.

'Hrimfaxi,' said Mustardseed, suddenly becoming very businesslike, 'told us that there was a gateway from here into the reality of Fairyland. I don't suppose, Robin, you know anything about it?'

'A place where reality clusters,' said Robin Goodfellow slowly. 'No, I can't say as I do. Come to think of it, if you're saying that I'm not actually completely real myself – although I feel so, sweet Joanna, let me reassure you of that – then how would I be recognizing things that were realer than me?' He stretched as if yawning, though his face was alert. 'I'm tired of all this heavy talk. The world was made for play and dance, and, though tomorrow may be made for thunderstorms to fill, perhaps the thunderstorms will be good enough to forget to come.'

A look of exasperation crossed Mustardseed's face, yet Joanna could see the handservant beginning to fall under Robin's sway. His playfulness was infectious: his bright eye had the power of command. Why, it seemed ever such a long time and even longer than that since her feet had danced . . .

'Those fish are real,' said Mr Dogg, bustling wetly through the grass. 'I've tested three of 'em now, and I'll give you my promise that there's none more palatably genuine.'

He broke the spell. Joanna looked at her extended legs as if she'd never seen them before. How had they got there? Who could have given them the notion that they should be ready for dancing? And Mustardseed reacted even more firmly: she clouted Robin Goodfellow about the ear, so that he went tumbling away into the grass, his cap and its feather flying.

THE FAR-ENOUGH WINDOW

'The stream,' said Mustardseed. 'Perhaps . . .?'

'It would be a start,' said Joanna hurriedly.

Mr Dogg said: 'It smells good when you jump into it, and its banks hide some most interesting secrets.'

'Tomorrow,' said Robin Goodfellow, picking himself up and stooping for his cap. 'I'll come with you three to see if this is a fool's errand – which is what I think it is, if the truth be told – or if the stream is a way into next year. But I won't do it tonight. The sun is riding low in the sky' – Joanna hadn't noticed this before, but it was true – 'and that's a sign for us all that it's time to rest our heads. Tomorrow will be as good a time as any for us to go looking at this stream of yours, Sir Mongrel.'

So they lit a fire using wood that Robin Goodfellow and Mr Dogg fetched, and as the night splashed shadows around them Robin and Mustardseed danced while Joanna and Mr Dogg cheered them on, and when the fire went out they curled around each other and fell asleep.

Dawn hung over the land. A light mist rose in the warmth of the sun. Joanna, still heavy from sleep, dawdled behind the others as they descended the hillside, Mr Dogg racing excitably ahead and then looping back to chivvy them along, as if they were recalcitrant sheep and he their sheepdog. The air around her was filled with the little whooshes and whines that betrayed the interest the little fairy-folk had discovered in her presence.

Running her tongue around her mouth, she yearned for a toothbrush – but was surprised by how little else she longed for of the comforts of home. The warm, good-morning hug of Mrs Ruggeley, perhaps, and certainly Knolly Mutton. Other than that – well, a bath might be welcome, and soft toilet paper, but these were merely the conveniences of home, not home itself. She was beginning, she realized, to think of Fairyland as home. It was proving remarkably easy to shake off seventeen years of living elsewhere.

The pain of Hrimfaxi's death – he had said it wasn't really a death, but her mind had come to refuse to recognize the distinction – was still sharp. Mustardseed and Mr Dogg seemed almost to have forgotten that the unicorn had ever existed, but to Joanna it was as if a part of her – a large part of her – had perished. She wondered if the natural bonding that all the legends said existed between unicorns and maidens were something more than that – if she and Hrimfaxi had together formed a sort of *ad hoc* symbiotic partnership. She recalled a notion she'd come across during her craze for reading books on mythology: that individual men and women are only half-creatures, and their life-quest is to discover their other half so as to form the complete being. Perhaps it had been the same with her and Hrimfaxi; now that he had gone she was cast back into her previous state of incompleteness, but haunted by the knowledge of what entirety felt like.

She had woken several times during the night with tears in her eyes, and now they came again.

'Buck up,' growled Mr Dogg, appearing at her side. 'Get a move on. We'll never get there at this rate.'

Obediently she quickened her pace, pushing aside the long grass ahead of her with Hrimfaxi's horn, and soon she was standing beside Mustardseed and Robin Goodfellow by the edge of a broad but swift-flowing stream. Little white flowers decorated both banks, and an uneven line of mossy stepping stones extended across the water. Splashes of cuckoo-spit embellished the longer reeds, and cobwebs – like spun silver in the dawn light – hung between them.

Mr Dogg leapt enthusiastically into the water and splashed about cheerfully, barking like a puppy.

'What's so special about this stream, then?' said Robin Goodfellow.

'It's full of fish,' said Mustardseed. 'Fuller than it should be.'

As if in confirmation, a silvery shape briefly broke the surface and fell back. Mr Dogg leapt after it, but the fish easily eluded him.

'That doesn't seem to argue for its being a place of greater reality than the rest of the world,' Robin observed. He knelt down and dangled his fingertips in the water. 'Colder than ice. It's a wonder our mongrel friend hasn't become a statue.'

Joanna's eye was caught by the sunlight on the ripples further upstream. The reflections formed a constantly changing tapestry of different coloured lights. Entranced, she wandered towards them, but the tapestry retreated in step with her. She was struck by the fancy that the pattern of dancing lights was leading her, but she didn't mind: she wanted it to lead her. She hardly noticed that she was rounding a bend in the stream's course, or that a little clump of overhanging willows was cutting her off from the view of her friends.

A brilliantly scarlet butterfly landed on the back of her hand, and stretched its wings. It was followed by a second, this one an almost metallic turquoise. Then came another, and another, and soon she was standing in the middle of a flock of fluttering wings. The insects landed with infinitesimal strokes on her exposed legs and arms, on her hair and her robe and her face and along the shaft of Hrimfaxi's horn. She felt she was breathing pure colour as, dressed in her living cloak, she continued to follow the pattern of ripples further upstream. Still more butterflies swarmed towards her from the nearby woods to join the throng, spiralling now high above her in a trailing polychromatic plume.

She walked slowly onwards, putting her feet down with deliberate delicacy for fear of crushing one of the creatures. The conviction came to her that she, too, had only a minuscule weight, that her steps were barely affecting the damp grasses and mosses of the stream's bank. She raised her arms to the sides and wondered if the merest of beats with her hands would raise her easily into the air, where she could circle and swirl, one more butterfly among the countless thousands. She glanced down at herself and saw nothing but wings: she had become a creature of colour. She flung her hair, and was surrounded by a halo of pulsing brightness as the butterflies clung to its strands.

She could hear nothing except the almost-silence of the fragile wings. Jerkily changing fringes of blurred colour encroached briefly on her vision before vanishing to be replaced by others.

Ahead of her a large spreading tree crouched over the water, blocking off the sunlight. At once the gleams of the ripples disappeared, and Joanna came to a halt, staring at the place where they had been. For the dozen yards or so where the water was in the shadow of the tree the surface seemed completely smooth, as if the darkness were pressing it flat.

She looked upwards and saw a wavering column of

brilliantly shifting colours reaching almost as far as the clouds. She stretched out her arms again and bent backwards, feeling the smooth curve of her spine. It would be so easy to join the butterflies in the green-tinged morning sky, so easy to shake off the pull of the world, and to rise into the cold newness of the day.

Her feet were still touching the ground, but not weighing upon it. She could feel the tiny moist filaments of the moss tickling her soles, and then she was floating clear, drifting upwards aimlessly in a haze of butterflies, feeling as if her soul were formed purely of light, as if her body were as weightless as that light.

'Come back!' cried a tiny voice from somewhere a million miles away. 'Joanna, come back!'

She listened to the beating of butterfly wings instead, the pulse which had become her own heart's. Words were heavy objects, seeking to drag her to the world's weight, but she was a creature of the aether.

And then there was a flurry of different wings around her, and a cascade of little squeals and yells. The cloth of colours covering her body seemed to coalesce, as if the butterflies were becoming leathery scales. She moved her arm, and dry, blood-coloured flakes cracked away, dropping lazily to the stream below. Her cloak was changing hue, its diversity ebbing towards a uniform rust-brown. She felt the weight of her body trying to pull her out of the air. She struggled against it, but all the movements of her limbs did was to shed more of the lifeless flakes. Above her the plume of butterflies was disintegrating, buffeting this way and that as if a tempest were loose within it. Battered butterfly corpses, their wings torn and their sticklike black bodies broken, fell in a rain around her.

And she too was falling.

She landed with a splash. A rounded boulder under the surface of the stream took her in the small of the back, arching her with shocking pain. She breathed water, pungent and icy in her nostrils, before her reflexes took over and she sat up screaming, coughing and spitting the liquid out of her. Despite the agony of her bruised back, she rolled over and got to her hands and knees, her vision no more than an anguished smear. All around her the water was the colour of blood as the flakes the butterflies had become dissolved. Dead insects floated downstream on the blood like a tiny, gaudy armada.

There was someone sloshing through the stream towards her. She looked up and saw saturated black cloth.

'We thought – ' Mustardseed began, then stopped, as if the thought were one too terrible to be spoken out loud. She knelt down beside Joanna and pummelled her shoulders, helping her cough up the water. Joanna clung to the Comelately's waist, pressing her ear between Mustardseed's hard little breasts, hearing Mustardseed's heart beating.

'What were they?' gasped Joanna at last. 'They were so very beautiful.'

Mustardseed said nothing. Joanna opened her eyes to see Robin Goodfellow perched on the bank, looking at her quizzically.

'You seem to be more important than I thought, mortal lady,' he said, 'though I can't for the life of me imagine why.'

'I never asked to be important,' said Joanna with a final splutter. She hauled herself up Mustardseed's body so that she was kneeling upright beside the handservant. 'It was you who brought me through the Far-Enough Window in the first place – you must know why you did so. Will do so,' she added lamely, remembering.

'It's a mystery to me,' said Robin acidly. 'If I had my future all over again I'd – '

She could hear Mr Dogg in the distance, growling and barking. He was pursuing something, but she couldn't guess what.

'The butterflies,' she said. 'What were they?'

The question snapped Robin's attention back to her. 'They were magic,' he said. 'But *whose* magic I don't know. It has to have been someone very powerful to have been able to summon that much magic into a single place. If you hadn't been holding this' – he raised Hrimfaxi's horn, which she must have dropped during her final fall – 'I doubt if anything we could have done would have saved you. But there's still enough of your erstwhile friend in this to give you some protection – enough that Mustardseed and I and our little airhead pals were able to break the spell.' Joanna remembered the sudden, invisible arrival of other wings. 'Otherwise you'd have been lost to the sky. You'd have become tonight's sunset.'

Joanna realized with a start that he meant this literally.

'A fine thing to become,' she breathed.

'Your spirit would have long gone by then,' he said angrily. 'You'd have known nothing about it. The blood of the dying day would have been your blood also.' He spat into the stream. 'Bah! Romantics are so despicable!'

'Thank you,' said Joanna meekly. 'Thank you all for saving me.'

The Comelately tightened her grip around Joanna's

shoulders. 'Think nothing of it, beloved friend of Mustardseed,' she said. 'Mustardseed would die to save the life of her friend Joanna.'

Joanna looked into the yellow, slitted eyes. They were too alien for her to be able to read any emotion in them, but she could tell the depth of Mustardseed's feeling from the lines of her purplish face and the stumbling of her speech back towards the cumbersome forms she had used when Joanna had first met her.

'Joanna would die to save the life of her friend Mustardseed,' she responded, and at least for that instant it was the truth. She threw her arm around the Comelately's shoulder and drew her into a close embrace, kissing her cheek and her pointy little ear.

'Very touching,' said Robin Goodfellow acidly. 'All we need now is a forest of violins – no! I didn't say that!' He jumped to his feet and shouted at the sky: 'I was not under any circumstances expressing a desire for a forest of violins!'

Joanna started to laugh but then, pulling away from Mustardseed, she saw that Robin was in deadly seriousness.

'What's he talking about?' she murmured to Mustardseed.

'Whatever – whoever – tried to seize you may still be near, listening to us,' she said. 'Although it'd hardly dare to launch an attack on Robin Goodfellow and myself, because that would be against all law, it might be able to harm us by granting a wish whose unforeseen consequences – unforeseen by us, I mean – would be disastrous. If ever it were taken to task by Oberon for causing our fates, it could argue, truthfully, that it had merely acceded to our expressed desire. So it is best for us not to say out loud that we wish for anything until we know we are well free of its presence.'

THE FAR-ENOUGH WINDOW

Joanna found it impossible, for a moment, to think of anything to say that didn't start with 'I wish'.

'Do we – you – not know anything about this, this – ?' She faltered.

'No, and it's probably a matter of the less we know about it the happier us being.' Mustardseed was choosing her words carefully. 'It is our best plan to try to shake ourselves free of its attentions, though this may not be easy: it must see you, Joanna, as a very grave threat indeed if it were prepared to move so openly to try to destroy you.'

'But *me*? How could I pose a threat to anybody?'

'Robin Goodfellow must have brought you into Fairyland for a very good purpose, even though none of us yet know what that might be.' Mustardseed got to her feet and waded to the bank, pulling Joanna by the hand.

'It was to reclaim Fairyland for the little Finefolk,' puffed Joanna as she climbed up onto the ground. Her soaking robe seemed to weigh a ton. 'But he didn't tell me how I was to help him do this, what part I could play – and I have no idea of my own.'

Robin had ceased gesticulating wrathfully at the sky, and was sitting on a fallen treetrunk, listening to them gloomily.

'What's that mutt of yours doing?' he said crossly.

'Chasing rabbits?' said Joanna. 'He said last night that he'd – '

'Mortals! Their dogs are as bad as their women!'

'I suppose he is all right, isn't he?' said Joanna, suddenly becoming anxious. 'How long is it since last you saw him?'

'Since about the time we realized you'd gone missing,' said Mustardseed slowly. She put back her head and let out a high whistle. There was a renewed volley of barking in the distance.

'Sounds like he's cornered something,' said Robin, heaving himself off the trunk. 'I suppose we'd better go and have a look. Here' – he raised Hrimfaxi's horn to Joanna – 'you'd better take this back. It's yours. You might need it again.'

She accepted the hard spike and caressed it. Robin had said that there still resided within it some essence of the unicorn's soulstuff. She wondered if there were enough of it to sense the love she felt for him.

Mustardseed led the way as they tramped through the vegetation in the direction of Mr Dogg's barking. The Comelately moved with a sort of easy tension, clearly alert to everything around her, her hands flexing lightly. Joanna began to see her in a new light: the Comelately was a huntress now. Although she'd wavered in the face of the nightmares they'd discovered within the Lair of Forgotten Fears, when she was moving in her own sort of territory, when she was confident of the nature of her surroundings – even though she did not like them, as here – she was impressive. Joanna was very glad that Mustardseed was on her side.

They found Mr Dogg in the middle of a natural lea. He was standing with his shoulders low and his forepaws splayed, yelping and snarling into the side of a little grassy mound.

'What've you found?' cried Joanna, running towards him.

'Stop!' Mustardseed called to her. 'You don't know what's there! It could be dangerous!'

Joanna ran on regardless, and threw herself to the grass alongside Mr Dogg. 'What've you found?' she repeated breathlessly. There was a dark hole in the mound. 'All this fuss for a rabbit?'

THE FAR-ENOUGH WINDOW

A voice came from the depths of the disused rabbit-hole. 'If ye'll call off this stupid great monster of yours, I'll be forever in your debt.'

'He's not stupid,' said Joanna tartly. *A talking rabbit?* she wondered. *With an Irish accent?*

'I don't care if he's a five-star genius,' said the voice waspishly. 'He's got teeth half as high as I am and a bellow that would waken the dead. Which is what he must have to use it for quite often if his breath is always like this.'

'You could make a little less noise,' said Joanna to Mr Dogg.

Mustardseed and Robin Goodfellow came rushing up from behind as Mr Dogg stopped snarling.

'Oh, no,' wailed the voice. 'Not *more* of ye's! I knew this whole enterprise smacked of disaster from the moment I clapped ears on it. "Leave the lassie be," I said to him, but he was having none of it. "Ye do as I say, Tamarary Pulkoon," he said, "or it'll turn out the worse for ye, seeing as how ye've still never repaid me for the good turn I did ye around the time of Christ when the demon drink had caused ye to commit such a folk's pass with that there Calpurnia." Such a lissome lovely she was, and I was convinced her virtue was no more than skin-deep right up until the time she rammed me face-first into the cloaca, where it was so dark I couldn't cast a shadow, just like here, so I had to call on himself – thinks he's so mighty! – for assistance.'

'Are you coming to the point?' said Joanna frostily. It was difficult to remain entirely polite towards someone who was apparently confessing to having tried to destroy her. She had her hand on Mr Dogg's collar and could feel him straining to be at the creature in the hole.

'To be sure, to be sure, and I'm getting there in God's own good time!'

'Let me at him,' growled Mr Dogg. 'Just five minutes alone with him, that's all I ask.'

'I could winkle him out of there with this,' Joanna said speculatively, hefting Hrimfaxi's horn, which suddenly seemed sharper than ever before.

'No! No!' said the little voice, rising in panic. 'Not with the unicorn spike! If it hadn't been for that bedamned pricker I'd have – I mean, how fortunate, sweet mortal lady with the silken hair, that ye were clutching that talisman to your fair – '

'Just come out of there, Tamarary Pulkoon,' said Robin flatly, stepping in front of Joanna and Mr Dogg. 'I'll keep the mortals off you. Come out of there and tell us what you've been up to.' He gestured them to retreat.

The being that crept shiftily from the rabbit-hole was only about half the size of Robin Goodfellow. He wore a blue pointed hat with a bell on it and a scowl that could have curdled milk. Something very like him but in porcelain and grinning playfully decorated a red-and-white-spotted toadstool, also in porcelain, in the vegetable garden back home.

'A leprechaun!' said Joanna.

'Not *a* leprechaun,' he said. '*The* leprechaun. Tamarary Pulkoon. My fame and the tales of my heroic doings have spread so far and wide that mortals reckon there must be a bushel of me, but indeed the world is only big enough for one. At your service.' He dropped a bow.

'I thought this might be the case,' said Robin Goodfellow grimly. He stabbed out with his foot and impaled Tamarary

THE FAR-ENOUGH WINDOW

Pulkoon's shadow on the grass. 'The leprechaun!' he said, wagging his finger in front of Joanna's nose. 'One of the very few things more troublesome than a mortal woman!'

'There's no need to get personal,' said Tamarary Pulkoon, tugging at his shadow. Robin's foot held it firm. 'We all have our different ways.'

Joanna was reminded of how Wendy had had to stitch back on Peter Pan's shadow for him. Tamarary Pulkoon's shadow seemed much the same: a material thing attached to his feet.

'And yours are the worst ways, Tamarary Pulkoon,' said Robin. 'Why were you trying to destroy my pretty young mortal friend here? Who put you up to it? Eh?'

Tamarary Pulkoon stopped pulling at his shadow and looked up at Robin in obvious consternation. 'To be sure, and ye don't think it's destroying or despoiling her I was after? As God is my witness, that's the last thing I would have been doing! I was told under pain of death – well, to be true, not death itself but a fate much worse than it – that I was to preserve every hair on her fair young body as careful as if it were one of my own. And' – he turned earnestly to Joanna – 'they don't make hairs much more precious than mine, I can tell ye.'

'Then what *were* you trying to do?' interposed Mustardseed. She was looking as if she'd like to pick up the leprechaun and wring the life from him.

'I was . . . I was . . . Look, can ye get your great clodhopper off my shadow, Robin Goodfellow?' The leprechaun began to dance with wrath and difficulty.

'No, Tamarary Pulkoon, that I will not do until you explain to me why you assailed this lady.' Robin turned to her. 'The leprechaun himself can do no more magic than you can, my dear one,' he said. 'But his shadow – ah, his shadow is a powerful sorcerer. If it were free it could conjure up a spell of darkness that might destroy us all.'

'It certainly wouldn't!' declared Tamarary Pulkoon. 'It's a nice, friendly shadow – a little misunderstood, that's all.'

'Who set you – *and* your shadow – on Joanna?' said Mustardseed loudly. She flexed her fingers, cracking her knuckles to most scarifying effect.

Tamarary Pulkoon sat down, the legs of his shadow tangled underneath him.

'It was the Great High King himself,' he said. 'Oberon.'

Robin Goodfellow paled. 'Matters have become even worse than I suspected,' he muttered. 'The day of the return of the Oldcomers cannot be far distant.'

'What's that ye're saying?' Tamarary Pulkoon keeked up at him.

'Nothing, nothing,' said Robin, waving the words away with his hand. 'And why should our revered monarch wish you to slay this innocent mortal, so newly come into our land?'

'I told ye before, Robin Goodfellow, that it was not my task to slay her! Had he demanded that of me then, debt of honour or no debt of honour, I, Tamarary Pulkoon, would have refused point-blank, at whatever the cost to my soul!' The leprechaun leapt to his feet and struck a pose, his fist on his chest. 'Almost certainly!' he added emphatically to Joanna. 'But it was not her life he sought, only her beauty.'

'Tell us a little bit more,' said Mustardseed quietly, coiling herself down beside him.

The leprechaun looked up at her face, so close to him,

decided he didn't like what he read in her eyes, and looked away hurriedly.

'He needs a bride,' he said. 'Titania has deserted him, and no one knows where she might have gone to. They seek her here, they seek her there, but nary a trace of her is there to be found anywhere. And what is a land whose king has no queen? Answer me no answer for that, because I've got an answer for ye: it's a dying land, is what kind of a land it is. A land that is headed for death as sure as any mortal king, without the temperance of a queen by his side, is headed for a bloody doom in battle over an inconsequence. Glory – yes, the king'd have that. For generations afterwards the minstrels would sing of his valour in slaughtering unarmed peasants. But doomed he'd be, just the same. And the same with a land whose king has no queen. Would ye like' – he glared fiercely up at Robin Goodfellow – 'this place to be a desert, all because Oberon has no one to keep him warm?'

'He wanted Joanna to take Titania's place,' said Mustardseed.

' "*Wanted*"? He most earnestly desired.' Tamarary Pulkoon sat down again. 'A hundred thousand blithe young fairies or more prepared to fill his bed at night, and what he wants is a mortal wench! "Oh," he says to me as soon as the news comes to him that there's a corn-haired mortal just arrived in the world. "I have heard she is surpassing fair, and none other can I contemplate in her place." So he sends me out to fetch her, by whatever means I can. And so I would have done had she not been clasping a unicorn spike, and had as her companion a hound from the depthmosts of hell!'

'So all you were doing was carrying me away to Oberon?' said Joanna. 'Why couldn't he come and ask me himself?'

She had gained the idea, from books and videos, that a proposal of marriage was a matter for candlelight and delicate, often misunderstood allusions.

'You don't know much about Oberon,' Mustardseed told her. 'If there's a stupid way of going about things, that's the one he'll take. Although I revere him,' she added hastily, 'as is the due of a liege-lord.'

'Then why don't we just go and see him and persuade him otherwise?' Joanna enquired.

'Because we're looking for the route that will take us out of this sham version of Fairyland,' said Mustardseed. 'Because it was very obvious, to me if not to you, that when you first met Oberon he'd never set eyes on you before. Oh, there are a hundred other reasons, Joanna.'

'A way out of Fairyland?' said Tamarary Pulkoon brightly. 'Is that what ye'd be looking after? Well, ye've come to the right person.'

They were back on the bank of the stream, and again Joanna was staring at the pattern of ripples on the water. The sun was by now high in the sky, but this didn't seem to make any difference to the kaleidoscope of reflections. The changed angle of the light, however, did bring out in relief the gossamer lines of the array of cobwebs spanning the rocks between her and the disturbed water.

'How *real* are you?' Joanna abruptly asked Tamarary Pulkoon.

Mustardseed laughed. 'He's as real as anything you'll ever find in Fairyland,' she said before the leprechaun could answer for himself. 'He's been a part of it through all eternity. There's no doubt he's a likelihood that'll be formed afresh into each new now. More's the pity,' she added affectionately, bending down to push Tamarary Pulkoon's conical cap over his eyes.

'Just 'cause ye have me at your mercy, ye great hulking brute of a besom,' he said crossly, straightening it. 'Ye just wait 'til the day comes when I – '

Mustardseed bent lower, and took the leprechaun's shadow in her hands. 'We'll just see about that,' she murmured.

Her fingers flew with lightning speed, and before Joanna could blink the Comelately had woven Tamarary Pulkoon's shadow into a curiously tangled ball, whose tiny knots seemed not entirely to be within the correct plane of actuality.

Tamarary Pulkoon was too apoplectic with misery and fury to speak.

'Well, Tamarary Pulkoon,' said Mustardseed, standing erect and putting her hands on her waist, 'now your shadow is tied into knots that it'll take you the rest of forever to unravel. What's the price you'll pay for the weaver herself to undo her weaving?' Her voice had taken on some of his Irish lilt, mocking him.

'Ye – Ye – ' he stammered.

'Me and Joanna and Mr Dogg and even Robin Goodfellow will be safe from your sorcery forever – is that what you're trying to say?' She stared at him; no smile was left on her face. 'Or, believe me, Tamarary Pulkoon, but I'll find you wherever you are and the least you'll have to fear will be me weaving your shadow again – because once I've done with it I'll do the same to you.'

The leprechaun let out a strangled squawk of anticipated

pain.

'And if anything's happened to stop me from attending to the matter personally, I shall have one of my sisters do it for me. They're not such good weavers as me, of course, so they'd be bound to make *lots* of mistakes.'

She bent over and swiftly unwove the shadow.

Robin Goodfellow had been watching all this with a surly expression on his face. 'Before we were distracted by the . . . the pantomime,' he said with heavy distaste, 'you were asking how *real* our scapegrace acquaintance Tamarary Pulkoon is. Mustardseed was right: he's as permanent as anything in Fairyland. And I'm the same: there's always been a Robin Goodfellow and there always will be. Your friend Hrimfaxi was right when he said you'd gather the real to you – that they'd find themselves driven to join you, much though I dislike the idea of having done anything except of my own free will. That must be why Oberon wanted you by his side, as soon as he heard about you – for he's as real as can be, too. We're the constants of Fairyland: Oberon, Tamarary Pulkoon and I – as was Titania until . . .' He shrugged. 'Until she went wherever she went.'

'And this place,' said Joanna to Tamarary Pulkoon once she had absorbed this, 'this stretch of stream – you say it's a gateway into Fairyland's present?'

'Yes,' said the leprechaun. He seemed to have decided he'd recovered most of his dignity. 'Ye were halfway to discovering it yourself when I sent my wingèd emissaries in an attempt to detain ye.'

The sound of wayward buzzings in the air immediately increased in intensity, becoming almost threatening, and Tamarary Pulkoon cowered. 'Not that I'd ever do any such thing again,' he said defensively. 'Not unless my name's not Tamarary Pulkoon.'

'What I still don't understand,' said Robin Goodfellow, 'is why I'm going to want to bring you into Fairyland through this Far-Enough Window you talk about. You say that this world of ours is soon going to be overwhelmed by the Comelatelies, and this I believe, for there have been many other signs of such a change – and our friend Mustardseed, exquisite as she is, is living evidence of such a change having taken place, for I remember her being like this, back in the days of the Oldcomers. Yet, for all that that's true, I cannot imagine how I'll think that you yourself – no offence meant, you understand, fair one? – can be of any help to us.'

'Perhaps you'll believe so,' said Mustardseed, 'because we'll have told you so.'

'It's really Hrimfaxi who's told you so.' Joanna was thoughtful. 'He said the whole point of our having journeyed into the Farness was so that we could re-enter Fairyland from somewhere in its might-have-been past. Perhaps the only reason we came here was so that we could tell you what your future holds, Robin Goodfellow, and what you must do there.'

'But I've never even heard of this Far-Enough Window of yours!' cried Robin. 'I haven't the first idea where I might be able to find it!'

'Far-Enough Window?' said Tamarary Pulkoon. 'And ye say ye can't find it? What in the name of our Dear Lord who died to save us all d'ye think ye're standing in front of?'

He pointed to the rippling reflections and the strands of gossamer crisscrossing in front of them.

'*That*'s the Far-Enough Window,' he said. 'The gateway

that leads to wherever ye want it to go to. All ye have to do is to be able to see far enough into it, ye great gouk!'

***

They had to lie down on the stream-bank before they could see it, and even then Joanna was the only one who could identify it for certain. There was a particular crossing of gossamer that echoed the leading of the Far-Enough Window she'd discovered in the topmost attic of the Lampeter Wing, and if one's eyes were at the precisely correct angle, one could see through it to the sole patch of dancing reflection that stayed still, whatever happened around it.

'It was a lot easier for me the last time,' she complained. 'I had *you* to guide my gaze, Robin Goodfellow – to help me see as far as was needed. Now I'm having to try to remember what it felt like – what it was that I did – and so much has happened since then . . .'

They were a fan of bodies on the mossy grass. Mr Dogg had given up trying to lie as flat as the other three, and was allowing his rump and tail to jut into the air; but his head was between his paws as he stared intently at the gossamer crosshatch.

Robin Goodfellow was alongside them, lying between Mustardseed and Joanna. They'd tried to tell him that it was impossible for him to go from the might-have-been past into the reality of the now, but he'd said that he wanted to try – wouldn't it be grand to meet himself, because there was no one else he'd rather meet?

Tamarary Pulkoon sat aloof. He looked disgusted with them all. Joanna didn't know whether this was a good sign or

THE FAR-ENOUGH WINDOW

a bad.

'Well, here goes,' she said. 'I'm going to give it my best try.'

And she focused not on the cross the cobweb-strands made, not on the grey light behind them, but on somewhere ineffably *beyond* – on the place that was far enough.

The world melted.

Eight

The Threefold Queen

All at once, a radiant form stood in the centre of the darkness, flashing a splendour on every side. Over a robe of soft white, her hair streamed in a cataract, black as the marble on which it fell. Her eyes were a luminous blackness; her arms and feet like warm ivory. She greeted me with the innocent smile of a girl – and in face, figure and motion seemed but now to have stepped over the threshold of womanhood.

– George MacDonald, *Lilith*, 1895

Total darkness, and a lot of dust. Joanna, on her hands and knees, was sneezing. Someone else was sneezing nearby. She couldn't at first imagine where she'd come to. She dropped something she'd been holding, and it tumbled away.

'Who's there?' she said when at last she had her voice under control.

The other person carried on sneezing, and the sound sparked Joanna off into a new set of convulsions.

When next both of them were silent, she croaked again: 'Who's there?'

'Mustardseed. Is that Joanna?'

'Yes.'

'Where are we? Are we back in the Lair of Forgotten Fears?'

'I don't know. I don't think so.'

Joanna felt around with her hands. She seemed to be on a filthy wooden floor. She sat back on her haunches and peered around her in the gloom.

As her eyes accustomed themselves, she discovered that the blackness wasn't entirely unrelieved. There was a faint glimmer at about the level of her head. Shuffling on her knees, she inched her way towards it.

Cold glass against her fingers. A circular shape, bulbous towards its lower part, with two hard linear shapes crossing it. Through the glass she could discern a milky grey landscape. Moonlight. Falling snow.

'We're back in my world,' she said. 'I know where we are. We're beside the Far-Enough Window. But when?' She could sense that it was now only a window, not the Far-Enough Window.

Mustardseed came up beside her. 'Let me see.'

'There isn't much to see. If only I could . . . I know I dropped a torch somewhere around here when first I came to the Lampeter Wing.'

She withdrew from the window a little and started patting the floor around her. Her hands encountered various objects, some of which she didn't want to know the identities of, but she didn't come across the smooth, plastic shape of the torch. Her search became more wide-ranging, and she almost fell through the hatch into the lower room. Now that she was looking directly down into it, she could see that there was a little more light there; the bulky stairway effectively blocked most of it off from the attic.

'Mustardseed,' she hissed. 'Over here.'

Muffled thuds and scrapes told her the Comelately was making her own, rather more confident way across the attic floor, and then Mustardseed was by her side, peering downwards.

'This is a strange place, this world of yours, Joanna.'

'It looks pretty strange to me, too, in this light. Come on – we'll be better off down there.' She swivelled around and put her legs through the opening, searching for a step. 'With luck, my torch may be there.'

'Torch? You have fire here?'

'No – it's a sort of portable lamp. It stays quite cold. You just press a button in it and light appears.'

'You want light?'

Joanna paused halfway down the steps. 'Mustardseed, you don't mean that – ?'

The Comelately made a clapping sound and at once her hands glowed a blinding white. Everything sprang into stark relief.

'It seems fairy magic works just as well in your world as it does in my own,' said Mustardseed calmly. 'I didn't know for certain.'

'Why didn't you try it before?' Joanna held up one of her own hands to show where it had been gashed on a nail.

'I forgot you couldn't see in the dark.'

Joanna said nothing, but hoped the *way* she said nothing spoke worlds.

By the light of Mustardseed's hands they searched the lower turret room, but could find no trace of Joanna's torch.

'I wonder where Mr Dogg is,' she mused out loud.

'He must be still with Robin Goodfellow, back in the past. Don't worry – Robin will see that he comes to no harm.'

That was when Joanna had the first flash that indicated to her that she was no longer merely a single individual: she had a vision of being herself, somewhere else, standing alongside Mustardseed as they both beat at the flames devouring the inner wall of Oberon's tent. Mr Dogg wasn't with them.

She assumed the vision was just some kind of daydream – although it seemed *realer* than a daydream. She said nothing of it to Mustardseed.

There was a gasp of horror from the Comelately. Joanna whipped around and saw that Mustardseed was standing in front of one of the room's filthy upright windows, looking aghast. 'How tall is this building we're in?' she said in a faint voice.

'A hundred feet?' Joanna guessed. 'This is the very tallest part of it – the tower over the northwestern wing.'

'So high,' Mustardseed whispered, still staring out of the window. 'So horribly high.'

'You must have flown far higher than this,' said Joanna in perplexity.

'Yes, but then I was flying. It's quite different.'

Joanna thought for a moment. 'Can you fly in this world?'

'I don't think so. In this form, I can't fly in Fairyland, so – ' She seemed to be making some tremendous mental effort; then her shoulders slumped. 'No. I haven't the power to do so here, either.'

'We can get closer to the ground quite easily,' Joanna said. 'There are more stairs – like the steps we've just come down, but made of stone. There are lots of them. They're very slippery, so we'll have to take care.'

With Joanna leading the way, they crept carefully down the long helical staircase. Mustardseed gave as much light as she could from the hand that wasn't clutching the rail. At the bottom they rested in the hall where Joanna had fantasized about taking over the Lampeter Wing as her own domain.

'This is a very grand place,' said Mustardseed, gazing around her. 'Do kings live here?'

Joanna smiled. 'No. No one lives here – no one has for a long time. And, as far as I know, never a king. This is just part of a very big house. We tend to build things on a larger scale, here in the mortal world, than you do in Fairyland.'

'Is this house as big as the Lair of Forgotten Fears?'

'No,' Joanna conceded. 'It's smaller than that. I shouldn't think there'll ever be any building in this world that can compare with the Lair.'

'Are we nearer the ground yet?'

'Yes, we've come down quite a long way – but there's still as far to go again, and a lot of it is very much more difficult than the bit we've done so far. We'll have to be twice as careful, and go twice as slowly.'

'Please don't take offence, dearest friend Joanna, but I do hope that I won't be confined to this world of mortals for long. It's very magnificent, but it's also very frightening. And there's a tang in the air that reminds me of the Fairyland we've just left.'

'You get used to our world, in time. Come on – I want to see what's happening in the rest of the house. I want to find Mrs Ruggeley.'

***

Joanna sneezed as she flailed at the burning cloth. She had suffered an almost debilitating shock of dislocation on returning here. Oberon's tent. Orange flames licked the wall of Mustardseed's chamber. At most a few seconds seemed to have passed in Fairyland since she and Mustardseed and Mr Dogg had taken off for the Farness on Hrimfaxi's back. What had happened to her body in the interim? Had she vanished and then reappeared? Or had 'someone else' – another self of hers – 'occupied' it?

There wasn't any time to think it out – if she and Mustardseed didn't get clear of this small chamber, it was a toss-up whether they'd be suffocated first or burnt alive. The cloth was as impenetrable as wood or stone when neither of them had an edged tool – a knife or blade of any kind – with which to cut through it.

A sharp edge. Ah –

'Your fingernails! Your claws!' she screamed at Mustardseed over the din from elsewhere in the tent. The Comelately turned and looked at her vacantly. Joanna grabbed her by the hand. She'd become so used to the Mustardseed who'd escaped the field of Oberon's thought-dampening power that she'd forgotten how stupid the old Mustardseed had been. 'You can claw us out of here!'

At last understanding seeped over Mustardseed's face. 'Joanna very clever, very right.'

'Quickly!'

Joanna, still holding the Comelately's hand, made a slashing motion with it at the opposite wall of the chamber.

Mustardseed took a couple of swift steps and chopped downwards with her outspread fingers. With an easy *zzzip!* the cloth tore. Mustardseed grabbed the three dangling strips she had produced and ripped them apart in the middle. 'Joanna go there,' she said hoarsely. 'Mustardseed follow.'

Joanna didn't hesitate but threw herself through the aperture to land in what she took for a washroom – there were basins on tripods and the cloying smell of stale hygiene. But even this stink was a merciful change from the acrid taste of burning cloth.

Mustardseed tumbled in beside her. Joanna mutely indicated the next wall, and the Comelately moved towards it. It couldn't be long before the whole tent went up in flames; nowhere inside it was safe. Even so, Joanna found that one of the basins was half full of scummy water, and she hurled it back the way they had come, hoping it would delay the flames an extra few seconds.

The Comelately seized her arm and dragged her through into a fresh chamber, larger than the previous two. Three or four other handservants, obviously in the final stages of mindless panic, were huddled in a corner. When they saw Joanna there was an immediate transformation, and they advanced towards her, hands grasping, lips pulled back from their evil-looking teeth.

Mustardseed snarled something incomprehensible at them and they fell back. When they saw her clawing at the wall they slowly – it was pitiful how slow-thinking they were – caught the idea, and followed suit. This time Joanna was the first to step through the curtain of tatters their efforts produced.

They were going away from the main chamber, and Joanna wondered quite how many walls they still had left to rip through before they reached the open air. None of the rooms was neatly rectangular, so it was difficult to know if they were going in a straight line. The pandemonium – the shouts and screams of Comelatelies in consternation – seemed to be coming from all around them. The handservants – yes, there were five of them, including Mustardseed – were at work on the next wall, shredding it almost completely in their eagerness. They shoved through in a group, shambling into some kind of dormitory. Joanna barely had time to take in the twin lines of low bed-heaps before she realized that grey twilight was filtering through the cloth in front of her.

'We're there!' she cried.

With a final flurry of clawed hands the Comelatelies burst through into the open. Joanna followed just in time to catch Mustardseed, who had tripped on a guy-rope.

This was the nearest Joanna had been to freedom since Peaseblossom had ensnared her with his wiles, and she didn't want to waste the moment. 'Quickly!' she shouted directly into Mustardseed's face. 'Remember – the whole encampment is a danger to me. Any of these folk might take it into their heads to kill me as a monster! If you want to preserve me for Oberon you must take me well clear of it.'

And indeed the place was in a complete turmoil. Comelatelies were trying to barge hither and thither, waving swords and screaming at each other. For the time being the little group of handservants, with Joanna at its centre, hadn't attracted attention in the mêlée, but surely it could be only a matter of moments before –

A Comelately warrior armed with an axe reared towards them.

Mustardseed's hand tore across his throat. Black blood sprayed. The other handservants fell back in horror. This was not death – it was hard to kill one of the Finefolk – but it was a close approximation. Mustardseed grabbed Joanna's arm again, just above the elbow, and started to drag her away.

'Mustardseed friend of Joanna,' the handservant was muttering in a steady litany. 'Joanna friend of Mustardseed. Oberon wants Mustardseed to keep Joanna safe.'

Another armed Comelately fell aside as the handservant's arm flashed.

Joanna felt as if she were being battered from every side. Part of it was the noise; but most of it was a genuine physical crushing as panicking Comelatelies lumbered against her. Their narrow eyes held no recognition of her: she was merely an obstacle. Mustardseed could perhaps continue to keep at bay those Comelatelies who saw the mortal woman and might wish to kill her as scapegoat for the terrors that had come into their midst; Joanna was far more frightened that one of them would kill her accidentally. Most of the males and some of the females were armed, and often they were whirling their swords and daggers at the air, as if it were somehow to blame for their misfortunes.

'Get me out of here!' she yelled at Mustardseed. There was no sign that the handservant had heard her.

The noise around her all at once seemed to escalate to such a pitch that it became silence. In that cocoon she suddenly knew she was clutching some kind of curved metal rail as she trod warily downwards into fitfully lit darkness. There was brightness behind her, but she dared not turn to look at it for fear of missing her step and falling headlong. The smell of musty disuse filled her nostrils.

And then she was back in the press, struggling after Mustardseed, who had her arm in an iron grip and was pushing ahead ruthlessly. That grip was bruising her cruelly. Tears of pain filled her eyes, but she refused to scream.

They broke free into emptiness at the edge of the encampment. They were at the base of the hillside upon which – so terribly long ago, it seemed! – they had sat together watching the Comelatelies swarm busily beneath them as they gathered for their meal. There were grey flowers among the grey grass; Joanna recognized them through the dusk as buttercups. The recognition was homely, reassuring.

'Climb, Mustardseed, climb!' she shrieked. 'We must get further away from your people! One of them might still chase after us!' She hoped that Oberon, who must be somewhere in the chaos behind them, wouldn't suddenly appear and beckon the pair of them back. Mustardseed would surely obey...

But Mustardseed was striding ahead up the hillside, lugging Joanna behind her.

A second abrupt flash of otherness. It was she, not Mustardseed, who was leading, and they were going downwards, not up. They were just entering a large space with carpets on its floors. The light was uncertain and constantly changing, but Joanna thought she could see the dark rectangles of framed pictures on the walls. She was confident: she was showing off this place to Mustardseed with some pride.

Then she was once more stumbling up a hillside in the twilight.

Of course she'd pottered about the house at night before, but it had never felt so devastatingly empty as it did just now.

THE FAR-ENOUGH WINDOW

She and Mustardseed stood in the great hall, at the foot of the stairs, looking upwards. Shafts of moonlight through glass created a weird frame around the house's front door. The Comelately had extinguished the luminescence of her hands some while ago: Joanna wanted to investigate the place before she risked waking up Mrs Ruggeley.

'I've been a prisoner here all my life,' said Joanna quietly to Mustardseed. 'I've been caged in this house by what other people – other people, never me – have chosen to call love. The first thing I ever saw through the Far-Enough Window was not Fairyland but the rest of my own world.'

'I was a prisoner of Oberon,' said Mustardseed. 'I thought there was no way I could ever be released from his thrall. You could be free of here, Joanna – if you really wanted to be.'

Joanna shook her head violently. 'This is my home,' she said.

'For how much longer?'

'I don't know.'

No sound except the moonlight brushing motes of dust.

'I need to ask Mrs Ruggeley what's going on,' Joanna said. 'Soon.'

'What makes you think she'll know?' said Mustardseed.

'She always knows,' said Joanna, 'everything.'

'She's a mortal,' said Mustardseed dismissively. 'She's never seen outside this mortal world of yours. You can't expect her to have any knowledge of Fairyland.'

'That's not what I want to know about.' Joanna felt a great reluctance to climb the stairs. 'I want to know why I've been imprisoned here. I want to know why I'm not allowed to experience the outside world. Mrs Ruggeley told me a little part of it, but I'm not sure I believe what she said. I want to know who my father really is, and where my mother has gone to. I want to discover who I am. I want to know so many things, Mustardseed. Travelling to Fairyland was hardly a marvel beside the mystery of my own life.'

She looked upwards. The stairs were a corrugation of greys, relieved where moonlight fell through small windows. The sight intimidated her.

'And I want,' she said quietly, 'to see my diary.'

They watched the encampment burn. Joanna was peeved to discover that Mustardseed had restored the handcuff-like link between them; it signified a lack of the mutual trust that Joanna had believed they had. She said as much to the handservant, but Mustardseed refused to talk about it.

The blazing tents lit up the night. The moon was lost in the angry light of the pyre. The screams of the Comelatelies seemed to come from all around the hills.

'I wish Mr Dogg were here.'

Mustardseed turned her head lethargically. Her scales shone a flickering orange. 'Who?'

'Never mind.'

Joanna was standing at the foot of the main staircase in her own home, looking upwards. There was someone beside her who she realized was Mustardseed.

She was back on the hillside.

'I wonder where Hrimfaxi's horn went to.'

'What Joanna talking about? Joanna acting very strange. Mustardseed concerned for Joanna.'

'The unicorn. He rescued us from' – Joanna waved at the leaping flames – 'all this. Before.'

THE FAR-ENOUGH WINDOW

Nothing but regular breathing from the handservant.

'Oh, of course,' said Joanna bitterly. 'You couldn't be expected to remember.'

She rested her chin in her hand glumly.

There was a tap on her shoulder.

'At last!' said Robin Goodfellow. 'I thought we might never find you.'

'Robin!'

'None other, and here at the service of the beautiful lady Joanna, than whose no praises should be sung higher.'

'And Dolly!' She threw out her arms and the little woman ran into them. 'And you, too, Lumpenkulder!'

Mustardseed was looking at the three newcomers suspiciously. She began to flex her fingers, and Joanna had a sickening memory of how easily the tentcloth had ripped. 'These are friends of Joanna's,' she said hurriedly. 'Any harm that comes to them would be a harm to Joanna.'

'I see Robin Goodfellow,' said the Comelately mechanically. 'I do not know these others.'

Joanna performed swift introductions. 'And where is Mr Dogg?' she asked Robin Goodfellow finally. 'Do you have him with you?'

'No,' said Robin, looking worried. 'I thought he would be with you. When I plucked away our ghosts from Oberon's tent Mr Dogg stayed behind to be at your side in case you needed him. That was part of the scheme, fair Joanna.'

'But I haven't seen him since I came through the Far-Enough Window. The last time, I mean. When I used it to reach the present from the past.'

Mustardseed was looking at Joanna as if she were mad. 'It's all perfectly easy to explain,' said Joanna in a hurried aside to her. 'But not now.'

'He disappeared *then* in the same moment that you did,' said Robin Goodfellow. 'I thought nothing of it at the time, and I never thought to ask Mr Dogg when you came back with him again. It was what Tamarary Pulkoon had led us to believe should happen. Oh, that leprechaun laughed at me when I was left there on the bank of the stream! "I told you so, Robin Goodfellow!" he kept crying, until I reminded him what your friend Mustardseed had said she would do to his shadow if he didn't behave himself. Not *this* Mustardseed' – with a jab of his head – 'of course, but the one who was with you then.'

Mustardseed stared at him as if he were a particularly revolting insect that she would like to squash flat. And then probably eat.

'This is getting very confusing,' said Joanna. She put her face in her hands.

'It gets much more confusing still,' said Robin Goodfellow, 'but now is not the right time to discuss it. Any moment now our good friend Oberon will notice that his new pet is missing and send his folk after you. We want to be far away and over the hill by the time that happens.'

Joanna got to her feet and felt the burden of the invisible bond on her wrist. 'Do you know yet why you brought me through the Far-Enough Window and into Fairyland?' she said. 'It was a question you couldn't answer the last time I saw you, and it's one you've never answered since first I met you.'

The Onskonsiders had started up the hill with Robin Goodfellow following them. Now he turned and shrugged. 'I came to fetch you because you told me I was going to,' he said. 'That was a good enough reason for me, darling lady

THE FAR-ENOUGH WINDOW

Joanna. And then, when I went to find you, *you* told me something of my purpose: that I was to bring you here to heal the wounds of Fairyland. But more than that I cannot tell you: my memory balks at the very notion, because things are not yet in their proper order.'

'When will they *ever* be?' said Joanna with a moan.

Mustardseed was still sitting stolidly on the grass, looking down at the burning encampment, ignoring the tugs Joanna was making on the line that linked them.

'Oberon not want to have his pet escape,' the Comelately said.

'Oberon not want to have his pet *die!*' snapped Joanna. 'Oberon want his pet taken out of danger! Mustardseed help take Oberon's pet far from those who would harm her! Joanna friend of Mustardseed: Joanna not deceive Mustardseed.'

The Comelately's shoulders, silhouetted against the blaze, expressed scepticism.

Just for a moment Joanna saw somewhere else where Mustardseed was hesitating. It was in a huge space where moonlight was playing with darkness. Joanna herself was standing a few steps higher than Mustardseed, and saying to her: 'And I want to see my diary.' The Comelately was looking up at her as if wanting to warn her of something yet unable to think of a good reason to do so.

As soon as it had arrived the image was gone, yet Joanna had recognized the hall at home, and the main staircase. 'I want to see my diary,' she said out loud on the hillside.

Mustardseed turned to stare at her. 'Diary?'

'No. I mean – At least, I *don't* mean – It's all so very, very *unfairly* confusing! Just come with me! *Please.* Come with me and my friends – because they're *your* friends as well, really, only you don't quite know it yet. And I'm sure Oberon would want this to happen, if only he knew what was going on! Please come! *Please.*'

Joanna put all her strength into a final jerk on the invisible rope.

Miraculously, it parted.

'Mustardseed cannot go with Joanna, but Mustardseed friend of Joanna so can let Joanna go without her.'

The dismissal – so curt and unexpected – revealed to Joanna how much she'd come to love the handservant, even in her slow-thinking aspect. She ran back and threw herself at the Comelately. 'Come with me!' she yelled. 'Come with me, you stupid blasted lump of reptile, or so help me I'll drag you the whole way!'

'Leave her,' said Robin Goodfellow, tugging at Joanna's back. 'You don't need her. She's just one of Oberon's catspaws.'

'I *can't* leave her!' cried Joanna, turning to look at him through a blur of tears. 'Don't you understand how much we need her if we're to regain Fairyland?'

'No,' said Robin, freezing. 'No, I don't. Perhaps you could tell me.'

'I – I can't explain right now.' Joanna wondered where the words had come from. She'd spoken them with total conviction, yet she didn't know why.

There was a shout from below. 'The monster!'

'They've noticed you've gone,' Robin hissed urgently, yanking her sleeve. 'Come on. Bring the wench if you can.'

'Mustardseed!' Joanna felt as if she were calling Mr Dogg to heel.

THE FAR-ENOUGH WINDOW

'Mustardseed will come with Joanna,' said the Comelately at last, obviously having been thinking hard all this time. She pushed herself heavily to her feet. 'Joanna greater friend of Mustardseed than Oberon is. Joanna cry when she think Mustardseed lost to her. Oberon never cry.'

The door swayed open almost silently, just the faint brush of its lower edge on the carpet betraying its movement. Joanna tiptoed into the room with Mustardseed right behind her.

'This is where I sleep,' she whispered.

'It's where you're sleeping now,' observed Mustardseed in the same low tone. 'Look.'

Joanna could hardly see the Comelately's pointing fingertip in the subdued moonlight, but she hardly needed to. On the bed there was a rounded heap of duvet and coverlet, snoring softly.

'That's *me*!' said Joanna, seeing the spray of moonlit hair on the pillow. She realized with horror that she'd spoken out loud, and pressed the back of her hand to her mouth.

'I shouldn't worry,' said Mustardseed nonchalantly. 'I think it's very doubtful that you could wake yourself up, even if you wanted to.' She went over to the window and stared out at the snow. 'Common sense is already being assailed grievously enough by there being two of you at large here in the past in the same world at the same time, without it being offended past repair by your meeting. I think we're here on sufferance, Joanna: permitted to explore the place as long as we don't affect it too much.'

'What makes you think we're here in the past?'

'I told you: there's something in the air that reminds me

of when we were in Fairyland's past. Besides, if this were the future you'd've stayed awake to welcome yourself, wouldn't you? Or at least you'd have tried.'

'I've got mixed up as to where exactly past and future *are* in relation to each other.' Joanna admitted. 'Just when I think I've got things sorted out in my head I find – '

'We can easily check by looking in your diary. Where is it?' Mustardseed made her hands start radiating unearthly white light again.

'I was planning to leave it on the dress– Yes, here it is.'

Joanna picked up the book, fiddled with the key on its chain around her neck, and opened the lock. There was no writing on the ruled pages until she'd riffled through nearly to the front.

One page had been filled in.

JANUARY 1: MONDAY

She cast her eyes down the tightly squeezed page of writing: the hand seemed very childish to her, although she recognized it as her own. One of her tutors had insisted that she learn to write exactly as it showed in a book – which book it had been Joanna couldn't remember – and the result was that her handwriting was as characterless as the fake handwriting of the endorsements in a magazine advertisement. The only declaration of independence she'd been able to make was to write in a tiny hand.

There were a lot of words on this single page, but Joanna was swiftly able to summarize their content:

THE FAR-ENOUGH WINDOW

January 1: Monday
Nothing much happened.

She glanced up to discover that Mustardseed had been reading over her shoulder.

'I'm sorry,' said Joanna, apologizing instinctively for the dullness of her life.

But another part of her, she realized, was doing something else entirely. The heavens were lit by the glare of a great conflagration, and Joanna was scrambling up a hillside away from it. Dolly Onskonsider and Lumpenkulder Onskonsider were there, and Mustardseed, and Robin Goodfellow too: they were all almost on hands and knees in their haste. Something dreadful – something that Joanna couldn't see but knew was dreadful – was pursuing them. A stitch was stabbing at her side. She had to stop, even if it meant being swallowed up by the relentless pursuer. The Comelately, just ahead of Joanna, reached back an arm and grabbed at the front of her robe, but missed. Joanna had to stop, had to –

'It's Oberon,' snarled Robin. 'Don't look behind you. Keep up with us!'

'Here!' cried Dolly Onskonsider, turning her head and making an odd shape in the air with her hand. 'This is yours!'

The pain of the stitch faded from Joanna's side, and she scampered up the hillside with a sudden renewal of energy . . .

She stood holding the diary. Her breathing was unnaturally loud. She felt as if she were still fleeing, although there was no other noise in the bedroom except herself – her *different* self – quietly snoring.

'There's no need to say you're sorry,' remarked Mustardseed. 'You and I both, we were locked away by other people. How could we have expected – have *been* expected – to lead interesting lives? We were trapped in the humdrum. The difference is that I allowed myself to be imprisoned: you didn't.'

'Yes, but really,' said Joanna, offering up the diary page in mute evidence. 'I mean, *really*.'

Mustardseed snatched her by the shoulders. The brightness of her hands made Joanna's vision reel.

'Don't you ever talk like that again,' said the Comelately, her mouth not an inch from Joanna's, 'or so help me I'll strangle the life right out of you! I mean it!'

Mustardseed's claws were digging into Joanna's throat. She could kill Joanna with a hiccup: there was no doubt.

'Don't ever again apologize for your life!' insisted Mustardseed. 'You were the one who was brave when we entered the Lair of Forgotten Fears – not I, not Mr Dogg, not the unicorn! It was *you* whom we followed. Don't you think that we wouldn't, one of us or all of us, even Hrimfaxi – most of all Hrimfaxi, perhaps, for all his size and apparent strength – have given up, rolled over, accepted our fate, if it hadn't been for you? Do you think we followed you for *nothing*? Do you want to insult us that much?'

'I – ' said Joanna.

'Look,' said Mustardseed. 'See.'

She waved her glowing hand over the page for JANUARY 1: MONDAY, and it was blank.

'See,' said Mustardseed, 'you can write yourself a whole new yesterday.'

THE FAR-ENOUGH WINDOW

The Onskonsiders led them to a cave far up the mountainside. Clearly they'd used the place before, because they moved around in it with an easy certainty as Lumpenkulder lit a fire and Dolly scrabbled among the provisions neatly stacked in cave's rear. Soon the five of them were warming themselves around a merry little blaze and eating leathery strips of some dried substance that tasted vaguely like smoked chicken but probably wasn't.

'What next?' said Joanna.

'Next we sleep the night here,' said Robin Goodfellow, 'and in the morning we try to get you as far away from Oberon as we possibly can. Dolly and Lumpenkulder can only move houses, not caves – for obvious reasons – so it'll be a question of going on foot.' He looked at Joanna's feet, which were bare and already much cut and bruised from the climb. Mustardseed was likewise unshod, but her tough soles looked as if they could take as much punishment as events might administer to them. 'Dolly may have some shoes stashed away somewhere. If not, we'll have to bind up your feet in cloths.'

'Where will we go to?' This was from Mustardseed, who was already showing some of the benefits of being distanced from the Great High King.

'Over the hills and far away,' said Robin Goodfellow with a smile, 'just as I told you. We have a whole world to choose from.'

'But the Great High King rules all of it. There's nowhere we'd be safe.'

'Yes there is,' said Joanna quickly. 'We could go back through the Far-Enough Window into *my* world. If you could guide us there, Robin . . .'

In the flickering of the fire she suddenly saw Knolly Mutton lying on her pillow at home. There was moonlight in the room, brightening his ever-outstretched arms; its whiteness was beautifully consonant with the mixed greys of the flames. She squinted, trying to bring the image into clearer focus, and saw that her own head was on the adjacent pillow. With a shock she realized that she was viewing this scene not from a cave in Fairyland but from the now-strange, now-foreign territory of her own bedroom. She turned her head back to look at her hand, which was holding her Osmiroid fountain-pen. She was about to write –

Her consciousness wavered, and she was back beside the fire. Earlier she had dismissed such slips of awareness as hallucinations – she was desperately tired and there had been so much else going on – but this time she was convinced that what she had seen was a genuine event, that she really was elsewhere – home – at the same time as she was *here*, in the cave, with Robin Goodfellow and the Onskonsiders and Mustardseed.

'Robin,' she whispered. 'There's something I think you ought to know . . .'

'. . . and anyway there's no place in your world for the likes of us,' Robin Goodfellow was saying. 'I could be everywhere in that world if you wanted me to be, but there's little difference, blithe one, between everywhere and nowhere.'

'No,' she said, her lips feeling numb. 'I agree we can't go there. But where? Back into the Farness? There's nowhere in Fairyland I'll be safe.'

'There's one place,' said Lumpenkulder Onskonsider

gravely. 'By the side of Oberon.' He stroked his face.

Joanna looked at him despairingly. 'As his *pet?*'

'As his queen.'

There was a silence broken only by the spitting of the fire and the noise of Mustardseed savaging a piece of the meat-that-was-not-meat.

Then Joanna snorted with mirth. 'You think that I could' – she searched for an expression that didn't sound too revolting – '*mate* with that creature.' She remembered him poised over her, his reptilian eyes upon her, the claws of his hands.

'No,' said Lumpenkulder. 'But the Oberon that there used to be . . .'

'The Oberon that used to be is a thing of the past,' said Dolly. 'He's a midsummer night's dream – no more than that.'

'He's an Oberon without a Titania,' said Robin Goodfellow with fresh enthusiasm.

Joanna remembered the odd feeling of *wanting* she'd known in Oberon's presence. She'd been disgusted by him – by his massiveness, by the scales he had in place of flesh – and yet she'd also been affected by the stark power of the Great High King. 'He's the most loathsome thing I've ever come across,' she said fiercely. 'Besides, we're fleeing from him. Don't you remember that?'

'I brought you through the Far-Enough Window and into Fairyland for some reason,' said Robin in a calculating tone. 'Your ghost said that I should do so – she said that I could restore Fairyland if only you were here. You said as much yourself, when we first met after your friend the unicorn had died. Maybe what both you and your ghost were thinking of was that – '

'No!' said Joanna. 'Do you think I'm just some kind of object to be farmed out? A breeding animal?'

'Not that at all,' said Lumpenkulder. 'Did you ever see Oberon the way he was, before the Comelatelies arrived to dominate the world?'

'Of course I didn't! He sent someone to seize me – a leprechaun called Tamarary Pulkoon – but I escaped him. Escaped him thanks to *you*, Robin Goodfellow, and *you*, Mustardseed! With your help I fled into the Far-Enough Window, and came back into the present, where . . .'

Her voice faltered. She was finishing the first line of writing on a ruled page, and she was squatting by the side of a fire. She was both places, and both people, at once.

The trouble was that she *had* seen the old Oberon. He'd been in a video. Only last year Mrs Ruggeley and Joanna's father had thought that the 1935 movie of *A Midsummer Night's Dream*, with James Cagney as Bottom, would be suitable viewing for her. An actor called Victor Jory, of whom she'd never heard, had been the fairy king. She couldn't remember who had been Titania.

Herself?

'But of course,' Robin Goodfellow whispered. 'You couldn't be expected to care for the Comelately version of Oberon, however much he might love you.'

'Love me?' She was horrified.

'Why do you think he didn't kill you?'

'Why should he have? I'd done him no harm.'

'Why shouldn't he have? You'd hurt him gravely simply by being here in Fairyland – for the kingdom is the king, after all, and you're an anomaly here: a mortal in a world of immortals. You were a danger, just through your presence. And you still are. You're a gallstone. You're something that should not be – and yet you are. Killing you would have been the easiest way for Oberon to solve the problem. But he didn't. He saw something of his lost Titania in you – no, that's doing you an injustice, for you're far more lovely than Titania ever was.'

'But he said I was ugly! He said all mortals were ugly!'

'And so they are – you are – to Oberon as he now is.' Robin Goodfellow was leaning towards her, marking each word with a jab of his forefinger. 'But not to the Oberon that once we knew. That was no warrior Oberon, holding his folk in the thrall of might and fear. The Oberon who ruled Fairyland between the demise of the Oldcomers and the advent of the Comelatelies was a king who believed in rule through happiness.

'For all of a hundred years we *played* here in Fairyland – played and enjoyed ourselves. We wished no harm to anyone: the worst we ever did was mischief, like Tamarary Pulkoon tried to do when he attempted to capture you for Oberon. I thought for a while that he was hoping to destroy you, because that was what it looked like; but that wasn't Fairyland's way, not in those days. Now – well, now it'd be a different matter.' Robin looked dark. 'The Oberon of now might have killed you as soon as looked at you – except that he, too, remembers the old times. He remembers Titania, and how she moved and was, and he still, in that great cold-blooded heart of his, feels the gape of her absence. And then he sees you . . .'

Robin leapt to his feet and pranced a crazy caper.

'Yes!' he said. 'This is the way it must have been! This is

surely why Oberon spared your life – far from killing you, he arranged to have you kept close to him while he toyed with the idea of – '

The fire flared as Dolly, unimpressed, threw another branch on it.

'*This* is how we can reclaim Fairyland for the Finefolk!' Robin declared.

'I *can't* just invent things that never happened to me,' said Joanna earnestly. 'What'll happen when she – when I' – she indicated the sleeping figure with a nod of her head – 'wakes up?'

'You already know what'll happen,' said Mustardseed. 'You woke up and read the page of your diary, and that drew you to find the Far-Enough Window.'

'Yes, but – '

It just didn't seem right to Joanna. If she hadn't gone to the Far-Enough Window she'd never have met Robin Goodfellow and been drawn though into Fairyland, and if she hadn't done that she wouldn't be sitting here now, preparing to pen exactly the words that had brought her here. The effect was the cause – surely that could not be?

She tried to explain to Mustardseed.

The Comelately wasn't convinced. 'What happens, happens,' she said. 'The ways the realms of the Farness work don't depend on whether or not you're able to explain them: they just *are*. Imagine the opposite: imagine what will happen if you *don't* create this new yesterday for yourself. The Far-Enough Window will just slumber on, undiscovered, at the top of its tower. Fairyland will be lost once more to a tyranny

THE FAR-ENOUGH WINDOW

– a tyranny that'll overspill into this mortal world of yours. And, most significantly, you'll never come back here to sit where you're sitting now! The consequence of your refusing to write what you're about to write would be that you weren't here at all! Can you believe it would be possible for you to both exist and not exist in the same moment?'

'I'd never have believed,' said Joanna, 'that I could exist *twice over* in the same moment.' Again she nodded towards the bed. 'Yet it's happened, hasn't it?'

'That's on a totally different *scale* of impossibility,' snapped Mustardseed. 'Now get writing, girl. If you can't remember the exact words, it doesn't matter. Just scribble down the sense of them.'

'But why?'

'Because,' said Mustardseed grimly, leaning down so that her face was only inches from Joanna's, 'if you don't you'll never go to Fairyland. And *then* where will you go to?'

Never going to Fairyland suddenly seemed to Joanna like quite an attractive proposition. All that her journey into the realms of the Farness had brought her were pain and loss and exhaustion. Yes, she reflected, but she'd also discovered the thrill of existence. She had been utterly miserable when Hrimfaxi had died in front of her, yet the very strength of the emotion had made her grief into something almost pleasurable – something honest. She'd known fear – fear alongside something else she didn't too much want to think about – when she'd been hauled in front of Oberon. There had been the horrible experience of being cramped by the tunnel in the Lair of Forgotten Fears, the terror of being lifted into the air by the tiny malevolent butterflies ... And yet all of these had been *real* emotions, unlike anything she'd ever felt before, cocooned as she'd been in the comfortable prison of home. She'd discovered that existence could have a sharp, thrilling edge to it.

In her earlier life she'd dwelt in merely two dimensions, like one of the people in the endless succession of bland videos she'd watched; now, having travelled through many dimensions, she had in consequence gained a third.

'And *then* where will you go to?' Mustardseed had said. It was a powerful question. The self that she was now couldn't simply disappear – and neither could her other self, the one that she sensed was still in Fairyland, a fugitive in a cave with Robin Goodfellow, the Onskonsiders and a different version of Mustardseed. If the sleeping Joanna were merely to rise tomorrow morning, discover when she glanced at her diary nothing more than the dreary confirmation that her life had passed another day without interest, she'd never think to go to the Lampeter Wing and find what it held for her; and the Joanna-in-Fairyland and the Joanna-sitting-here-with-an-Osmiroid-in-her-hand would be cast adrift from their origin. Lost. Drifting away to become, eventually, unlikely likelihoods that had never chanced to come into reality. They'd be part of an unsuccessful version of the past.

'So hurry up,' Mustardseed said, 'and then we can go and see this Mrs Ruggeley of yours and be out of here.'

Joanna nodded, still with doubts lingering in her mind, and bent to her task.

She ran into the night, tripping and falling and picking herself up again. Fearful equally of the Great High King's encampment and the cave from which she had fled, she cut across the mountainside. The Comelatelies had quelled the blaze below her, so that all she could see of it was a collection of individual glows like a handful of semi-precious stones thrown onto an ink-black table.

Oberon. Robin Goodfellow had wanted to deliver her into the hands of Oberon so that the Great High King would take her as his bride. Although the notion repelled Joanna, made her stomach feel queasy, at the same time she could appreciate its logic. In order to love her physically the Great High King would have to take on his alternate form, so that he resembled a beautiful mortal. In such a state he would surely choose to surround himself not with the massive denizens of Faerie but, once more, with the little Finefolk of Fairyland – with the little beings who had come to Cottingley, who had been painted so lovingly by Arthur Rackham, who had inspired the affectionate venom of J.M. Barrie. Yes, in this way the Fairyland after which Robin Goodfellow yearned could be brought back into existence – but at what cost!

Little enough, Joanna conceded, in terms of all the multitudinous realities of the Farness; but inasmuch as she herself was concerned the cost was her own life, her own being.

How valuable was that being? She recalled the life she'd been leading before the false entry in her diary –

– no, it wasn't a false entry, it had been written by herself, she could sense herself writing it at this very moment, Mustardseed leaning over her shoulder to watch the words take shape –

– had led her to the Lampeter Wing and through its must and moulderiness to the attic where the Far-Enough Window had beckoned her, where Robin Goodfellow had lured her with his buoyant amicability even though, at the time, he'd been totally in the dark about his own motivations. Who had she been before that time? (She was tripped by a lowflung stem of gorse and thrown flat on her stomach. For a moment all she could see were flashing lights. Then she picked herself up and stumbled onwards.) The Joanna who'd lived in the stately house whose estates had represented the limits of her world: who had that person been?

She knew the answer, of course, but didn't like to acknowledge it. The old Joanna had been little more than a cipher, living – if living it could be called – in a state of artificiality. Really! People didn't lock away their children from the outside world – not in the twenty-first century they didn't! Perhaps in a Victorian novel, or in a Disney movie ...

She fell again, and this time she felt something snap in her ankle. Her mind singing with pain, she looked back to see what had this time caused her downfall.

Robin Goodfellow's hand, jutting up from the dark grass.

She tugged it out by the roots, pain forgotten, and scrambled back upright. The arm fell away from her, rolling off down the hillside: it had the watery gravitas of a courgette.

Again she looked back the way she had come, seeing nothing but night. If Robin Goodfellow and the Onskonsiders and Mustardseed (no, surely not Mustardseed, who of all of them was the one in whose friendship Joanna most trusted) were pursuing her, there were no signs of them.

How bad would it be to be Oberon's bride?

Worse than limping with a sprained and possibly broken ankle across a hostile hillside?

What virtue would she be sacrificing? What, if *anything*,

would she be sacrificing? The barrenness of the existence she had known, back in the mortal world: easy living, with nothing demanded of her, but no progression from one day to the next. She could exist a century or more in that life, knowing the passage of time only through the wrinkles around her eyes, and never really start to *live*.

(Somewhere else, her ankle started to throb. Without noticing what she was doing, Joanna uncrossed her feet and then crossed them the other way. Her pen was writing: '... full of old junk. I tried on a hat made of straw with a broken feather sticking out of it, but as I pushed it down on my head the crown disintagrated, so I threw it away and had a lot of trouble getting the bits out of my hair. But most' – score that out and correct – '~~most~~ *more* important than that . . .')

A stream had cut a steep-edged groove into the hillside. Joanna found herself careering down the almost vertical slope, her arms wide. She kept her balance for a surprisingly long time; the jumbled boulders along the stream's side were her eventual undoing, and she fell into a splash of cold. She surfaced, spluttering. As if reminded by the freezing water, the bruise at the base of her spine started to pulse again.

What would be so terrible about being the Queen of Fairyland? How much would it differ from her previous life, in the mortal world? Instead of being catered to by Mrs Ruggeley she'd have a thousand willing servants flitting to the tune of her whim: it would be her job to be vacuous, to be an essence of empty-headed prettiness – but hadn't that been her fate already? Her thoughts would doubtless be very limited, very trivial in scope – but hadn't that all along been the case, with a world confined inside the gardens' tall stone walls?

She dragged herself painfully out of the stream. Her back and her ankle were sharp, icy daggers.

She would have to learn to accept – her mind searched the pages of the dimly recollected novels of Jane Austen for a suitable euphemism and discovered nothing – the *physical attentions* of the Great High King, but would those be so intolerably ghastly? Everything she had ever known, not least the descriptions offered to her by Robin Goodfellow and Mustardseed, told her that Oberon, in his almost-human guise, was like an exquisitely lovely man . . .

As Titania was an exquisitely lovely almost-woman.

Not 'was'. Had been.

Titania was gone: no longer a part of Fairyland.

Fairyland needed a queen. There was a vacant ecological niche.

'I feel just exactly like a vacant ecological niche,' Joanna muttered to herself as she surmounted a new ridge. Still there was no sound of pursuit.

She plopped herself down on a little mound, hoping it wasn't an anthill, and asked herself how much she wanted to continue her flight. The various agonies in her body made her eyes blur. If Robin Goodfellow had it right, she could trade this freezing cold misery very swiftly for a life of luxury, dwelling throughout eternity in a pleasant glade, with tiny worshippers flying to and fro to bring her the freshest berries and the daintiest sweetmeats.

Was she –

– she finished writing the new page of her diary: '. . . learned it's name of the Far-Enough Window, like he said. But tonight I am tired and I am getting to the bottom of the page so I will stop now, dear reader, and tell you more tomorrow when I hope there is more to tell.' She had more to tell, all right – whole volumes more to tell! – but Mustardseed was pulling at her arm. Joanna gave a last sad look at the girl who was sleeping beside Knolly Mutton, wishing she could wake her and talk to her of the Farness, and of the exhilaration, the smack of ozone in the nostrils as one ventured into it, but –

– crazy? The Joanna she once had been had dreamt of nothing finer than –

'I feel like a burglar,' said Joanna as they crept into Mrs Ruggeley's bedroom. Mustardseed silently closed the door behind them.

'We could still go back,' whispered the Comelately. 'We could go all the way back to the Far-Enough Window and get out of this realm. In a way that's what I'd best like to do.' She'd muted the glare of her hands again.

'No,' said Joanna. 'Forward. There isn't any other way but forward.'

Mrs Ruggeley's bed had been vast the last time she'd been here – an almost limitless acreage of pale-gleaming linen and heavy scent, ample room for a small child to discover respite from bad dreams. Now it looked like a narrow cot: how could there ever have been space for she and Mrs Ruggeley to sleep in each other's arms?

She reached out to pull the sheet away from Mrs Ruggeley's face.

The housekeeper's eyes opened.

They didn't open far. They couldn't. They were slits that shone green-yellow in the dim light from Mustardseed's hands. Each eye was divided in the centre by a vertical line of black.

This is how Mrs Ruggeley has always looked, Joanna realized, even as she staggered back from the bedside, *and I've never noticed it before. I've always seen and known her as a cuddly old woman, because that's the way she's wanted me to see and know her.*

Mrs Ruggeley sat up. The effect was of a pupating insect breaking out of its prison as the bedclothes fell away from about her shoulders.

Mustardseed's hands flared.

'You!' said Mrs Ruggeley.

Joanna realized the housekeeper – no, that was the trouble, Mrs Ruggeley wasn't a housekeeper, never had been – was talking not to her but to Mustardseed.

'*You!*' said Mustardseed.

The two Comelatelies stared at each other. The light from Mustardseed's hands dipped briefly, then the glare increased to an even greater intensity.

And Mustardseed fell to her knees, holding up her supplicatory hands so that they became a brilliant white flower.

'You!' she repeated.

She could still just see the embers of the encampment in the distance beneath her. The night air was piercingly cold: she felt as if she looked like an ice-clad spectre as she cleaved through it. Oberon must still be there – surely he would still be there – he *must* be there. Her feet moved one after the other, downslope over the unseen grass, without her knowledge: even from this distance she was obeying the inexorable lure of the Great High King.

She watched herself from afar, wondering how much her thoughts were being controlled by the monarch. At one moment she had been determined to flee from him, finding the very notion of his presence repellent; now she was complaisantly walking towards him, not so much resigned to him as rushing eagerly to him. Had he reached out his mind to change her thoughts, the way he had changed those of the Finefolk who would be his courtiers? Or had it been Robin Goodfellow's words that had finally prevailed, persuading her that if she went to Oberon she would save Fairyland from the tyrant?

Or was she at last acknowledging the ambivalence she'd felt when she'd stood before the Great High King's throne, the simultaneous revulsion and attraction?

How much did it matter? How free had her thoughts ever been? A few days ago she'd have claimed at once that she had total freedom, living as she did in an environment where her every wish was almost certain to be granted. Now she recognized that her wishes had been constrained by the limits of the life she'd been permitted – like Mustardseed, she'd been allowed to think only very small thoughts. Oberon had said that he wanted her as a plaything, a pet: although she'd told herself that she was according with his wish only because that was the best escape strategy, wasn't it the truth that secretly she *wanted* to be his pet?

Bride. Pet. The two words seemed to have identical meaning.

She had gone more than halfway towards the Great High King's encampment without realizing it.

'You may be making a great mistake,' said Dolly

Onskonsider, or an illusion of her, appearing suddenly ahead. 'Being queen isn't such a fine thing. It's not all it's cracked up to be, dearie. Self-sacrifice doesn't comfort you when you wake up in the middle of the night realizing how dismally unhappy you've allowed yourself to become. You might feel grand whenever you remember that you've restored the little Finefolk to Fairyland, but there's only a limited amount of pleasure to be had from selflessness – not enough to last you a lifetime, especially a lifetime that endures for eternity.'

'It's the dream of all the girls to meet a handsome king and become his consort,' said Joanna crisply, continuing on her way.

Dolly Onskonsider faded reluctantly from her sight. If Joanna returned to the mortal world she could become just like Dolly Onskonsider, as the years added folds of flesh to her waist. But in Fairyland – ah, in Fairyland she'd remain forever young.

'Mr Dogg died, you know,' announced Robin Goodfellow, springing into being beside her and running to keep pace with her. 'I didn't want to tell you before – I was prepared to lie about it – because I knew it would upset you so much. He saw you and Mustardseed vanish towards the Far-Enough Window and he tried to follow you, but instead he was captured by the ripples and dragged down to drowning. It was an unjust death – he deserved far better – and I'd have stopped it had I could. But he was a mortal trespassing in Fairyland: Fairyland treats mortals with arbitrary cruelty. And the fate Fairyland has reserved for you is far crueller than the death Mr Dogg met.'

'You brought me here,' she replied, never ceasing the

tramp of her feet. 'You brought me here to reclaim Fairyland for you and your kind. You told me just now, not half an hour ago, how I could go about it. And yet here you are trying to dissuade me.'

'Whatever makes you think it was I who brought you here?' said Robin Goodfellow. 'Hasn't it been evident for a very long time that it was *you* who took you through the Far-Enough Window? It was *you* who wanted to preserve the Fairyland you'd always known! The me you're talking to just now – that's you, too, if only you'd acknowledge it.'

'In that case,' said Joanna, 'it was me, too, who decided that I should offer myself to Oberon as his queen. Don't try to turn me back, Robin Goodfellow. I thought all this while that I was merely an instrument in your hands, not understanding the purpose to which you intended to put me. Now I discover that I was following my own inclinations all along. You cannot begin to understand the joy this sense of *empowering* gives me.'

Was it her own mind that was making her lips and her tongue move to sound the words, or was it the Great High King's? She didn't know. If she had become the Great High King's puppet it was because she wanted to be so – in which case, who was the puppeteer?

'Leave me now, Robin Goodfellow,' she said. 'When next we meet, you shall be my subject, I your queen.'

Robin Goodfellow dissolved from her sight between the start of one leap and its end. She was alone again, drawing ever closer to the encampment where her lover – her true and fairy lover – was restoring order to the aftermath of the inferno. Oberon would welcome her as part of that order – as a healing of the wound that Titania had inflicted on

Fairyland when she'd left him.

(Titania was an old woman in front of her. Naked in wavering light, clad in the wrinkles of age, the queen was still a queen. But the queen was dead to Oberon: long live Oberon's queen.)

Lumpenkulder Onskonsider stood in front of her, one palm raised to halt her. She kept walking, so that he had to leap aside or be trampled under. He seemed to be trying to radiate towards her an impression of stately paternalism, difficult in view of his pell-mell loss of dignity.

'Listen to one who's wise in the ways of Fairyland,' he pleaded. His voice no longer sounded like the voice she knew – more like her own, if anything. 'The course you're taking is irreversible! We – that is, me and Dolly, and Robin Goodfellow – we'd rather have you as our friend Joanna and let this realm go to rot than know that you were suffering for our sakes!'

'You never said as much, back in the cave.'

'Back in the cave? What are you talking about?'

'When Robin Goodfellow sat with us by the fire and discovered the reason why I'd been taken through the Far-Enough Window. He wanted – although now he says the opposite – to use me as a poultice to heal the Great High King and hence the world. I never heard you speak against him, Lumpenkulder Onskonsider: you seemed much more concerned about your supper than with me!'

'I – '

'You were happy for me to become merely an object, just so long as it suited Robin Goodfellow's purposes – and yours, and Dolly's. You never thought of what *I* might think. And now that I've decided that yes, I'd like to spend forever as the queen of a world where magic lurks in every crevice of the landscape – now that it's *me* who's determined that this is what I want – you're flying into a frenzy trying to stop me! Why? What makes you think that I'll listen to you?'

Lumpenkulder Onskonsider suddenly stopped, and Joanna felt herself stop with him.

'All the things you did in your old life, Joanna,' he said, 'were the choices of other people. When you came into Fairyland, you expected to find freedom, but found none. I want Fairyland to be reclaimed as the place it until recently was – yes, I'd be a liar if I said anything else – yet more than that I want to give you, at the very last, an option to exercise *choice* over what befalls you.'

'I chose,' said Joanna. They were almost at the outskirts of the Great High King's encampment. 'I chose a while ago, when I was standing dripping water so cold it hurt me more than ice ever could, when the night gripped me, when all the friends I'd thought I had were wanting just to *use* me ... That's when I made my decision – *my* decision, do you hear? *My* choice.

'I was in a cage, once – a cage whose bars were forged of false love. The love that Oberon will have for me will be true – for nothing else would be possible in the Fairyland over which he and I will reign. His love will cage me, once again – don't you think I know that? But' – she picked up a weightless, textureless Lumpenkulder Onskonsider by the front of his jerkin and shook him – '*I'm moving to a much more comfortable cage.* That's *my* choice!'

She threw him away from her.

The flailing of his limbs as he fell turned into another face she knew well.

'Mustardseed,' she said. 'The truest of all my friends, unless it were Mr Dogg. Please don't try to dissuade me. I'm following the plot of a story that was written a very long time ago, even though I've only just devised it.'

The Comelately shrugged. Who was she, after all, but a ghost of Joanna herself?

'Mustardseed content to think only very little thoughts.'

When the woman spat she became the entire room: the chasm of her throat was the end wall; the rest of her body was spread over the ceiling and walls and floor. Joanna and Mustardseed cowered by the bed, seeming at the very heart of her.

'Titania,' said Mustardseed. 'She had to flee somewhere.'

Mrs Ruggeley – Harriet – Tettie – Titania. Joanna's mind made the link. But Titania was supposed to be a beautiful woman, the delight of all Fairyland – not the monstrous thing which now surrounded them. The queen had departed Oberon knowing that the era of the little Finefolk was drifting to its end, that Fairyland was abandoning its beauty, and yet what had she herself become? A plump late-middle-aged mortal woman: no beauty – although Joanna acknowledged that her own ideas of beauty might be circumscribed. Or Titania was the monstrosity who now shrieked at them from all the room's perimeters: no beauty in this, only ugliness.

'I will not return!' screamed the room. 'My life is here.'

Neither Joanna nor Mustardseed had words with which to respond.

'I bred you!' cried Titania. 'I bred you, Joanna – and for

why? Because Oberon needed a queen, and I was no longer prepared to play that rôle. He needed beauty, so I created beauty for him. I gave the Far-Enough Window to Fairyland so that I could escape here, and then I gave the Far-Enough Window to this world also, so that eventually you would find it, and use it. How could Oberon fail to love you when I, who knew his mind better than any other, had made you for him?'

'I – ' Joanna stammered, 'I don't wish to force you back to Fairyland, if you don't want to go there. That isn't what I came to you in search of. If I'd known who you really were, I'd have asked you to remain forever Mrs Ruggeley – *my* Mrs Ruggeley. What I wanted was . . .'

The room seemed to gather itself in. '*What?*'

'To find out who I am.' Joanna stood up to her full height. 'That is my *right!*'

The form of Titania concentrated itself, so that she was once more a withered Comelately seated on the bed. Mustardseed retreated to a distant corner, holding her hands up in front of her face.

'Do you remember your mother, Joanna?' said Titania in a rush of soft sibilance that was difficult to unravel.

'Yes. Well, I remember things about her. I can recall her warmth, and the softness of her embrace.'

'And can you remember your father?'

'Daddy? Of course I can! He was here only . . .'

Joanna stopped, appalled. Yes, she had a clear picture of her father in her mind, only now she came to look for it she discovered she couldn't find it. He was . . . he was . . .

And then she remembered the shifting columns and blobs of light that had momentarily so terrified her in the Lair of Forgotten Fears. 'His name is Aubrey and he drives a car,' she said weakly. The electronic keyboard. The videotapes. A collection of copies of *The Sound of Music*. 'And he gives me things at Christmas and birthdays.' He was here last summer . . . but how *long* ago was last summer?

Aubrey, she suddenly recognized. *The name is only a hairsbreadth away from Auberon. Auberon. Oberon . . .*

'I brought him here with me,' said Titania. 'Or, at least, enough of him to father you. Enough of him to give you something you could remember as having been your father. Just as over the years I told you fragments about a mother you had had, until in the end you could remember the feeling of being in her arms. You could remember the emptiness when she went – except that all she did was change what she revealed to you. Your father slowly dissipated out of this reality – the fraction of Oberon that I'd brought with me was weak by my design, because I no longer wished to suffer under his dominion. Too weak, as I eventually discovered. Its . . . his . . . toehold on this reality – in this world, this realm of the Farness – was too insecure for him to be able to stay here long. Yet he survived until he'd sparked your life in me, and then for some years more. And I grieved when he . . . went . . .'

'You're my mother?' said Joanna, incredulous. 'I'm the daughter of Titania? And now you want to marry me off to my own father, so that you don't have to be his consort yourself any longer?'

'Haven't you understood? I bred you for exactly that purpose,' said the queen coldly. 'Why else would I have allowed my body to give you birth?'

'You must loathe Oberon very greatly.' Joanna found herself sitting on the bed beside Titania; at times of distress

THE FAR-ENOUGH WINDOW

she'd always reached out to Mrs Ruggeley for comfort and now she was trying to do so again. Except that Mrs Ruggeley wasn't Mrs Ruggeley any more – had never been Mrs Ruggeley – and the scaly creature next to Joanna was someone impossible to hug: Titania's mind was a million miles remote from Joanna's own.

'Loathe him?' said Titania. 'Why, I suppose I do. And yet I must love him at the same time. What other reason could I have had to go to such great lengths to heal his grief?'

'But you gave up everything just to be away from him.'

'I saw that he was leading Fairyland back to ugliness. I saw how the Oldcomer faces of ourselves were to return, and how Fairyland would once again become a realm dominated by cruelty, subject to my husband's tyranny. If I could not preserve the land's beauty – and I have never been able directly to thwart my husband – then at least I could preserve my own.'

'But it wasn't Oberon's wishes that were taking Fairyland back to the way it had been before,' complained Joanna. 'It was the way we mortals thought of Fairyland – *that* was what was Thinning the little Finefolk's Fairyland, and *that* was what was restoring the Siddhe. And you haven't preserved your own beauty . . .'

Her voice trickled away. For the being sitting beside her was indeed beautiful. Joanna had found Mustardseed horrifically ugly at first, but then had discovered how beautiful her friend really was. Now she was making the same voyage of discovery about Titania. All that Joanna had ever been taught to recognize as human beauty suddenly seemed very vapid, very dilute to her: in the wrinkles and scales of Titania there was a strength of form that defied definitions.

But Joanna herself was not ugly either. Her beauty and Titania's – and Mustardseed's – were not mutually exclusive.

Except in Oberon's mind.

She remembered his beautiful power as he'd sat above her in his tent.

He had thought her ugly, then. And yet he had loved her for her beauty. But for him to be able to encompass that beauty he would have to change – he would have to become a handsome prince.

(The knowledge came to her that at this very moment she was standing in front of him once again, and that he was reaching out his great clawed hand almost shyly to touch her on the shoulder. At the moment of his touch her mortal beauty would start to suffuse into him, transforming first him and then, sluggishly, the realm of the Farness that was called Fairyland. The territory would be regained, just as Robin Goodfellow had – No, just as Joanna had – No: as *Titania* had wished.

(Smoke stinging her eyes, she was watching Oberon's hand descend on her shoulder.

('Father,' she said.)

As they slowly climbed the stone stairs of the Lampeter Wing, moving in single file by the light of Mustardseed's hands, Joanna began to reassess the way she had perceived the central elements of her life. She had seen everything – everyone – not as themselves but in terms of the rôles they played, of the functions they performed. It was necessary to her sense of selfness that she had a father, so she as much as Mrs Ruggeley (or Titania) had created the fragmentary recollections of a man who was successful and handsome, who was remote from her not because he wanted to be but because that was the way his lifestyle forced him to be, who had visited her whenever he could – but always in the past or possibly in the future: had never been with her in the present, not since her furthest infancy. And Titania – Titania had served the function of a housekeeper, a mother-who-was-not-a-mother, and so Joanna had seen her as such: as a frumpy elderly lady, Mrs Ruggeley, whose kitchen was always full of good things.

Yet Mrs Ruggeley had never been like that, outside Joanna's own perceptions of her: she had been instead a mother who held no real love for her child; it had been in a quite different sense that she had been a mother-who-was-not-a-mother.

And Joanna had gone a stage further, equipping the house with a gardener, Mudgett, because after all weren't stately houses supposed to have gardeners? They always did in books. They always did in movies. But Mudgett hadn't served any real purpose in the existence she had created for herself except to be there as a token of stability, a sign that all was right with the world. He wasn't really a human being at all: he was . . .

'Mr Dogg!' she cried, halting abruptly. 'Whatever happened to Mr Dogg?'

'He's around somewhere,' said Titania, irritated. 'Why do you choose a time like this to ask, child?'

'Because it's important to me,' said Joanna, refusing to move. '*He*'s important to me.'

'He was settled in his basket in the kitchen the last time I saw him,' said Titania. 'He'll be there still.'

'But he didn't bark when Mustardseed and I were prowling around downstairs! He didn't come to greet us! He didn't come to rescue us when you were filling the house with your screams!'

'He's an old dog,' said Titania. 'He probably slept through everything. You've written him a tiring day for tomorrow: you've sent us all sledging in the snow. He needs as much rest as he can get in preparation for it.'

'But – '

'Please keep going, Joanna,' said Mustardseed. 'Once we're back in Fairyland we can sort all these things out.'

'No!' Joanna shouted. The echoes bounced away down the gloomy spiral stairway. 'I'm not going there!'

'You must,' said Titania. 'Otherwise what would be the point in my having groomed you for this?'

'I'm already there! I know it! I feel it! Already I've wedded Oberon: the betrothal is complete, the marriage ceremony already performed by a consenting in our hearts! I am healing him! The wound you inflicted on him, Titania, is no longer bleeding – I've staunched it!'

'I don't believe you,' said Titania, gripping Joanna's wrist and starting to drag her up the stone steps. 'Come on, Mustardseed: I command you to help me with this stupid wench.'

'Mustardseed is a friend of Joanna. Mustardseed not like to do what Joanna doesn't wish.'

'Mustardseed is also a loyal subject of her monarchs!' the queen snapped. 'Help me!'

But Joanna wasn't resisting any longer. She was filled with a sense of inevitability. No: she wasn't going to return to Fairyland, because indeed she was already there. Whatever

THE FAR-ENOUGH WINDOW

Titania – her mother-who-was-not-a-mother – did wouldn't change that fact. Something would happen to frustrate the queen's intention. Joanna didn't need to fight what was going on. The problem had already been solved.

Something would happen.

Something marvellous.

The three of them stood in front of the Far-Enough Window, watching it. The last time Joanna and Mustardseed had seen it – only a couple of hours ago – it had been devoid of any potential to be other than a window, but now Joanna could sense it pulsing with the infinite possibilities of the Farness hidden behind the glass.

And there was something else there, too. Something achingly familiar, dropped in her confusion when all she'd been able to see was darkness.

Hrimfaxi's horn. It still contained enough of him to help protect her, Robin Goodfellow had said.

'Robin,' she called silently. Neither of the others saw her lips move. 'Robin!'

And he was there, crouched in the frame of the window, looking at her.

'I don't make a habit of coming when ghosts call me,' he said crossly. 'Who are you?'

Then his gaze moved, and he saw Titania.

'My queen!' he breathed. He tried to bow from his precarious sitting position, and tumbled out of the window-frame onto the floor. 'My apologies,' he said, becoming visibly angrier as he picked himself up and dusted himself off. 'You caught me unawares, my lady.'

'What are you doing here, Robin Goodfellow?' snarled Titania. 'I never summoned you!'

'I – I'm sorry again, my lady,' said Robin Goodfellow, this time successfully executing a neat little bow. 'But the person whose wish brought me to this place is the ghost standing beside you. And yet – And yet her command was irresistible because it was that of my queen.' He pushed back his cap to scratch his forehead. 'If I weren't a creature of common sense,' he mused, 'I'd be tempted to think that I'd gone from having no queen to having two. But such a thing can't be possible.' He turned once more to Joanna and repeated: 'Who are you?'

'Already I'm becoming your queen, Robin Goodfellow, and you and my good friends the Onskonsiders are becoming my faithfulest subjects. You don't know this yet, because it's happening some little while in your future. But I can sense it: I know that these events are taking place. They're taking place because tomorrow you will come here again for the express purpose of leading me – the other me, not the one who stands before you – through the Far-Enough Window and into Fairyland, whose healing queen she shall become.'

Brushing off Titania's hand, Joanna strode across the floor to bend down and pick up Hrimfaxi's horn.

'This is mine,' she said quietly. 'It was given to me by someone who died in love of me, and it is forever a part of me.' She held it across her breast. The horn shimmered, the same colour as the moonlight slanting in through the Far-Enough Window.

'Watch,' she said, suddenly knowing what was going to happen.

She felt no physical change at all, although there was a

sudden ecstatic leap in her mind. The horn moved, moulding itself to the contours of her body, pressing itself against her; and then slowly, almost imperceptibly slowly, it melted, passing its substance piecemeal through her borrowed Fairyland robe to become a part of her. Something of it had done this once before, just after Hrimfaxi had died: now the rest of the horn was following.

'I am a human being,' she said to Titania and Robin Goodfellow; Mustardseed wouldn't look at her. 'There is no place for someone like me in Fairyland – no place at all. The person you both want to become Oberon's queen is someone else entirely: she is sleeping in her room downstairs at the moment, unaware of any of this, and she is also already reigning over your realm at Oberon's side. You'll meet her here tomorrow, Robin Goodfellow, because I, your queen, command that it should be so.

'You' – she addressed Titania directly – 'have voluntarily abdicated your throne: either through cowardice or through selfishness you have abandoned Fairyland to its fate, putting another in your place and forcing her to accept the responsibility of healing the realm. You seem to have forgotten that, in giving up the duties of monarchy, you gave up also its entitlements. Robin Goodfellow is no longer your subject to instruct, and neither is Mustardseed, and neither am I. Rather, you have placed yourself under the sovereignty of Oberon's new queen – his threefold queen, who is part the naïve, two-dimensional girl sleeping downstairs, part the woman who has willingly prostituted herself to Oberon in order to restore Fairyland, and part the person who stands in front of you.

'As one of the aspects of the Queen of Fairyland, I

command you to spend the rest of your life – which will be of only mortal span, for that is what you have condemned yourself to – to spend that life as something genuine for once: a fussy old housekeeper with a bosom of starched linen and a devotion to her kitchen. You are no longer Titania, except perhaps in your inmost heart: you are Mrs Ruggeley, because my *life* requires you to be so.'

Robin Goodfellow looked back and forth between them in manifest consternation. If what Joanna had said was true, he was in the presence of two queens, and owed his liege to both. If what she had said was . . .

Titania seemed to shrink, becoming squatter. The polygonal patterning of the scales on her body lost discipline, becoming randomly curved creases. For the first time since Joanna and Mustardseed had awakened her she became aware of her nakedness, and in a blind panic she seized the nearest item of junk – an old lampshade – and held it up to her body, attempting pathetically to cover herself.

'Well I never did!' said Mrs Ruggeley. 'Well I . . . I just never did, that's all.'

Joanna dismissed the housekeeper's concerns with a wave of her hand.

'Mustardseed,' she said.

The Comelately, crouched against the far wall, looked up apprehensively at her.

'You have the choice,' said Joanna, 'between Fairyland and this mortal realm. You can become like me, a mortal with a slice of the marvellous in her – a woman with the horn of a unicorn at her core – or you can leave here to re-enter the realm of the immortal, of the wholly marvellous. The choice is yours, finest of all friends. You can go with Robin

THE FAR-ENOUGH WINDOW

Goodfellow now, or you can come back downstairs with me and help me put Mrs Ruggeley to bed. You, Mustardseed, are the one person of all Fairyland whom I have no right to command.'

They didn't find Mr Dogg in his basket, and he didn't come to them, no matter how they shouted his name in the hall and upstairs.

'He must be still on the other side of the Far-Enough Window,' said Mustardseed, putting her arm around Joanna's shoulders.

The old Joanna would have crumpled into tears at the loss of her friend. The Joanna-who-now-was thought of the old mongrel having a whole new world of smells to explore, broad plains filled with rabbits to chase, friends like Robin Goodfellow and the Onskonsiders to cherish him. And in Fairyland he would be immortal ...

She sniffed a couple of times, but recognized that her unhappiness was for herself.

Nothing loops, thought Joanna a little later, packing, *exactly*.

She wondered where the thought had come from – but only briefly: there wasn't time.

Dawn was only vaguely thinking of breaking as they left the house.

'I don't know where we're going to go to,' said Joanna nervously. The suitcase of books she held seemed too heavy to carry; she hefted it against her thigh. 'I don't know how we're going to live, or where. There's still time for you to change your mind, Mustardseed.'

'Hey, I'm your friend, remember?' the larger woman said. She was dressed in an old black raincoat several sizes too big for her, and had an ancient tweed fishing trilby, complete with tied flies in its band, crammed down on her head. She was clutching a collection of carrier bags filled with clothes for the two of them. Joanna worried that Mustardseed's attire might draw unwelcome attention to them at some point in the future ... but the future hadn't been written yet, so couldn't be worth her concern.

At least, not after the next few hours. The next few hours would see the knot unravelled and everything restored to its proper order at last. Not just Fairyland but the ordering of the story, the smooth progress of the now, would be reclaimed.

'I don't think I'll ever get used to the way you mortals live,' said Mustardseed. 'It seems odd to make stones into roads and houses when what they really want to be is bits of mountains.'

Joanna breathed free air, and looked back at the house where she'd spent all her life. She wasn't at all surprised to see that it was one of the centre houses in a terrace of two-up-two-downs. She and Mustardseed were no longer standing on the gravel of an eloquently curving drive – had probably never been – but trod a road of patchy tarmac. There was a light drizzle in the grey air. In the distance a milk float hummed into new motion. A brown and black mongrel – yes, assuredly it was Mr Dogg, *this* world's Mr Dogg – rounded the end of the terrace and came leaping towards her, his tongue flopping in delight.

'I'm the Queen of Fairyland,' said Joanna. 'And I'll make them believe me.'

THE END

Also Available from BeWrite Books

Horror
Chill   Terri Pine, Peter Lee,
                                     Andrew Müller

Fantasy
Zolin – A Rockin' Good Wizard   Barry Ireland

Crime/Humour
Sweet Molly Maguire   Terry Houston

Crime
Porlock Counterpoint   Sam Smith
Marks   Sam Smith
The Knotted Cord   Alistair Kinnon

Thriller
Blood Money   Azam Gill

Coming Soon

The Hundredfold Problem   John Grant

All the above titles are available from

www.bewrite.net

Printed in the United Kingdom
by Lightning Source UK Ltd.
92943